ST. MARTIN'S

MINOTAUR

MYSTERIES

D0204027

The Man in the Brown Suit

AGATHA CHRISTIE

The Man in the Brown Suit

St. Martin's Paperbacks

ISBN: 0-312-97948-7

Printed in the United States of America

St. Martin's Paperbacks edition / September 2001

St. Martin's Paperbacks are published by St. Martin's Press, 175 Fifth Avenue, New York, NY 10010.

10 9 8 7 6 5 4 3 2

To E.A.B.

In memory of a journey, some lion stories and a request that I should some day write the "Mystery of the Mill House"

The Man in the Brown Suit

PROLOGUE

Nadina, the Russian dancer who had taken Paris by storm, swayed to the sound of the applause, bowed and bowed again. Her narrow black eyes narrowed themselves still more, the long line of her scarlet mouth curved faintly upwards. Enthusiastic Frenchmen continued to beat the ground appreciatively as the curtain fell with a swish, hiding the reds and blues and magentas of the bizarre *décors*. In a swirl of blue and orange draperies the dancer left the stage. A bearded gentleman received her enthusiastically in his arms. It was the Manager.

"*Magnificent, petite*, magnificent," he cried. "Tonight you have surpassed yourself." He kissed her gallantly on both cheeks in a somewhat matter-of-fact manner.

Madame Nadina accepted the tribute with the ease of long habit and passed on to her dressing-room, where bouquets were heaped carelessly everywhere, marvellous garments of futuristic design with the scent of the massed blossoms and with more sophisticated perfumes and essences. Jeanne, the dresser, ministered to her mistress, talking incessantly and pouring out a stream of fulsome compliments.

A knock at the door interrupted the flow. Jeanne went to answer it, and returned with a card in her hand.

"Madame will receive?"

"Let me see."

The dancer stretched out a languid hand, but at the sight of the name on the card, "Count Sergius Paulovitch," a sudden flicker of interest came into her eyes.

"I will see him. The maize *peignoir*, Jeanne, and quickly. And when the Count comes you may go."

"Bien, Madame."

Jeanne brought the *peignoir*, an exquisite wisp of corn-coloured chiffon and ermine. Nadina slipped into it, and sat smiling to herself, whilst one long white hand beat a slow tattoo on the glass of the dressing-table.

The Count was prompt to avail himself of the privilege accorded to him—a man of medium height, very slim, very elegant, very pale, extraordinarily weary. In feature, little to take hold of, a man difficult to recognize again if one left his mannerisms out of account. He bowed over the dancer's hand with exaggerated courtliness.

"Madame, this is a pleasure indeed."

So much Jeanne heard before she went out closing the door behind her. Alone with her visitor, a subtle change came over Nadina's smile.

"Compatriots though we are, we will not speak Russian, I think," she observed.

"Since we neither of us know a word of the language, it might be as well," agreed her guest.

By common consent, they dropped into English, and nobody, now that the Count's mannerisms had dropped from him, could doubt that it was his native language. He had, indeed, started life as a quick-change music-hall artiste in London.

"You had a great success to-night," he remarked. "I congratulate you."

"All the same," said the woman, "I am disturbed. My position is not what it was. The suspicions aroused during the War have never died down. I am continually watched and spied upon."

"But no charge of espionage was ever brought against you?"

"Our chief lays his plans too carefully for that."

"Long life to the 'Colonel,' " said the Count, smiling. "Amazing news, is it not, that he means to retire? To retire! Just like a doctor, or a butcher, or a plumber—"

"Or any other business man," finished Nadina. "It should not surprise us. That is what the 'Colonel' has always been—an excellent man of business. He has organized crime as another man might organize a boot factory. Without committing himself, he has planned and directed a series of stupendous *coups*, embracing every branch of what we might call his 'profession.' Jewel robberies, forgery, espionage (the latter very profitable in war-time), sabotage, discreet assassination, there is hardly anything he has not touched. Wisest of all, he knows when to stop. The game begins to be dangerous?—he retires gracefully—with an enormous fortune!"

"H'm!" said the Count doubtfully. "It is rather—upsetting for all of us. We are at a loose end, as it were."

"But we are being paid off—on a most generous scale!" Something, some undercurrent of mockery in her tone, made the man look at her sharply. She was smiling to herself, and the quality of her smile aroused his curiosity. But he proceeded diplomatically:

"Yes, the 'Colonel' has always been a generous paymaster. I attribute much of his success to that—and to his invariable plan of providing a suitable scapegoat. A great brain, undoubtedly a great brain! And an apostle of the maxim, 'If you want a thing done safely, do not do it yourself!' Here we are, every one of us incriminated up to the hilt and absolutely in his power, and not one of us has anything on him."

He paused, almost as though he were expecting her to disagree with him, but she remained silent, smiling to herself as before.

"Not one of us," he mused. "Still, you know, he is superstitious, the old man. Years ago, I believe, he went to one of these fortune-telling people. She prophesied a lifetime of success, but declared that his downfall would be brought about through a woman."

He had interested her now. She looked up eagerly.

"That is strange, very strange! Through a woman, you say?"

He smiled and shrugged his shoulders.

"Doubtless, now that he has—retired, he will marry. Some young society beauty, who will disperse his millions faster than he acquired them."

Nadina shook her head.

"No, no, that is not the way of it. Listen, my friend, tomorrow I go to London."

"But your contract here?"

"I shall be away only one night. And I go incognito, like Royalty. No one will ever know that I have left France. And why do you think that I go?"

"Hardly for pleasure at this time of year. January, a detestable foggy month! It must be for profit, eh?"

"Exactly." She rose and stood in front of him, every graceful line of her arrogant with pride. "You said just now that none of us had anything on the chief. You were wrong. I have. I, a woman, have had the wit and, yes, the courage—for it needs courage—to double-cross him. You remember the De Beer diamonds?"

"Yes, I remember. At Kimberley, just before the War broke out? I had nothing to do with it, and I never heard the details, the case was hushed up for some reason, was it not? A fine haul too."

"A hundred thousand pounds worth of stones. Two of us worked it—under the 'Colonel's' orders, of course. And it was then that I saw my chance. You see, the plan was to substitute some of the De Beer diamonds for some sample diamonds brought from South America by two young prospectors who happened to be in Kimberley at the time. Suspicion was then bound to fall on them."

"Very clever," interpolated the Count approvingly.

"The 'Colonel' is always clever. Well, I did my part—but I also did one thing which the 'Colonel' had not foreseen. I kept back some of the South American stones—one or two are unique and could easily be proved never to have passed through De Beer's hands. With these diamonds in my possession, I have the whip-hand of my esteemed chief. Once the two young men are cleared, his part in the matter is bound to be suspected. I have said nothing all these years, I have been content to know that I had this weapon in reserve, but now matters are different. I want my price—and it will be a big, I might almost say a staggering price."

"Extraordinary," said the Count. "And doubtless you carry these diamonds about with you everywhere?"

His eyes roamed gently round the disordered room.

Nadina laughed softly. "You need suppose nothing of the sort. I am not a fool. The diamonds are in a safe place where no one will dream of looking for them."

"I never thought you a fool, my dear lady, but may I venture to suggest that you are somewhat foolhardy? The 'Colonel' is not the type of man to take kindly to being blackmailed, you know."

"I am not afraid of him," she laughed. "There is only one man I have ever feared—and he is dead."

The man looked at her curiously.

"Let us hope that he will not come to life again, then," he remarked lightly.

"What do you mean?" cried the dancer sharply.

The Count looked slightly surprised.

"I only meant that a resurrection would be awkward for you," he explained. "A foolish joke."

She gave a sigh of relief.

"Oh, no, he is dead all right. Killed in the War. He was a man who once—loved me."

"In South Africa?" asked the Count negligently.

"Yes, since you ask it, in South Africa."

"That is your native country, is it not?"

She nodded. Her visitor rose and reached for his hat.

"Well," he remarked, "you know your own business best, but, if I were you, I should fear the 'Colonel' far more than any disillusioned lover. He is a man whom it is particularly easy to—underestimate."

She laughed scornfully.

"As if I did not know him after all these years!"

"I wonder if you do?" he said softly. "I very much wonder if you do."

"Oh, I am not a fool! And I am not alone in this. The South African mail-boat docks at Southampton to-morrow, and on board her is a man who has come specially from Africa at my request and who has carried out certain orders of mine. The 'Colonel' will have not one of us to deal with, but two."

"Is that wise?"

"It is necessary."

"You are sure of this man?"

A rather peculiar smile played over the dancer's face.

"I am quite sure of him. He is inefficient, but perfectly trustworthy." She paused, and then added in an indifferent tone of voice: "As a matter of fact, he happens to be my husband."

Everybody has been at me, right and left, to write this story from the great (represented by Lord Nasby) to the small (represented by our late maid of all work, Emily, whom I saw when I was last in England. "Lor', miss, what a beyewtiful book you might make out of it all—just like the pictures!").

I'll admit that I've certain qualifications for the task. I was mixed up in the affair from the very beginning, I was in the thick of it all through, and I was triumphantly "in at the death." Very fortunately, too, the gaps that I cannot supply from my own knowledge are amply covered by Sir Eustace Pedler's diary, of which he has kindly begged me to make use.

So here goes. Anne Beddingfeld starts to narrate her adventures.

I'd always longed for adventures. You see, my life had such a dreadful sameness. My father, Professor Beddingfeld, was one of England's greatest living authorities on Primitive Man. He really was a genius—every one admits that. His mind dwelt in Palæolithic times, and the inconvenience of life for him was that his body inhabited the modern world. Papa did not care for modern man—even Neolithic Man he despised as a mere herder of cattle, and he did not rise to enthusiasm until he reached the Mousterian period.

Unfortunately one cannot entirely dispense with modern men. One is forced to have some kind of truck with butchers and bakers and milkmen and greengrocers. Therefore, Papa being immersed in the past, Mamma having died when I was a baby, it fell to me to undertake the practical side of living. Frankly, I hate Palæolithic Man, be he Aurignacian, Mousterian, Chellian, or anything else, and though I typed and revised most of Papa's *Neanderthal Man and his Ancestors*, Neanderthal men themselves fill me with loathing, and I always reflect what a fortunate circumstance it was that they became extinct in remote ages.

I do not know whether Papa guessed my feelings on the subject, probably not, and in any case he would not have been interested. The opinion of other people never interested him in the slightest degree. I think it was really a sign of his greatness. In the same way, he lived quite detached from the necessities of daily life. He ate what was put before him in an exemplary fashion, but seemed mildly pained when the question of paying for it arose. We never seemed to have any money. His celebrity was not of the kind that brought in a cash return. Although he was a fellow of almost every important society, and had rows of letters after his name, the general public scarcely knew of his existence, and his long learned books, though adding signally to the sum-total of human knowledge, had no attraction for the masses. Only on one occasion did he leap into the public gaze. He had read a paper before some society on the subject of the young of the chimpanzee. The young of the human race show some anthropoid features, whereas the young of the chimpanzee approach more nearly to the human than the adult chimpanzee does. That seems to show that whereas our ancestors were more Simian than we are, the chimpanzee's were of a higher type than the present species—in other words, the chimpanzee is a degenerate. That enterprising newspaper, the *Daily Budget*, being hard up for something spicy, immediately brought itself out with large headlines. "*We* are not descended from monkeys, but are monkeys descended from *us?* Eminent Professor says chimpanzees are decadent humans." Shortly afterwards a reporter called to see Papa, and endeavoured to induce him to write a series of popular articles on the theory. I have seldom seen Papa so angry. He turned the reporter out of the house with scant ceremony, much to my secret sorrow, as we were particularly short of money at the moment. In fact, for a moment I meditated running after the young man and informing him that my father had changed his mind and would send the articles in question. I could easily have written them myself, and the probabilities were that Papa would never have learnt of the transaction, not being a reader of the *Daily Budget*. However, I rejected this course as being too risky, so I merely put on my best hat and went sadly down the village to interview our justly irate grocer.

The reporter from the *Daily Budget* was the only young man who ever came to our house. There were times when I envied Emily, our little servant, who "walked out" whenever occasion offered with a large sailor to whom she was affianced. In between times, to "keep her hand in" as she expressed it, she walked out with the greengrocer's young man, and the chemist's assistant. I reflected sadly that I had no one to "keep my hand in" with. All Papa's friends were aged Professors— usually with long beards. It is true that Professor Peterson once clasped me affectionately and said I had a "neat little waist" and then tried to kiss me. The phrase alone dated him hopelessly. No self-respecting female has had a "neat little waist" since I was in my cradle.

I yearned for adventure, for love, for romance, and I seemed condemned to an existence of drab utility. The village possessed a lending library, full of tattered works of fiction, and I enjoyed perils and love-making at second hand, and went to sleep dreaming of stern, silent Rhodesians, and of strong men who always "felled their opponent with a single blow." There was no one in the village who even looked as though he could "fell" an opponent, with a single blow or with several.

There was the Kinema too, with a weekly episode of "The Perils of Pamela." Pamela was a magnificent young woman. Nothing daunted her. She fell out of aeroplanes, adventured in submarines, climbed skyscrapers and crept about in the Underworld without turning a hair. She was not really clever, the Master Criminal of the Underworld caught her each time, but as he seemed loath to knock her on the head in a simple way, and always doomed her to death in a sewer-gas chamber or by some new and marvellous means, the hero was always able to rescue her at the beginning of the following week's episode. I used to come out with my head in a delirious whirl—and then I would get home and find a notice from the Gas Company threatening to cut us off if the outstanding account was not paid!

And yet, though I did not suspect it, every moment was bringing adventure nearer to me.

It is possible that there are many people in the world who have never heard of the finding of an antique skull at the Broken Hill Mine in Northern Rhodesia. I came down one morning to find Papa excited to the point of apoplexy. He poured out the whole story to me.

"You understand, Anne? There are undoubtedly certain resemblances to the Java skull, but superficial—superficial only. No, here we have what I have always maintained—the ancestral form of the Neanderthal race.

You grant that the Gibraltar skull is the most primitive of the Neanderthal skulls found? Why? The cradle of the race was in Africa. They passed to Europe——"

"Not marmalade on kippers, papa," I said hastily, arresting my parent's absent-minded hand. "Yes, you were saying?"

"They passed to Europe on——"

Here he broke down with a bad fit of choking, the result of an immoderate mouthful of kipper-bones.

"But we must start at once," he declared, as he rose to his feet at the conclusion of the meal. "There is no time to be lost. We must be on the spot—there are doubtless incalculable finds to be found in the neighbourhood. I shall be interested to note whether the implements are typical of the Mousterian period—there will be the remains of the primitive ox, I should say, but not those of the woolly rhinoceros. Yes, a little army will be starting soon. We must get ahead of them. You will write to Cook's to-day, Anne?"

"What about money, papa?" I hinted delicately.

He turned a reproachful eye upon me.

"Your point of view always depresses me, my child. We must not be sordid. No, no, in the cause of science one must not be sordid."

"I feel Cook's might be sordid, papa."

Papa looked pained.

"My dear Anne, you will pay them in ready money."

"I haven't got any ready money."

Papa looked thoroughly exasperated.

"My child, I really cannot be bothered with these vulgar money details. The bank—I had something from the Manager yesterday, saying I had twenty-seven pounds."

"That's your overdraft, I fancy."

"Ah, I have it! Write to my publishers."

I acquiesced doubtfully, Papa's books bringing in more glory than money. I liked the idea of going to Rhodesia immensely. "Stern silent men," I murmured to myself in an ecstasy. Then something in my parent's appearance struck me as unusual.

"You have odd boots on, papa," I said. "Take off the brown one and put on the other black one. And don't forget your muffler. It's a very cold day."

In a few minutes Papa stalked off, correctly booted and well mufflered.

He returned late that evening, and, to my dismay, I saw his muffler and overcoat were missing.

"Dear me, Anne, you are quite right. I took them off to go into the cavern. One gets so dirty there."

I nodded feelingly, remembering an occasion when Papa had returned literally plastered from head to foot with rich Pleiocene clay.

Our principal reason for settling in Little Hampsly had been the neighbourhood of Hampsly Cavern, a buried cave rich in deposits of the Aurignacian culture. We had a tiny Museum in the village, and the curator and Papa spent most of their days messing about underground and bringing to light portions of woolly rhinoceros and cave bear.

Papa coughed badly all the evening, and the following morning I saw he had a temperature and sent for the doctor.

Poor Papa, he never had a chance. It was double pneumonia. He died four days later.

2

Everyone was very kind to me. Dazed as I was, I appreciated that. I felt no overwhelming grief. Papa had never loved me, I knew that well enough. If he had, I might have loved him in return. No, there had not been love between us, but we had belonged together, and I had looked after him, and had secretly admired his learning and his uncompromising devotion to science. And it hurt me that Papa should have died just when the interest of life was at its height for him. I should have felt happier if I could have buried him in a cave, with paintings of reindeer and flint implements, but the force of public opinion constrained a neat tomb (with marble slab) in our hideous local churchyard. The vicar's consolations, though well meant, did not console me in the least.

It took some time to dawn upon me that the thing I had always longed for—freedom—was at last mine. I was an orphan, and practically penniless, but free. At the same time I realized the extraordinary kindness of all these good people. The vicar did his best to persuade me that his wife was in urgent need of companion help. Our tiny local library suddenly made up its mind to have an assistant librarian. Finally, the doctor called upon me, and after making various ridiculous excuses for failing to send in a proper bill, he hummed and hawed a good deal and suddenly suggested that I should marry him.

I was very much astonished. The doctor was nearer forty than thirty, and a round, tubby little man. He was not at all like the hero of "The Perils of Pamela," and even less like a stern and silent Rhodesian. I reflected a minute and then asked him why he wanted to marry me. That seemed to fluster him a good deal, and he murmured that a wife was a great help to a General Practitioner. The position seemed even more unromantic than before, and yet something in me urged towards its acceptance. Safety, that was what I was being offered. Safety—and a Comfortable Home. Thinking it over now, I believe I did the little man an injustice. He was honestly in love with me, but a mistaken delicacy prevented him from pressing his suit on those lines. Anyway, my love of romance rebelled.

"It's extremely kind of you," I said. "But it's impossible. I could never marry a man unless I loved him madly."

"You don't think——?"

"No, I don't," I said firmly.

He sighed.

"But, my dear child, what do you propose to do?"

"Have adventures and see the world," I replied, without the least hesitation.

"Miss Anne, you are very much of a child still. You don't understand——"

"The practical difficulties? Yes, I do, doctor. I'm not a sentimental schoolgirl—I'm a hard-headed mercenary shrew! You'd know it if you married me!"

"I wish you would reconsider——"

"I can't."

He sighed again.

"I have another proposal to make. An aunt of mine who lives in Wales is in want of a young lady to help her. How would that suit you?"

"No, doctor, I'm going to London. If things happen anywhere, they happen in London. I shall keep my eyes open and you'll see, something will turn up! You'll hear of me next in China or Timbuctoo."

My next visitor was Mr. Flemming, Papa's London solicitor. He came down specially from town to see me. An ardent anthropologist himself, he was a great admirer of Papa's works. He was a tall, spare man with a thin face and grey hair. He rose to meet me as I entered the room and, taking both my hands in his, patted them affectionately.

"My poor child," he said. "My poor, poor child."

Without conscious hypocrisy, I found myself assuming the demeanour of a bereaved orphan. He hypnotized me into it. He was benignant, kind and fatherly—and without the least doubt he regarded me as a perfect fool of a girl left adrift to face an unkind world. From the first I felt that it was quite useless to try to convince him of the contrary. As things turned out, perhaps it was just as well I didn't.

"My dear child, do you think you can listen to me whilst I try to make a few things clear to you?"

"Oh, yes."

"Your father, as you know, was a very great man. Posterity will appreciate him. But he was not a good man of business."

I knew that quite as well, if not better than Mr. Flemming, but I restrained myself from saying so. He continued:

"I do not suppose you understand much of these matters. I will try to explain as clearly as I can."

He explained at unnecessary length. The upshot seemed to be that I was left to face life with the sum of £87, 17s. 4d. It seemed a strangely unsatisfying amount. I waited in some trepidation for what was coming next.

I feared that Mr. Flemming would be sure to have an aunt in Scotland who was in want of a bright young companion. Apparently, however, he didn't.

"The question is," he went on, "the future. I understand you have no living relatives?"

"I'm alone in the world," I said, and was struck anew by my likeness to a film heroine.

"You have friends?"

"Every one has been very kind to me," I said gratefully.

"Who would not be kind to one so young and charming?" said Mr. Flemming gallantly. "Well, well, my dear, we must see what can be done." He hesitated a minute, and then said: "Supposing—how would it be if you came to us for a time?"

I jumped at the chance. London! The place for things to happen.

"It's awfully kind of you," I said. "Might I really? Just while I'm looking round. I must start out to earn my living, you know?"

"Yes, yes, my dear child. I quite understand. We will look round for something—suitable."

I felt instinctively that Mr. Flemming's ideas of "something suitable" and mine were likely to be widely divergent, but it was certainly not the moment to air my views.

"That is settled then. Why not return with me today?"

"Oh, thank you, but will Mrs. Flemming——"

"My wife will be delighted to welcome you."

I wonder if husbands know as much about their wives as they think they do. If I had a husband, I should hate him to bring home orphans without consulting me first.

"We will send her a wire from the station," continued the lawyer.

My few personal belongings were soon packed. I contemplated my hat sadly before putting it on. It had originally been what I call a "Mary" hat, meaning by that the kind of hat a housemaid ought to wear on her day out—but doesn't! A limp thing of black straw with a suitably depressed brim. With the inspiration of genius, I had kicked it once, punched it twice, dented in the crown and affixed to it a thing like a cubist's dream of a jazz carrot. The result had been distinctly chic. The carrot I had already removed, of course, and now I proceeded to undo the rest of my handiwork. The "Mary" hat resumed its former status with an additional battered appearance which made it even more depressing than formerly. I might as well look as much like the popular conception of an orphan as possible. I was just a shade nervous of Mrs. Flemming's reception, but hoped my appearance might have a sufficiently disarming effect.

Mr. Flemming was nervous too. I realized that as we went up the stairs of the tall house in a quiet Kensington Square. Mrs. Flemming greeted me pleasantly enough. She was a stout, pleasant woman of the "good wife and mother" type. She took me up to a spotless chintz-hung bedroom, hoped I had everything I wanted, informed me that tea would be ready in about a quarter of an hour, and left me to my own devices.

I heard her voice, slightly raised, as she entered the drawing-room below on the first floor.

"Well, Henry, why on earth——" I lost the rest, but the acerbity of the tone was evident. And a few minutes later another phrase floated up to me, in an even more acid voice:

"I agree with you! She is certainly *very* good-looking."

It is really a hard life. Men will not be nice to you if you are not good-looking, and women will not be nice to you if you are.

With a deep sigh I proceeded to do things to my hair. I have nice hair. It is black—a real black, not dark brown, and it grows well back from my forehead and down over the ears. With a ruthless hand I dragged it upwards. As ears, my ears are quite all right, but there is no doubt about it, ears are *démodé* nowadays. They are like the "Queen of Spain's legs" in Professor Peterson's young day. When I had finished I looked almost unbelievably like the kind of orphan that walks out in a queue with a little bonnet and a red cloak.

I noticed when I went down that Mrs. Flemming's eyes rested on my exposed ears with quite a kindly glance. Mr. Flemming seemed puzzled. I had no doubt that he was saying to himself, "What *has* the child done to herself?"

On the whole the rest of the day passed off well. It was settled that I was to start at once to look for something to do.

When I went to bed, I stared earnestly at my face in the glass. Was I really good-looking? Honestly, I couldn't say I thought so! I hadn't got a straight Grecian nose, or a rosebud mouth, or any of the things you ought to have. It is true that a curate once told me that my eyes were like "imprisoned sunshine in a dark, dark wood"—but curates always know so many quotations, and fire them off at random. I'd much prefer to have Irish blue eyes than dark green ones with yellow flecks! Still, green is a good colour for adventuresses.

I wound a black garment tightly round me, leaving my arms and shoulders bare. Then I brushed back my hair and pulled it well down over my ears again. I put a lot of powder on my face, so that the skin seemed even whiter than usual. I fished about until I found some old lip-salve, and I put oceans of it on my lips. Then I did under my eyes with burnt cork. Finally, I draped a red ribbon over my bare shoulder, stuck a scarlet feather in my hair, and placed a cigarette in one corner of my mouth. The whole effect pleased me very much.

"Anna the Adventuress," I said aloud, nodding at my reflection. "Anna the Adventuress. Episode I, 'The House in Kensington'!"

Girls are foolish things.

3

In the succeeding weeks I was a good deal bored. Mrs. Flemming and her friends seemed to me to be supremely uninteresting. They talked for hours of themselves and their children and of the difficulties of getting good milk for the children and of what they said to the Dairy when the milk wasn't good. Then they would go on to servants, and the difficulties of getting good servants and of what they had said to the woman at the Registry Office and of what the woman at the Registry Office had said to them. They never seemed to read the papers or to care about what went on in the world. They disliked travelling—everything was so different to England. The Riviera was all right, of course, because one met all one's friends there.

I listened and contained myself with difficulty. Most of these women were rich. The whole wide beautiful world was theirs to wander in and they deliberately stayed in dirty dull London and talked about milkmen and servants! I think now, looking back, that I was perhaps a shade intolerant. But they *were* stupid—stupid even at their chosen job: most of them kept the most extraordinarily inadequate and muddled housekeeping accounts.

My affairs did not progress very fast. The house and furniture had been sold, and the amount realized had just covered our debts. As yet, I had not been successful in finding a post. Not that I really wanted one! I had the firm conviction that, if I went about looking for adventure, adventure would meet me halfway. It is a theory of mine that one always gets what one wants.

My theory was about to be proved in practice.

It was early in January—the 8th, to be exact. I was returning from an unsuccessful interview with a lady who said she wanted a secretary-companion, but really seemed to require a strong charwoman who would work twelve hours a day for £25 a year. Having parted with mutual veiled impoliteness, I walked down Edgware Road (the interview had taken place in a house in St. John's Wood) and across Hyde Park to St. George's Hospital. There I entered Hyde Park Corner Tube Station and took a ticket to Gloucester Road.

Once on the platform I walked to the extreme end of it. My inquiring mind wished to satisfy itself as to whether there really *were* points and an opening between the two tunnels just beyond the station in the direction of Down Street. I was foolishly pleased to find I was right. There were not many people on the platform, and at the extreme end there was only myself and one man. As I passed him, I sniffed dubiously. If there is one smell I cannot bear it is that of moth balls! This man's heavy overcoat simply reeked of them. And yet most men begin to wear their winter overcoats before January, and consequently by this time the smell ought to have worn off. The man was beyond me, standing close to the edge of the tunnel. He seemed lost in thought, and I was able to stare at him without rudeness. He was a small thin man, very brown of face, with light blue eyes and a small dark beard.

"Just come from abroad," I deduced. "That's why his overcoat smells so. He's come from India. Not an officer, or he wouldn't have a beard. Perhaps a tea-planter."

At this moment the man turned as though to retrace his steps along the platform. He glanced at me and then his eyes went on to something behind me, and his face changed. It was distorted by fear—almost panic. He stood a step backwards as though involuntarily recoiling from some danger, forgetting that he was standing on the extreme edge of the platform, and went down and over.

There was a vivid flash from the rails and a crackling sound. I shrieked. People came running up. Two station officials seemed to materialize from nowhere and took command.

I remained where I was, rooted to the spot by a sort of horrible fascination. Part of me was appalled at the sudden disaster, and another part of me was coolly and dispassionately interested in the methods employed for lifting the man off the live rail and back onto the platform.

"Let me pass, please. I am a medical man."

A tall man with a brown beard pressed past me and bent over the motionless body.

As he examined it, a curious sense of unreality seemed to possess me. The thing wasn't real—couldn't be. Finally, the doctor stood upright and shook his head.

"Dead as a door-nail. Nothing to be done."

We had all crowded nearer, and an aggrieved porter raised his voice.

"Now then, stand back there, will you? What's the sense in crowding round."

A sudden nausea seized me, and I turned blindly and ran up the stairs towards the lift. I felt that it was too horrible. I must get out into the open air. The doctor who had examined the body was just ahead of me. The lift was just about to go up, another having descended, and he broke into a run. As he did so, he dropped a piece of paper.

I stopped, picked it up, and and ran after him. But the lift gates clanged in my face, and I was left holding the paper in my hand. By the time the second lift reached the street level, there was no sign of my quarry. I hoped it was nothing important that he had lost, and for the first time I examined it.

It was a plain half-sheet of notepaper with some figures and words scrawled upon it in pencil. This is a facsimile of it:

$$1\ 7 \cdot 1\ 2\ 2 \quad \text{Kilmorden Castle}$$

On the face of it, it certainly did not appear to be of any importance. Still, I hesitated to throw it away. As I stood there holding it, I involuntarily wrinkled my nose in displeasure. Moth balls again! I held the paper gingerly to my nose. Yes, it smelt strongly of them. But, then——

I folded up the paper carefully and put it in my bag. I walked home slowly and did a good deal of thinking.

I explained to Mrs. Flemming that I had witnessed a nasty accident in the Tube and that I was rather upset and would go to my room and lie down. The kind woman insisted on my having a cup of tea. After that I was left to my own devices, and I proceeded to carry out a plan I had formed coming home. I wanted to know what it was that had produced that curious feeling of unreality whilst I was watching the doctor examine the body. First I lay down on the floor in the attitude of the corpse, then I laid a bolster down in my stead, and proceeded to duplicate, so far as I could remember, every motion and gesture of the doctor. When I had finished I had got what I wanted. I sat back on my heels and frowned at the opposite walls.

There was a brief notice in the evening papers that a man had been killed in the Tube, and a doubt was expressed whether it was suicide or accident. That seemed to me to make my duty clear, and when Mr. Flemming heard my story he quite agreed with me.

"Undoubtedly you will be wanted at the inquest. You say no one else was near enough to see what happened?"

"I had the feeling some one was coming up behind me, but I can't be sure—and, anyway, they wouldn't be as near as I was."

The inquest was held. Mr. Flemming made all the arrangements and took me there with him. He seemed to fear that it would be a great ordeal to me, and I had to conceal from him my complete composure.

The deceased had been identified as L. B. Carton. Nothing had been found in his pockets except a house-agent's order to view a house on the river near Marlow. It was in the name of L. B. Carton, Russell Hotel. The bureau clerk from the hotel identified the man as having arrived the day before and booked a room under that name. He had registered as L. B. Carton, Kimberley, South Africa. He had evidently come straight off the steamer.

I was the only person who had seen anything of the affair.

"You think it was an accident?" the coroner asked me.

"I am positive of it. Something alarmed him, and he stepped backwards blindly without thinking what he was doing."

"But what could have alarmed him?"

"That I don't know. But there was something. He looked panic-stricken."

A stolid juryman suggested that some men were terrified of cats. The man might have seen a cat. I didn't think his suggestion a very brilliant one, but it seemed to pass muster with the jury, who were obviously impatient to get home and only too pleased at being able to give a verdict of accident as opposed to suicide.

"It is extraordinary to me," said the coroner, "that the doctor who first examined the body has not come forward. His name and address should have been taken at the time. It was most irregular not to do so."

I smiled to myself. I had my own theory in regard to the doctor. In pursuance of it, I determined to make a call upon Scotland Yard at an early date.

But the next morning brought a surprise. The Flemmings took in the *Daily Budget*, and the *Daily Budget* was having a day after its own heart.

EXTRAORDINARY SEQUEL TO TUBE ACCIDENT.
WOMAN FOUND STRANGLED IN LONELY
HOUSE.

I read eagerly.

"A sensational discovery was made yesterday at the Mill House, Marlow. The Mill House, which is the property of Sir Eustace Pedler, M.P., is to be let unfurnished, and an order to view this property was found in the pocket of the man who was at first thought to have committed suicide by throwing himself on the live rail at Hyde Park Corner Tube Station. In an upper room of the Mill House the body of a beautiful young woman was discovered yesterday, strangled. She is thought to be a foreigner, but so far has not been identified. The police are reported to have a clue. Sir Eustace Pedler, the owner of the Mill House, is wintering on the Riviera."

Nobody came forward to identify the dead woman. The inquest elicited the following facts.

Shortly after one o'clock on January 8th, a well-dressed woman with a slight foreign accent had entered the offices of Messrs. Butler and Park, house-agents, in Knightsbridge. She explained that she wanted to rent or purchase a house on the Thames within easy reach of London. The particulars of several were given to her, including those of the Mill House. She gave the name of Mrs. de Castina and her address as the Ritz, but there proved to be no one of that name staying there, and the hotel people failed to identify the body.

Mrs. James, the wife of Sir Eustace Pedler's gardener, who acted as caretaker to the Mill House and inhabited the small lodge opening on the main road, gave evidence. About three o'clock that afternoon, a lady came to see over the house. She produced an order from the house-agents, and, as was the usual custom, Mrs. James gave her the keys of the house. It was situated at some distance from the lodge, and she was not in the habit of accompanying prospective tenants. A few minutes later a young man arrived. Mrs. James described him as tall and broad-shouldered, with a bronzed face and light grey eyes. He was clean-shaven and was wearing a brown suit. He explained to Mrs. James that he was a friend of the lady who had come to look over the house, but had stopped at the post office to send a telegram. She directed him to the house, and thought no more about the matter.

Five minutes later he reappeared, handed her back the keys and explained that he feared the house would not suit them. Mrs. James did not see the lady, but thought that she had gone on ahead. What she did notice was that the young man seemed very much upset about something. "He looked like a man who'd seen a ghost. I thought he was taken ill."

On the following day another lady and gentleman came to see the property and discovered the body lying on the floor in one of the upstairs rooms. Mrs. James identified it as that of the lady who had come the day before. The house-agents also recognized it as that of "Mrs. de Castina." The police surgeon gave it as his opinion that the woman had been dead about twenty-four hours. The *Daily Budget* had jumped to the conclusion that the man in the Tube had murdered the woman and afterwards committed suicide. However, as the Tube victim was dead at two o'clock, and the woman was alive and well at three o'clock, the only logical conclusion to come to was that the two occurrences had nothing to do with each other, and that the order to view the house at Marlow found in the dead man's pocket was merely one of those coincidences which so often occur in this life.

A verdict of "Wilful Murder against some person or persons unknown," was returned, and the police (and the *Daily Budget*) were left to look for "the man in the brown suit." Since Mrs. James was positive that there was no one in the house when the lady entered it, and that nobody except the young man in question entered it until the following afternoon, it seemed only logical to conclude that he was the murderer of the unfortunate

Mrs. de Castina. She had been strangled with a piece of stout black cord, and had evidently been caught unawares with no time to cry out. The black silk handbag which she carried contained a well-filled notecase and some loose change, a fine lace handkerchief, unmarked, and the return half of a first-class ticket to London. Nothing much there to go upon.

Such were the details published broadcast by the *Daily Budget*, and "Find the Man in the Brown Suit" was their daily war-cry. On an average about five hundred people wrote daily to announce their success in the quest, and tall young men with well-tanned faces cursed the day when their tailors had persuaded them to a brown suit. The accident in the Tube, dismissed as a coincidence, faded out of the public mind.

Was it a coincidence? I was not so sure. No doubt I was prejudiced—the Tube incident was my own pet mystery—but there certainly seemed to me to be a connection of some kind between the two fatalities. In each there was a man with a tanned face—evidently an Englishman living abroad, and there were other things. It was the consideration of these other things that finally impelled me to what I considered a dashing step. I presented myself at Scotland Yard and demanded to see whoever was in charge of the Mill House case.

My request took some time to understand, as I had inadvertently selected the department for lost umbrellas, but eventually I was ushered into a small room and presented to Detective Inspector Meadows.

Inspector Meadows was a small man with a ginger head and what I considered a peculiarly irritating manner. A satellite, also in plain clothes, sat unobtrusively in a corner.

"Good morning," I said nervously.

"Good morning. Will you take a seat? I understand you've something to tell me that you think may be of use to us."

His tone seemed to indicate that such a thing was unlikely in the extreme. I felt my temper stirred.

"Of course you know about the man who was killed in the Tube? The man who had an order to view this same house at Marlow in his pocket."

"Ah!" said the inspector. "You are the Miss Bedding-feld who gave evidence at the inquest. Certainly the man had an order in his pocket. A lot of other people may have had too—only they didn't happen to be killed."

I rallied my forces.

"You didn't think it odd that this man had no ticket in his pocket?"

"Easiest thing in the world to drop your ticket. Done it myself."

"And no money."

"He had some loose change in his trousers pocket."

"But no notecase."

"Some men don't carry a pocket-book or notecase of any kind."

I tried another tack.

"You don't think it's odd that the doctor never came forward afterwards?"

"A busy medical man very often doesn't read the papers. He probably forgot all about the accident."

"In fact, inspector, you are determined to find nothing odd," I said sweetly.

"Well, I'm inclined to think you're a little too fond of the word, Miss Beddingfeld. Young ladies are romantic. I know—fond of mysteries and such-like. But as I'm a busy man—"

I took the hint and rose.

The man in the corner raised a meek voice.

"Perhaps the young lady would tell us briefly what her ideas really are on the subject, inspector?"

The inspector fell in with the suggestion readily enough.

"Yes, come now, Miss Beddingfeld, don't be offended. You've asked questions and hinted things. Just say straight out what it is you've got in your head."

I wavered between injured dignity and the overwhelming desire to express my theories. Injured dignity went to the wall.

"You said at the inquest you were positive it wasn't suicide?"

"Yes, I'm quite certain of that. The man was frightened. What frightened him? It wasn't me. But some one might have been walking up the platform towards us—some one he recognized."

"You didn't see any one?"

"No," I admitted. "I didn't turn my head. Then, as soon as the body was recovered from the line, a man pushed forward to examine it, saying he was a doctor."

"Nothing unusual in that," said the inspector dryly.

"But he wasn't a doctor."

"What?"

"He wasn't a doctor," I repeated.

"How do you know that, Miss Beddingfeld?"

"It's difficult to say, exactly. I've worked in Hospital during the war, and I've seen doctors handle bodies. There's a sort of deft professional callousness that this man hadn't got. Besides, a doctor doesn't usually feel for the heart on the right side of the body."

"He did that?"

"Yes, I didn't notice it specially at the time—except that I felt there was something wrong. But I worked it out when I got home, and then I saw why the whole thing had looked so unhandy to me at the time."

"H'm," said the inspector. He was reaching slowly for pen and paper.

"In running his hands over the upper part of the man's body he would have ample opportunity to take anything he wanted from the pockets."

"Doesn't sound likely to me," said the inspector. "But—well, can you describe him at all?"

"He was tall and broad-shouldered, wore a dark overcoat and black boots, a bowler hat. He had a dark pointed beard and gold-rimmed eyeglasses."

"Take away the overcoat, the beard and the eyeglasses, and there wouldn't be much to know him by," grumbled the inspector. "He could alter his appearance easy enough in five minutes if he wanted to—which he would do if he's the swell pickpocket you suggest."

I had not intended to suggest anything of the kind. But from this moment I gave the inspector up as hopeless.

"Nothing more you can tell us about him?" he demanded, as I rose to depart.

"Yes," I said. I seized my opportunity to fire a parting shot. "His head was markedly brachycephalic. He will not find it so easy to alter that."

I observed with pleasure that Inspector Meadow's pen wavered. It was clear that he did not know how to spell brachycephalic.

In the first heat of indignation I found my next step unexpectedly easy to tackle. I had had a half-formed plan in my head when I went into Scotland Yard. One to be carried out if my interview there was unsatisfactory (it had been profoundly unsatisfactory). That is, if I had the nerve to go through with it.

Things that one would shrink from attempting normally are easily tackled in a flush of anger. Without giving myself time to reflect, I walked straight to the house of Lord Nasby.

Lord Nasby was the millionaire owner of the *Daily Budget*. He owned other papers—several of them, but the *Daily Budget* was his special child. It was as the owner of the *Daily Budget* that he was known to every householder in the United Kingdom. Owing to the fact that an itinerary of the great man's daily proceedings had just been published, I knew exactly where to find him at this moment. It was his hour for dictating to his secretary in his own house.

I did not, of course, suppose that any young woman who chose to come and ask for him would be at once admitted to the august presence. But I had attended to that side of the matter. In the card-tray in the hall of the Flemmings' house I had observed the card of the Marquis of Loamsley, England's most famous sporting peer. I had removed the card, cleaned it carefully with breadcrumbs, and pencilled upon it the words: "Please give Miss Beddingfeld a few moments of your time." Adventuresses must not be too scrupulous in their methods.

The thing worked. A powdered footman received the card and bore it away. Presently a pale secretary appeared. I fenced with him successfully. He retired defeated. He again reappeared and begged me to follow him. I did so. I entered a large room, a frightened-looking shorthand-typist fled past me like a visitant from the spirit-world. Then the door shut and I was face to face with Lord Nasby.

A big man. Big head. Big face. Big moustache. Big stomach. I pulled myself together. I had not come here to comment on Lord Nasby's stomach. He was already roaring at me.

"Well, what is it? What does Loamsley want? You his secretary? What's it all about?"

"To begin with," I said with as great an appearance of coolness as I could manage, "I don't know Lord Loamsley, and he certainly knows nothing about me. I took his card from the tray in the house of the people I'm staying with, and I wrote those words on it myself. It was important that I should see you."

For a moment it appeared to be a toss up as to whether Lord Nasby had apoplexy or not. In the end, he swallowed twice and got over it.

"I admire your coolness, young woman. Well, you see me! If you interest me, you will continue to see me for exactly two minutes longer."

"That will be ample," I replied. "And I shall interest you. It's the Mill House Mystery."

"If you've found 'The Man in the Brown Suit,' write to the Editor," he interrupted hastily.

"If you will interrupt, I shall be more than two minutes," I said sternly. "I haven't found 'The Man in the Brown Suit,' but I'm quite likely to do so."

In as few words as possible I put the facts of the Tube accident and the conclusions I had drawn from them before him. When I had finished he said unexpectedly:

"What do you know of brachycephalic heads?"

I mentioned Papa.

"The Monkey Man? Eh? Well, you seem to have a head of some kind upon your own shoulders, young woman. But it's all pretty thin, you know. Not much to go upon. And no use to us—as it stands."

"I'm perfectly aware of that."

"What d'you want, then?"

"I want a job on your paper to investigate this matter."

"Can't do that. We've got our own special man on it."

"And I've got my own special knowledge."

"What you've just told me, eh?"

"Oh, no, Lord Nasby. I've still got something up my sleeve."

"Oh, you have, have you? You seem a bright sort of girl. Well, what is it?"

"When this so-called doctor got into the lift, he dropped a piece of paper. I picked it up. It smelt of moth balls. So did the dead man. The doctor didn't. So I saw at once that the doctor must have taken it off the body. It had two words written on it and some figures."

"Let's see it."

Lord Nasby stretched out a careless hand.

"I think not," I said, smiling. "It's my find, you see."

"I'm right. You *are* a bright girl. Quite right to hang on to it. No scruples about not handing it over to the police?"

"I went there to do so this morning. They persisted in regarding the whole thing as having nothing to do with the Marlow affair, so I thought that in the circumstances I was justified in retaining the paper. Besides, the inspector put my back up."

"Short-sighted man. Well, my dear girl, here's all I can do for you. Go on working on this line of yours. If you get anything—anything that's publishable—send it along and you shall have your chance. There's always room for real talent on the *Daily Budget*. But you've got to make good first. See?"

I thanked him and apologized for my methods.

"Don't mention it. I rather like cheek—for a pretty girl. By the way, you said two minutes and you've been three, allowing for interruptions. For a woman, that's quite remarkable! Must be your scientific training."

I was in the street again, breathing hard as though I had been running. I found Lord Nasby rather wearing as a new acquaintance.

I went home with a feeling of exultation. My scheme had succeeded far better than I could possibly have hoped. Lord Nasby had been positively genial. It only now remained for me to "Make good," as he expressed it. Once locked in my own room, I took out my precious piece of paper and studied it attentively. Here was the clue to the mystery.

To begin with, what did the figures represent? There were five of them, and a dot after the first two. "Seventeen—one hundred and twenty-two," I murmured.

That did not seem to lead to anything.

Next I added them up. That is often done in works of fiction and leads to surprising deductions.

"One and seven make eight and one is nine and two are eleven and two are thirteen."

Thirteen! Fateful number! Was this a warning to me to leave the whole thing alone? Very possibly. Anyway, except as a warning, it seemed to be singularly useless. I declined to believe that any conspirator would take that way of writing thirteen in real life. If he meant thirteen, he would write thirteen. "13"—like that.

There was a space between the one and the two. I accordingly subtracted twenty-two from a hundred and seventy-one. The result was a hundred and fifty-nine. I did it again and made it a hundred and forty-nine. These arithmetical exercises were doubtless excellent practice, but as regarded the solution of the mystery, they seemed totally ineffectual. I left arithmetic alone, not attempting fancy division or multiplication, and went on to the words.

Kilmorden Castle. That was something definite. A place. Probably the cradle of an aristocratic family. (Missing heir? Claimant to title?) Or possibly a picturesque ruin. (Buried treasure?)

Yes, on the whole I inclined to the theory of buried treasure. Figures always go with buried treasure. One pace to the right, seven paces to the left, dig one foot, descend twenty-two steps. That sort of idea. I could work out that later. The thing was to get to Kilmorden Castle as quickly as possible.

I made a strategic sally from my room and returned laden with books of reference. *Who's Who*, Whitaker, a Gazetteer, a History of Scotch Ancestral Homes, and Somebody or other's British Isles.

Time passed. I searched diligently, but with growing annoyance. Finally, I shut the last book with a bang. There appeared to be no such place as Kilmorden Castle. Here was an unexpected check. There *must* be such a place. Why should any one invent a name like that and write it down on a piece of paper? Absurd!

Another idea occurred to me. Possibly it was a castellated abomination in the suburbs with a high-sounding name invented by its owner. But if so, it was going to be extraordinarily hard to find. I sat back gloomily on my heels (I always sit on the floor to do anything really important) and wondered how on earth I was to set about it.

Was there any other line I could follow? I reflected earnestly and then sprang to my feet delightedly. Of course! I must visit the "scene of the crime." Always done by the best sleuths! And no matter how long afterwards it may be, they always find something that the police have overlooked. My course was clear. I must go to Marlow.

But how was I to get into the house? I discarded several adventurous methods, and plumped for stern simplicity. The house had been to let—presumably was still to let. I would be a prospective tenant.

I also decided on attacking the local house-agents, as having fewer houses on their books.

Here, however, I reckoned without my host. A pleasant clerk produced particulars of about half a dozen desirable properties. It took all my ingenuity to find objections to them. In the end I feared I had drawn a blank.

"And you've really nothing else?" I asked, gazing pathetically into the clerk's eyes. "Something right on the river, and with a fair amount of garden and a small lodge," I added, summing up the main points of the Mill House, as I had gathered them from the papers.

"Well, of course there's Sir Eustace Pedler's place," said the man doubtfully. "The Mill House, you know."

"Not—not where——" I faltered. (Really, faltering is getting to be my strong point.)

"That's it! Where the murder took place. But perhaps you wouldn't like——"

"Oh, I don't think I should mind," I said with an appearance of rallying. I felt my *bona fides* were not quite established. "And perhaps I might get it cheap—in the circumstances."

A master touch, I thought.

"Well, it's possible. There's no pretending that it will be easy to let now—servants and all that, you know. If you like the place after you've seen it, I should advise you to make an offer. Shall I write you out an order?"

"If you please."

A quarter of an hour later I was at the lodge of the Mill House. In answer to my knock, the door flew open and a tall middle-aged woman literally bounced out.

"Nobody can go into the house, do you hear that? Fairly sick of you reporters, I am. Sir Eustace's orders are——"

"I understand the house was to let," I said freezingly, holding out my order. "Of course, if it's already taken——"

"Oh, I'm sure I beg your pardon, miss. I've been fairly pestered with these newspaper people. Not a minute's peace. No, the house isn't let—nor likely to be now."

"Are the drains wrong?" I asked in an anxious whisper.

"Oh, Lord, miss, the *drains* is all right! But surely you've heard about that foreign lady as was done to death here?"

"I believe I did read something about it in the papers," I said carelessly.

My indifference piqued the good woman. If I had betrayed any interest, she would probably have closed up like an oyster. As it was, she positively bridled.

"I should say you did, miss! It's been in all the newspapers. The *Daily Budget's* out still to catch the man who did it. It seems, according to them, as our police are no good at all. Well, I hope they'll get him—although a nice-looking young fellow he was and no mistake. A kind of soldierly look about him—ah, well, I dare say he'd been wounded in the war, and sometimes they go a bit queer afterwards, my sister's boy did. Perhaps she'd used him bad—they're a bad lot, those foreigners. Though she was a fine-looking woman. Stood there where you're standing now."

"Was she dark or fair?" I ventured. "You can't tell from these newspaper portraits."

"Dark hair, and a very white face—too white for nature, I thought, and her lips reddened something cruel. I don't like to see it—a little powder now and then is quite another thing."

We were conversing like old friends now. I put another question.

"Did she seem nervous or upset at all?"

"Not a bit. She was smiling to herself, quiet like, as though she was amused at something. That's why you could have knocked me down with a feather when, the next afternoon, those people came running out calling for the police and saying there'd been a murder done. I shall never get over it, and as for setting foot in that house after dark I wouldn't do it, not if it was ever so. Why, I wouldn't even stay here at the lodge, if Sir Eustace hadn't been down on his bended knees to me."

"I thought Sir Eustace Pedler was at Cannes?"

"So he was, miss. He come back to England when he heard the news, and, as to the bended knees, that was a figure of speech, his secretary, Mr. Pagett, having offered us double pay to stay on, and, as my John says, money is money nowadays."

I concurred heartily with John's by no means original remarks.

"The young man now," said Mrs. James, reverting suddenly to a former point in the conversation. "He *was* upset. His eyes, light eyes, they were, I noticed them particular, was all shining. Excited, *I* thought. But I never dreamt of anything being wrong. Not even when he came out again looking all queer."

"How long was he in the house?"

"Oh, not long, a matter of five minutes maybe."

"How tall was he, do you think? About six foot?"

"I should say so maybe."

"He was clean-shaven, you say?"

"Yes, miss—not even one of these toothbrush moustaches."

"Was his chin at all shiny?" I asked on a sudden impulse.

Mrs. James stared at me with awe.

"Well, now you come to mention it, miss, it *was*. However did you know?"

"It's a curious thing, but murderers often have shiny chins," I explained wildly.

Mrs. James accepted the statement in all good faith.

"Really, now, miss. I never heard that before."

"You didn't notice what kind of a head he had, I suppose?"

"Just the ordinary kind, miss. I'll fetch you the keys, shall I?"

I accepted them, and went on my way to the Mill House. My reconstructions so far I considered good. All along I had realized that the differences between the man Mrs. James had described and my Tube "doctor" were those of non-essentials. An overcoat, a beard, gold-rimmed eyeglasses. The "doctor" had appeared middle-aged, but I remembered that he had stooped over the body like a comparatively young man. There had been a suppleness which told of young joints.

The victim of the accident (the Moth Ball man, as I called him to myself) and the foreign woman, Mrs. de Castina, or whatever her real name was, had had an assignation to meet at the Mill House. That was how I pieced the thing together. Either because they feared they were being watched or for some other reason, they chose the rather ingenious method of both getting an order to view the same house. Thus their meeting there might have the appearance of pure chance.

That the Moth Ball man had suddenly caught sight of the "doctor," and that the meeting was totally unexpected and alarming to him, was another fact of which I was fairly sure. What had happened next? The "doctor" had removed his disguise and followed the woman to Marlow. But it was possible that had he removed it rather hastily traces of spirit-gum might still linger on his chin. Hence my question to Mrs. James.

Whilst occupied with my thoughts I had arrived at the low old-fashioned door of the Mill House. Unlocking it with the key, I passed inside. The hall was low and dark, the place smelt forlorn and mildewy. In spite of myself, I shivered. Did the woman who had come here "smiling to herself" a few days ago feel no chill of premonition as she entered this house? I wondered. Did the smile fade from her lips, and did a nameless dread close round her heart? Or had she gone upstairs, smiling still, unconscious of the doom that was so soon to overtake her? My heart beat a little faster. Was the house really empty? Was doom waiting for me in it also? For the first time, I understood the meaning of the much-used word, "atmosphere." There was an atmosphere in this house, an atmosphere of cruelty, of menace, of evil.

7

Shaking off the feelings that oppressed me, I went quickly upstairs. I had no difficulty in finding the room of the tragedy. On the day the body was discovered it had rained heavily, and large muddy boots had trampled the uncarpeted floor in every direction. I wondered if the murderer had left any footmarks the previous day. It was likely that the police would be reticent on the subject if he had, but on consideration I decided it was unlikely. The weather had been fine and dry.

There was nothing of interest about the room. It was almost square with two big bay windows, plain white walls and a bare floor, the boards being stained round the edges where the carpet had ceased. I searched it carefully, but there was not so much as a pin lying about. The gifted young detective did not seem likely to discover a neglected clue.

I had brought with me a pencil and notebook. There did not seem much to note, but I duly dotted down a brief sketch of the room to cover my disappointment at the failure of my quest. As I was in the act of returning the pencil to my bag, it slipped from my fingers and rolled along the floor.

The Mill House was really old, and the floors were very uneven. The pencil rolled steadily, with increasing momentum, until it came to rest under one of the windows. In the recess of each window there was a broad window-seat, underneath which there was a cupboard. My pencil was lying right against the cupboard door. The cupboard was shut, but it suddenly occurred to me that if it had been open my pencil would have rolled inside. I opened the door, and my pencil immediately rolled in and sheltered modestly in the farthest corner. I retrieved it, noting as I did so that owing to the lack of light and the peculiar formation of the cupboard one could not see it, but had to feel for it. Apart from my pencil the cupboard was empty, but being thorough by nature I tried the one under the opposite window.

At first sight, it looked as though that also was empty, but I grubbed about perseveringly, and was rewarded by feeling my hand close on a hard paper cylinder which lay in a sort of trough, or depression, in the far corner of the cupboard. As soon as I had it in my hand, I knew what it was. A roll of Kodak films. Here was a find!

I realized, of course, that these films might very well be an old roll belonging to Sir Eustace Pedler which had rolled in here and had not been found when the cupboard was emptied. But I did not think so. The red paper was far too fresh-looking. It was just as dusty as it would have been had it laid there for two or three days—that is to say, since the murder. Had it been there for any length of time, it would have been thickly coated.

Who had dropped it? The woman or the man? I remembered that the contents of her handbag had appeared to be intact. If it had been jerked open in the struggle and the roll of films had fallen out, surely some of the loose money would have been scattered about also? No, it was not the woman who had dropped the films.

I sniffed suddenly and suspiciously. Was the smell of moth balls becoming an obsession with me? I could swear that the roll of films smelt of it also? I held them under my nose. They had, as usual, a strong smell of their own, but apart from that I could clearly detect the odour I disliked so much. I soon found the cause. A minute shred of cloth had caught on a rough edge of the centre wood, and that shred was strongly impregnated with moth balls. At some time or another the films had been carried in the overcoat pocket of the man who was killed in the Tube. Was it he who had dropped them here? Hardly. His movements were all accounted for.

No, it was the other man, the "doctor." He had taken the films when he had taken the paper. It was he who had dropped them here during his struggle with the woman.

I had got my clue! I would have the roll developed, and then I would have further developments to work upon.

Very elated, I left the house, returned the keys to Mrs. James and made my way as quickly as possible to the station. On the way back to town, I took out my paper and studied it afresh. Suddenly the figures took on a new significance. Suppose they were a date? 17 1 22. The 17th of January, 1922. Surely that must be it! Idiot that I was not to have thought of it before. But in that case I *must* find out the whereabouts of Kilmorden Castle, for to-day was actually the 14th. Three days. Little enough— almost hopeless when one had no idea of where to look!

It was too late to hand in my roll to-day. I had to hurry home to Kensington so as not to be late for dinner. It occurred to me that there was an easy way of verifying whether some of my conclusions were correct. I asked Mr. Flemming whether there had been a camera amongst the dead man's belongings. I knew that he had taken an interest in the case and was conversant with all the details.

To my surprise and annoyance he replied that there had been no camera. All Carton's effects had been gone over very carefully in the hopes of finding something that might throw light upon his state of mind. He was positive that there had been no photographic apparatus of any kind.

That was rather a set-back to my theory. If he had no camera, why should he be carrying a roll of films?

I set out early next morning to take my precious roll to be developed. I was so fussy that I went all the way to Regent Street to the big Kodak place. I handed it in and asked for a print of each film. The man finished stacking together a heap of films packed in yellow tin cylinders for the tropics, and picked up my roll.

He looked at me.

"You've made a mistake, I think," he said, smiling.

"Oh, no," I said. "I'm sure I haven't."

"You've given me the wrong roll. This is an *unexposed* one."

I walked out with what dignity I could muster. I dare say it is good for one now and again to realize what an idiot one can be! But nobody relishes the process.

And then, just as I was passing one of the big shipping offices, I came to a sudden halt. In the window was a beautiful model of one of the company's boats, and it was labelled "Kenilworth Castle." A wild idea shot through my brain. I pushed the door open and went in. I went up to the counter and in faltering voice (genuine this time!) I murmured:

"Kilmorden Castle?"

"On the 17th from Southampton. Cape Town? First or second class?"

"How much is it?"

"First class, eighty-seven pounds——"

I interrupted him. The coincidence was too much for me. Exactly the amount of my legacy! I would put all my eggs in one basket.

"First class," I said.

I was now definitely committed to the adventure.

8

It is an extraordinary thing that I never seem to get any peace. I am a man who likes a quiet life. I like my Club, my rubber of Bridge, a well-cooked meal, a sound wine. I like England in the summer, and the Riviera in the winter. I have no desire to participate in sensational happenings. Sometimes, in front of a good fire, I do not object to reading about them in the newspaper. But that is as far as I am willing to go. My object in life is to be thoroughly comfortable. I have devoted a certain amount of thought, and a considerable amount of money, to further that end. But I cannot say that I always succeed. If things do not actually happen to me, they happen round me, and frequently, in spite of myself, I become involved. I hate being involved.

All this because Guy Pagett came into my bedroom this morning with a telegram in his hand and a face as long as a mute at a funeral.

Guy Pagett is my secretary, a zealous, painstaking, hard-working fellow, admirable in every respect. I know no one who annoys me more. For a long time I have been racking my brains as to how to get rid of him. But you cannot very well dismiss a secretary because he prefers work to play, likes getting up early in the morning, and has positively no vices. The only amusing thing about the fellow is his face. He has the face of a fourteenth-century poisoner—the sort of man the Borgias got to do their odd jobs for them.

I wouldn't mind so much if Pagett didn't make me work too. My idea of work is something that should be undertaken lightly and airily—trifled with, in fact! I doubt if Guy Pagett has ever trifled with anything in his life. He takes everything seriously. That is what makes him so difficult to live with.

Last week I had the brilliant idea of sending him off to Florence. He talked about Florence and how much he wanted to go there.

"My dear fellow," I cried, "you shall go to-morrow. I will pay all your expenses."

January isn't the usual time for going to Florence, but it would be all one to Pagett. I could imagine him going about, guide-book in hand, religiously doing all the picture galleries. And a week's freedom was cheap to me at the price.

It has been a delightful week. I have done everything I wanted to, and nothing that I did not want to do. But when I blinked my eyes open, and perceived Pagett standing between me and the light at the unearthly hour of 9 A.M. this morning, I realized that freedom was over.

"My dear fellow," I said, "has the funeral already taken place, or is it for later in the morning?"

Pagett does not appreciate dry humour. He merely stared.

"So you know, Sir Eustace?"

"Know what?" I said crossly. "From the expression of your face I inferred that one of your near and dear relatives was to be interred this morning."

Pagett ignored the sally as far as possible.

"I thought you couldn't know about this." He tapped the telegram. "I know you dislike being aroused early—

but it *is* nine o'clock"—Pagett insists on regarding 9 A.M. as practically the middle of the day—"and I thought that under the circumstances——" He tapped the telegram again.

"What is that thing?" I asked.

"It's a telegram from the police at Marlow. A woman has been murdered in your house."

That aroused me in earnest.

"What colossal cheek," I exclaimed. "Why in *my* house? Who murdered her?"

"They don't say. I suppose we shall go back to England at once, Sir Eustace?"

"You need suppose nothing of the kind. Why should we go back?"

"The police——"

"What on earth have I to do with the police?"

"Well, it was your house."

"That," I said, "appears to be more my misfortune than my fault."

Guy Pagett shook his head gloomily.

"It will have a very unfortunate effect upon the constituency," he remarked lugubriously.

I don't see why it should have—and yet I have a feeling that in such matters Pagett's instincts are always right. On the face of it, a Member of Parliament will be none the less efficient because a stray young woman comes and gets herself murdered in an empty house that belongs to him—but there is no accounting for the view the respectable British public takes of a matter.

"She's a foreigner too, and that makes it worse," continued Pagett gloomily.

Again I believe he is right. If it is disreputable to have a woman murdered in your house, it becomes more disreputable if the woman is a foreigner. Another idea struck me.

"Good heavens," I exclaimed, "I hope this won't upset Caroline."

Caroline is the lady who cooks for me. Incidentally she is the wife of my gardener. What kind of a wife she makes I do not know, but she is an excellent cook. James, on the other hand, is not a good gardener—but I support him in idleness and give him the lodge to live in solely on account of Caroline's cooking.

"I don't suppose she'll stay after this," said Pagett.

"You always were a cheerful fellow," I said.

I expect I shall have to go back to England. Pagett clearly intends that I shall. And there is Caroline to pacify.

THREE DAYS LATER.

It is incredible to me that any one who can get away from England in winter does not do so! It is an abominable climate. All this trouble is very annoying. The house-agents say it will be next to impossible to let the Mill House after all the publicity. Caroline has been pacified—with double pay. We could have sent her a cable to that effect from Cannes. In fact, as I have said all along, there was no earthly purpose to serve by our coming over. I shall go back to-morrow.

ONE DAY LATER.

Several very surprising things have occurred. To begin with, I met Augustus Milray, the most perfect example of an old ass the present Government has produced. His manner oozed diplomatic secrecy as he drew me aside in the Club into a quiet corner. He talked a good deal. About South Africa and the industrial situation there. About the growing rumours of a strike on the Rand. Of the secret causes actuating that strike. I listened as patiently as I could. Finally, he dropped his voice to a whisper and explained that certain documents had come to light which ought to be placed in the hands of General Smuts.

"I've no doubt you're quite right," I said, stifling a yawn.

"But how are we to get them to him? Our position in the matter is delicate—very delicate."

"What's wrong with the post?" I said cheerfully. "Put a two-penny stamp on and drop 'em in the nearest letter-box."

He seemed quite shocked at the suggestion.

"My dear Pedler! The common post!"

It has always been a mystery to me why Governments employ Kings' Messengers and draw such attention to their confidential documents.

"If you don't like the post, send one of your young Foreign Office fellows. He'll enjoy the trip."

"Impossible," said Milray, wagging his head in a senile fashion. "There are reasons, my dear Pedler—I assure you there are reasons."

"Well," I said, rising, "all this is very interesting, but I must be off——"

"One minute, my dear Pedler, one minute, I beg of you. Now tell me, in confidence, is it not true that you intend visiting South Africa shortly yourself? You have large interests in Rhodesia, I know, and the question of Rhodesia joining in the Union is one in which you have a vital interest."

"Well, I had thought of going out in about a month's time."

"You couldn't possibly make it sooner? This month? This week, in fact?"

"I could," I said, eyeing him with some interest. "But I don't know that I particularly want to."

"You would be doing the Government a great service—a very great service. You would not find them—er—ungrateful."

"Meaning, you want me to be the postman?"

"Exactly. Your position is an unofficial one, your journey is *bona fide*. Everything would be eminently satisfactory."

"Well," I said slowly, "I don't mind if I do. The one thing I am anxious to do is to get out of England again as soon as possible."

"You will find the climate of South Africa delightful—quite delightful."

"My dear fellow, I know all about the climate. I was out there shortly before the war."

"I am really much obliged to you, Pedler. I will send you round the package by messenger. To be placed in General Smuts's own hands, you understand? The *Kilmorden Castle* sails on Saturday—quite a good boat."

I accompanied him a short way along Pall Mall before we parted. He shook me warmly by the hand, and thanked me again effusively.

I walked home reflecting on the curious by-ways of Governmental policy.

It was the following evening that Jarvis, my butler, informed me that a gentleman wished to see me on private business, but declined to give his name. I have always a lively apprehension of insurance touts, so told Jarvis to say I could not see him. Guy Pagett, unfortunately, when he might for once have been of real use, was laid up with a bilious attack. These earnest, hard-working young men with weak stomachs are always liable to bilious attacks.

Jarvis returned.

"The gentleman asked me to tell you, Sir Eustace, that he comes to you from Mr. Milray."

That altered the complexion of things. A few minutes later I was confronting my visitor in the library. He was a well-built young fellow with a deeply tanned face. A scar ran diagonally from the corner of his eye to the jaw, disfiguring what would otherwise have been a handsome though somewhat reckless countenance.

"Well," I said, "what's the matter?"

"Mr. Milray sent me to you, Sir Eustace. I am to accompany you to South Africa as your secretary."

"My dear fellow," I said, "I've got a secretary already. I don't want another."

"I think you do, Sir Eustace. Where is your secretary now?"

"He's down with a bilious attack," I explained.

"You are sure it's only a bilious attack?"

"Of course it is. He's subject to them."

My visitor smiled.

"It may or may not be a bilious attack. Time will show. But I can tell you this, Sir Eustace, Mr. Milray would not be surprised if an attempt were made to get your secretary out of the way. Oh, you need have no fear for yourself"—I suppose a momentary alarm had flickered across my face—"you are not threatened. Your secretary out of the way, access to you would be easier. In any case, Mr. Milray wishes me to accompany you. The passage-money will be our affair, of course, but you will take the necessary steps about the passport, as though you had decided that you needed the services of a second secretary."

He seemed a determined young man. We stared at each other and he stared me down.

"Very well," I said feebly.

"You will say nothing to any one as to my accompanying you."

"Very well," I said again.

After all, perhaps it was better to have this fellow with me, but I had a premonition that I was getting into deep waters. Just when I thought I had attained peace!

I stopped my visitor as he was turning to depart.

"It might be just as well if I knew my new secretary's name," I observed sarcastically.

He considered for a minute.

"Harry Rayburn seems quite a suitable name," he observed.

It was a curious way of putting it.

"Very well," I said for the third time.

9

(Anne's Narrative Resumed)

It is most undignified for a heroine to be sea-sick. In books the more it rolls and tosses, the better she likes it. When everybody else is ill, she alone staggers along the deck, braving the elements and positively rejoicing in the storm. I regret to say that at the first roll the *Kilmorden* gave, I turned pale and hastened below. A sympathetic stewardess received me. She suggested dry toast and ginger ale.

I remained groaning in my cabin for three days. Forgotten was my quest. I had no longer any interest in solving mysteries. I was a totally different Anne to the one who had rushed back to the South Kensington square so jubilantly from the shipping office.

I smile now as I remember my abrupt entry into the drawing-room. Mrs. Flemming was alone there. She turned her head as I entered.

"Is that you, Anne, my dear? There is something I want to talk over with you."

"Yes?" I said, curbing my impatience.

"Miss Emery is leaving me." Miss Emery was the governess. "As you have not yet succeeded in finding anything, I wondered if you would care—it would be so nice if you remained with us altogether?"

I was touched. She didn't want me, I knew. It was sheer Christian charity that prompted the offer. I felt remorseful for my secret criticism of her. Getting up, I ran impulsively across the room and flung my arms round her neck.

"You're a dear," I said. "A dear, a dear, a dear! And thank you ever so much. But it's all right, I'm off to South Africa on Saturday."

My abrupt onslaught had startled the good lady. She was not used to sudden demonstrations of affection. My words startled her still more.

"To South Africa? My dear Anne. We would have to look into anything of that kind very carefully."

That was the last thing I wanted. I explained that I had already taken my passage, and that upon arrival I proposed to take up the duties of a parlourmaid. It was the only thing I could think of on the spur of the moment. There was, I said, a great demand for parlourmaids in South Africa. I assured her that I was equal to taking care of myself, and in the end, with a sigh of relief at getting me off her hands, she accepted the project without further query. At parting, she slipped an envelope into my hand. Inside it I found five new crisp five-pound notes and the words: "I hope you will not be offended and will accept this with my love." She was a very good, kind woman. I could not have continued to live in the same house with her, but I did recognize her intrinsic worth.

So here I was, with twenty-five pounds in my pocket, facing the world and pursuing my adventure.

It was on the fourth day that the stewardess finally urged me up on deck. Under the impression that I should die quicker below, I had steadfastly refused to leave my bunk. She now tempted me with the advent of Madeira. Hope rose in my breast. I could leave the boat and go ashore and be a parlourmaid there. Anything for dry land.

Muffled in coats and rugs, and weak as a kitten on my legs, I was hauled up and deposited, an inert mass, on a deck-chair. I lay there with my eyes closed, hating life. The purser, a fair-haired young man, with a round boyish face, came and sat down beside me.

"Hullo! Feeling rather sorry for yourself, eh?"

"Yes," I replied, hating him.

"Ah, you won't know yourself in another day or two. We've had rather a nasty dusting in the Bay, but there's smooth weather ahead. I'll be taking you on at quoits to-morrow."

I did not reply.

"Think you'll never recover, eh? But I've seen people much worse than you, and two days later they were the life and soul of the ship. You'll be the same."

I did not feel sufficiently pugnacious to tell him out-right that he was a liar. I endeavoured to convey it by a glance. He chatted pleasantly for a few minutes more, then he mercifully departed. People passed and repassed, brisk couples "exercising," curveting children, laughing young people. A few other pallid sufferers lay, like myself, in deck-chairs.

The air was pleasant, crisp, not too cold, and the sun was shining brightly. Insensibly, I felt a little cheered. I began to watch the people. One woman in particular attracted me. She was about thirty, of medium height and very fair with a round dimpled face and very blue eyes. Her clothes, though perfectly plain, had that in-definable air of "cut" about them which spoke of Paris. Also, in a pleasant but self-possessed way, she seemed to own the ship!

Deck stewards ran to and fro obeying her commands. She had a special deck-chair, and an apparently inexhaustible supply of cushions. She changed her mind three times as to where she would like it placed. Throughout everything she remained attractive and charming. She appeared to be one of those rare people in the world who know what they want, see that they get it, and manage to do so without being offensive. I decided that if I ever recovered—but of course I shouldn't—it would amuse me to talk to her.

We reached Madeira about midday. I was still too inert to move, but I enjoyed the picturesque-looking merchants who came on board and spread their merchandise about the decks. There were flowers too. I buried my nose in an enormous bunch of sweet wet violets and felt distinctly better. In fact, I thought I might just possibly last out the end of the voyage. When my stewardess spoke of the attractions of a little chicken broth, I only protested feebly. When it came I enjoyed it.

My attractive woman had been ashore. She came back escorted by a tall, soldierly-looking man with dark hair and a bronzed face whom I had noticed striding up and down the deck earlier in the day. I put him down at once as one of the strong, silent men of Rhodesia. He was about forty, with a touch of greying hair at either temple, and was easily the best-looking man on board.

When the stewardess brought me up an extra rug, I asked her if she knew who my attractive woman was.

"That's a well-known society lady, the Hon. Mrs. Clarence Blair. You must have read about her in the papers."

I nodded, looking at her with renewed interest. Mrs. Blair was very well known indeed as one of the smartest women of the day. I observed, with some amusement, that she was the centre of a good deal of attention. Several people essayed to scrape acquaintance with the pleasant informality that a boat allows. I admired the polite way that Mrs. Blair snubbed them. She appeared to have adopted the strong, silent man as her special cavalier, and he seemed duly sensible of the privilege accorded him.

The following morning, to my surprise, after taking a few turns round the deck with her attentive companion, Mrs. Blair came to a halt by my chair.

"Feeling better this morning?"

I thanked her, and said I felt slightly more like a human being.

"You did look ill yesterday. Colonel Race and I decided that we should have the excitement of a funeral at sea—but you've disappointed us."

I laughed.

"Being up in the air has done me good."

"Nothing like fresh air," said Colonel Race, smiling.

"Being shut up in those stuffy cabins would kill any one," declared Mrs. Blair, dropping into a seat by my side and dismissing her companion with a little nod. "You've got an outside, I hope?"

I shook my head.

"My dear girl! Why don't you change? There's plenty of room. A lot of people got off at Madeira, and the boat's very empty. Talk to the purser about it. He's a nice little boy—he changed me into a beautiful cabin because I didn't care for the one I'd got. You talk to him at lunch-time when you go down."

I shuddered.

"I couldn't move."

"Don't be silly. Come and take a walk now with me."

She dimpled at me encouragingly. I felt very weak on my legs at first, but as we walked briskly up and down I began to feel a brighter and better being.

After a turn or two, Colonel Race joined us again.

"You can see the Grand Peak of Tenerife from the other side."

"Can we? Can I get a photograph of it, do you think?"

"No—but that won't deter you from snapping off at it."

Mrs. Blair laughed.

"You are unkind. Some of my photographs are very good."

"About three per cent effective, I should say."

We all went round to the other side of the deck. There glimmering white and snowy, enveloped in a delicate rose-coloured mist, rose the glistening pinnacle. I uttered an exclamation of delight. Mrs. Blair ran for her camera.

Undeterred by Colonel Race's sardonic comments, she snapped vigorously:

"There, that's the end of the roll. Oh," her tone changed to one of chagrin, "I've had the thing at 'bulb' all the time."

"I always like to see a child with a new toy," murmured the Colonel.

"How horrid you are—but I've got another roll."

She produced it in triumph from the pocket of her sweater. A sudden roll of the boat upset her balance, and as she caught at the rail to steady herself the roll of films flashed over the side.

"Oh!" cried Mrs. Blair, comically dismayed. She leaned over. "Do you think they have gone overboard?"

"No, you may have been fortunate enough to brain an unlucky steward in the deck below."

A small boy who had arrived unobserved a few paces to our rear blew a deafening blast on a bugle.

"Lunch," declared Mrs. Blair ecstatically. "I've had nothing to eat since breakfast, except two cups of beef-tea. Lunch, Miss Beddingfeld?"

"Well," I said waveringly. "Yes, I *do* feel rather hungry."

"Splendid. You're sitting at the purser's table, I know. Tackle him about the cabin."

I found my way down to the saloon, began to eat gingerly, and finished by consuming an enormous meal. My friend of yesterday congratulated me on my recovery. Every one was changing cabins to-day, he told me and he promised that my things should be moved to an outside one without delay.

There were only four at our table, myself, a couple of elderly ladies, and a missionary who talked a lot about "our poor black brothers."

I looked round at the other tables. Mrs. Blair was sitting at the Captain's table, Colonel Race next to her. On the other side of the Captain was a distinguished-looking, grey-haired man. A good many people I had already noticed on deck, but there was one man who had not previously appeared. Had he done so, he could hardly have escaped my notice. He was tall and dark, and had such a peculiarly sinister type of countenance that I was quite startled. I asked the purser, with some curiosity, who he was.

"That man? Oh, that's Sir Eustace Pedler's secretary. Been very sea-sick, poor chap, and not appeared before. Sir Eustace has got two secretaries with him, and the sea's been too much for both of them. The other fellow hasn't turned up yet. This man's name is Pagett."

So Sir Eustace Pedler, the owner of the Mill House, was on board. Probably only a coincidence, and yet——

"That's Sir Eustace," my informant continued, "sitting next to the Captain. Pompous old ass."

The more I studied the secretary's face, the less I liked it. Its even pallor, the secretive, heavy-lidded eyes, the curiously flattened head—it all gave me a feeling of distaste, of apprehension.

Leaving the saloon at the same time as he did, I was close behind him as he went up on deck. He was speaking to Sir Eustace, and I overheard a fragment or two.

"I'll see about the cabin at once then, shall I? Its impossible to work in yours, with all your trunks."

"My dear fellow," Sir Eustace replied. "My cabin is intended *(a)* for me to sleep in, and *(b)* to attempt to dress in. I never had any intentions of allowing you to sprawl about the place making an infernal clicking with that typewriter of yours."

"That's just what I say, Sir Eustace, we must have somewhere to work——"

Here I parted company from them, and went below to see if my removal was in progress. I found my steward busy at the task.

"Very nice cabin, miss. On D deck. No. 13."

"Oh, no!" I cried. "*Not* 13."

Thirteen is the one thing I am superstitious about. It was a nice cabin too. I inspected it, wavered, but a foolish superstition prevailed. I appealed almost tearfully to the steward.

"Isn't there any other cabin I can have?"

The steward reflected.

"Well, there's 17, just along on the starboard side. That was empty this morning, but I rather fancy it's been allotted to some one. Still, as the gentleman's things aren't in yet, and as gentlemen aren't anything like so superstitious as ladies, I dare say he wouldn't mind changing."

I hailed the proposition gratefully, and the steward departed to obtain permission from the purser. He returned grinning.

"That's all right, miss. We can go along."

He led the way to 17. It was not quite as large as No. 13, but I found it eminently satisfactory.

"I'll fetch your things right away, miss," said the steward.

But at that moment, the man with the sinister face (as I had nicknamed him) appeared in the doorway.

"Excuse me," he said, "but this cabin is reserved for the use of Sir Eustace Pedler."

"That's all right, sir," explained the steward. "We're fitting up No. 13 instead."

"No, it was No. 17 I was to have."

"No. 13 is a better cabin, sir—larger."

"I specially selected No. 17, and the purser said I could have it."

"I'm sorry," I said coldly. "But No. 17 has been allotted to me."

"I can't agree to that."

The steward put in his oar.

"The other cabin's just the same, only better."

"I want No. 17."

"What's all this?" demanded a new voice. "Steward, put my things in here. This is my cabin."

It was my neighbor at lunch, the Rev. Edward Chichester.

"I beg your pardon," I said. "It's my cabin."

"It is allotted to Sir Eustace Pedler," said Mr. Pagett.

We were all getting rather heated.

"I'm sorry to have to dispute the matter," said Chichester with a meek smile which failed to mask his determination to get his own way. Meek men are always obstinate, I have noticed.

He edged himself sideways into the doorway.

"You're to have No. 28 on the port side," said the steward. "A very good cabin, sir."

"I am afraid that I must insist. No. 17 was the cabin promised to me."

We had come to an impasse. Each one of us was determined not to give way. Strictly speaking, I, at any rate, might have retired from the contest and eased matters by offering to accept Cabin 28. So long as I did not have 13 it was immaterial to me what other cabin I had. But my blood was up. I had not the least intention of being the first to give way. And I disliked Chichester. He had false teeth which clicked when he ate. Many men have been hated for less.

We all said the same things over again. The steward assured us, even more strongly, that both the other cabins were better cabins. None of us paid any attention to him.

Pagett began to lose his temper. Chichester kept his serenely. With an effort I also kept mine. And still none of us would give way an inch.

A wink and a whispered word from the steward gave me my cue. I faded unobtrusively from the scene. I was lucky enough to encounter the purser almost immediately.

"Oh, please," I said, "you did say I could have Cabin 17? And the others won't go away. Mr. Chichester and Mr. Pagett. You *will* let me have it, won't you?"

I always say that there are no people like sailors for being nice to women. My little purser came to the scratch splendidly. He strode to the scene, informed the disputants that No. 17 was my cabin, they could have Nos. 13 and 28 respectively or stay where they were— whichever they chose.

I permitted my eyes to tell him what a hero he was and then installed myself in my new domain. The encounter had done me worlds of good. The sea was smooth, the weather growing daily warmer. Sea-sickness was a thing of the past!

I went up on deck and was initiated into the mysteries of deck-quoits. I entered my name for various sports. Tea was served on deck, and I ate heartily. After tea, I played shovel-board with some pleasant young men. They were extraordinarily nice to me. I felt that life was satisfactory and delightful.

The dressing bugle came as a surprise and I hurried to my new cabin. The stewardess was awaiting me with a troubled face.

"There's a terrible smell in your cabin, miss. What it is, I'm sure I can't think, but I doubt if you'll be able to sleep here. There's a deck cabin up on C deck, I believe. You might move into that—just for the night, anyway."

The smell really was pretty bad—quite nauseating. I told the stewardess I would think over the question of moving whilst I dressed. I hurried over my toilet, sniffing distastefully as I did so.

What *was* the smell? Dead rat? No, worse than that—and quite different. Yet I knew it! It was something I had smelt before. Something——Ah! I had got it. Asafœtida! I had worked in a Hospital dispensary during the war for a short time and had become acquainted with various nauseous drugs.

Asafœtida, that was it. But how——

I sank down on the sofa, suddenly realizing the thing. Somebody had put a pinch of asafœtida in my cabin. Why? So that I should vacate it? Why were they so anxious to get me out? I thought of the scene this afternoon from a rather different point of view. What was there about Cabin 17 that made so many people anxious to get hold of it? The other two cabins were better cabins, why had both men insisted on sticking to 17?

17. How the number persisted. It was on the 17th I had sailed from Southampton. It was a 17—I stopped with a sudden gasp. Quickly I unlocked my suit-case, and took my precious paper from its place of concealment in some rolled stockings.

17 1 22—I had taken that for a date, the date of departure of the *Kilmorden Castle*. Supposing I was wrong. When I came to think of it, would any one, writing down a date, think it necessary to put the year as well as the month? Supposing 17 meant *Cabin* 17? And 1? The time—one o'clock. Then 22 must be the date. I looked up at my little almanac.

To-morrow was the 22nd!

10

I was violently excited. I was sure that I had hit on the right trail at last. One thing was clear, I must not move out of the cabin. The asafœtida had got to be borne. I examined my facts again.

To-morrow was the 22nd, and at 1 A.M. or 1 P.M. something would happen. I plumped for 1 A.M. It was now seven o'clock. In six hours I should know.

I don't know how I got through the evening. I retired to my cabin fairly early. I had told the stewardess that I had a cold in the head and didn't mind smells. She still seemed distressed, but I was firm.

The evening seemed interminable. I duly retired to bed, but in view of emergencies I swathed myself in a thick flannel dressing-gown, and encased my feet in slippers. Thus attired I felt that I could spring up and take an active part in anything that happened.

What did I expect to happen? I hardly knew. Vague fancies, most of them wildly improbable, flitted through my brain. But one thing I was firmly convinced of, at one o'clock *something* would happen.

At various times, I heard my fellow-passengers coming to bed. Fragments of conversation, laughing good-nights, floated in through the open transom. Then, silence. Most of the lights went out. There was still one in the passage outside, and there was therefore a certain amount of light in my cabin. I heard eight bells go. The hour that followed seemed the longest I had ever known. I consulted my watch surreptitiously to be sure I had not overshot the time.

If my deductions were wrong, if nothing happened at one o'clock, I should have made a fool of myself, and spent all the money I had in the world on a mare's-nest. My heart beat painfully.

Two bells went overhead. One o'clock! And nothing. Wait—what was that? I heard the quick light patter of feet running—running along the passage.

Then with the suddenness of a bombshell my cabin door burst open and a man almost fell inside.

"Save me," he said hoarsely. "They're after me."

It was not a moment for argument or explanation. I could hear footsteps outside. I had about forty seconds in which to act. I had sprung to my feet and was standing facing the stranger in the middle of the cabin.

A cabin does not abound in hiding-places for a six-foot man. With one arm I pulled out my cabin trunk. He slipped down behind it under the bunk. I raised the lid. At the same time, with the other hand I pulled down the wash-basin. A deft movement and my hair was screwed into a tiny knot on the top of my head. From the point of view of appearance it was inartistic, from another standpoint it was supremely artistic. A lady, with her hair screwed into an unbecoming knob and in the act of removing a piece of soap from her trunk with which, apparently to wash her neck, could hardly be suspected of harbouring a fugitive.

There was a knock at the door, and without waiting for me to say, "Come in," it was pushed open.

I don't know what I expected to see. I think I had vague ideas of Mr. Pagett brandishing a revolver. Or my missionary friend with a sandbag, or some other lethal weapon. But certainly I did not expect to see a night stewardess, with an inquiring face and looking the essence of respectability.

"I beg your pardon, miss, I thought you called out."

"No," I said, "I didn't."

"I'm sorry for interrupting you."

"That's all right," I said. "I couldn't sleep. I thought a wash would do me good." It sounded rather as though it was a thing I never had as a general rule.

"I'm sorry, miss," said the stewardess again. "But there's a gentleman about who's rather drunk, and we are afraid he might get into one of the ladies' cabins and frighten them."

"How dreadful," I said, looking alarmed. "He won't come in here, will he?"

"Oh, I don't think so, miss. Ring the bell if he does. Good night."

"Good night."

I opened the door and peeped down the corridor. Except for the retreating form of the stewardess, there was nobody in sight.

Drunk! So that was the explanation of it. My histrionic talents had been wasted. I pulled the cabin trunk out a little farther and said:

"Come out at once, please," in an acid voice.

There was no answer. I peered under the bunk. My visitor lay immovable. He seemed to be asleep. I tugged at his shoulder. He did not move.

"Dead drunk," I thought vexedly. "What *am* I to do?"

Then I saw something that made me catch my breath, a small scarlet spot on the floor.

Using all my strength, I succeeded in dragging the man out into the middle of the cabin. The dead whiteness of his face showed that he had fainted. I found the cause of his fainting easily enough. He had been stabbed under the left shoulder-blade—a nasty deep wound. I got his coat off and set to work to attend to it.

At the sting of the cold water he stirred, then sat up.

"Keep still, please," I said.

He was the kind of young man who recovers his faculties very quickly. He pulled himself to his feet and stood there swaying a little.

"Thank you, I don't need anything done for me."

His manner was defiant, almost aggressive. Not a word of thanks—or even common gratitude!

"That is a nasty wound. You must let me dress it."

"You will do nothing of the kind."

He flung the words in my face as though I had been begging a favour of him. My temper, never placid, rose.

"I cannot congratulate you upon your manners," I said coldly.

"I can at least relieve you of my presence." He started for the door, but reeled as he did so. With an abrupt movement I pushed him down upon the sofa.

"Don't be a fool," I said unceremoniously. "You don't want to go bleeding all over the ship, do you?"

He seemed to see the sense of that, for he sat quietly whilst I bandaged up the wound as best I could.

"There," I said, bestowing a pat on my handiwork, "that will have to do for the present. Are you better tempered now and do you feel inclined to tell me what it's all about?"

"I'm sorry that I can't satisfy your very natural curiosity."

"Why not?" I said, chagrined.

He smiled nastily.

"If you want a thing broadcasted, tell a woman. Otherwise keep your mouth shut."

"Don't you think I could keep a secret?"

"I don't think—I know."

He rose to his feet.

"At any rate," I said spitefully, "I shall be able to do a little broadcasting about the events of this evening."

"I've no doubt you will too," he said indifferently.

"How dare you?" I cried angrily.

We were facing each other, glaring at each other with the ferocity of bitter enemies. For the first time, I took in the details of his appearance, the close-cropped dark head, the lean jaw, the scar on the brown cheek, the curious light grey eyes that looked into mine with a sort of reckless mockery hard to describe. There was something dangerous about him.

"You haven't thanked me yet for saving your life?" I said with false sweetness.

I hit him there. I saw him flinch distinctly. Intuitively I knew that he hated above all to be reminded that he owed his life to me. I didn't care. I wanted to hurt him. I had never wanted to hurt any one so much.

"I wish to God you hadn't!" he said explosively. "I'd be better dead and out of it."

"I'm glad you acknowledge the debt. You can't get out of it. I saved your life and I'm waiting for you to say 'Thank you.' "

If looks could have killed, I think he would have liked to kill me then. He pushed roughly past me. At the door he turned back, and spoke over his shoulder.

"I shall not thank you—now or at any other time. But I acknowledge the debt. Some day I will pay it."

He was gone, leaving me with clenched hands, and my heart beating like a mill race.

11

There were no further excitements that night. I had breakfast in bed and got up late the next morning. Mrs. Blair hailed me as I came on deck.

"Good-morning, Gipsy girl, sit down here by me. You look as though you hadn't slept well."

"Why do you call me that?" I asked, as I sat down obediently.

"Do you mind? It suits you somehow. I've called you that in my own mind from the beginning. It's the gipsy element in you that makes you so different from any one else. I decided in my own mind that you and Colonel Race were the only two people on board who wouldn't bore me to death to talk to."

"That's funny," I said, "I thought the same about you—only it's more understandable in your case. You're—you're such an exquisitely finished product."

"Not badly put," said Mrs. Blair, nodding her head. "Tell me all about yourself, Gipsy girl. Why are you going to South Africa?"

I told her something about Papa's life work.

"So you're Charles Beddingfeld's daughter? I thought you weren't a mere provincial Miss! Are you going to Broken Hill to grub up more skulls?"

"I may," I said cautiously. "I've got other plans as well."

"What a mysterious minx you are. But you do look tired this morning. Didn't you sleep well? I can't keep awake on board a boat. Ten hours' sleep for a fool, they say! I could do with twenty!"

She yawned, looking like a sleepy kitten. "An idiot of a steward woke me up in the middle of the night to return me that roll of films I dropped yesterday. He did it in the most melodramatic manner, stuck his arm through the ventilator and dropped them nearly in the middle of my tummy. I thought it was a bomb for a moment!"

"Here's your Colonel," I said, as the tall soldierly figure of Colonel Race appeared on the deck.

"He's not my Colonel particularly. In fact he admires *you* very much, Gipsy girl. So don't run away."

"I want to tie something round my head. It will be more comfortable than a hat."

I slipped quickly away. For some reason or other I was uncomfortable with Colonel Race. He was one of the few people who were capable of making me feel shy.

I went down to my cabin and began looking for a broad band of ribbon, or a motor-veil, with which I could restrain my rebellious locks. Now I am a tidy person, I like my things always arranged in a certain way and I keep them so. I had no sooner opened my drawer than I realized that somebody had been disarranging my things. Everything had been turned over and scattered. I looked in the other drawers and the small hanging cupboard. They told me the same tale. It was as though some one had been making a hurried and ineffectual search for something.

I sat down on the edge of the bunk with a grave face. Who had been searching my cabin and what had they been looking for? Was it the half-sheet of paper with scribbled figures and words? I shook my head, dissatisfied. Surely that was past history now. But what else could there be?

I wanted to think. The events of last night, though exciting, had not really done anything to elucidate matters. Who was the young man who had burst into my cabin so abruptly? I had not seen him on board previously, either on deck or in the saloon. Was he one of the ship's company or was he a passenger? Who had stabbed him? Why had they stabbed him? And why, in the name of goodness, should Cabin No. 17 figure so prominently? It was all a mystery, but there was no doubt that some very peculiar occurrences were taking place on the *Kilmorden Castle*.

I counted off on my fingers the people on whom it behoved me to keep a watch.

Setting aside my visitor of the night before, but promising myself that I would discover him on board before another day had passed, I selected the following persons as worthy of my notice.

(1) Sir Eustace Pedler. He was the owner of the Mill House and his presence on the *Kilmorden Castle* seemed something of a coincidence.

(2) Mr. Pagett, the sinister-looking secretary, whose eagerness to obtain Cabin 17 had been so very marked. N.B. Find out whether he had accompanied Sir Eustace to Cannes.

(3) The Rev. Edward Chichester. All I had against him was his obstinacy over Cabin 17, and that might be entirely due to his own peculiar temperament. Obstinacy can be an amazing thing.

But a little conversation with Mr. Chichester would not come amiss, I decided. Hastily tying a handkerchief round my rebellious locks, I went up on deck again, full of purpose. I was in luck. My quarry was leaning against the rail, drinking beef tea. I went up to him.

"I hope you've forgiven me over Cabin 17," I said, with my best smile.

"I consider it unchristian to bear a grudge," said Mr. Chichester coldly. "But the purser had distinctly promised me that cabin."

"Pursers are such busy men, aren't they?" I said vaguely. "I suppose they're bound to forget sometimes."

Mr. Chichester did not reply.

"Is this your first visit to Africa?" I inquired conversationally.

"To South Africa, yes. But I have worked for the last two years amongst the cannibal tribes in the interior of East Africa."

"How thrilling! Have you had many narrow escapes?"

"Escapes?"

"Of being eaten, I mean?"

"You should not treat sacred subjects with levity, Miss Beddingfeld."

"I didn't know that cannibalism was a sacred subject," I retorted, stung.

As the words left my lips, another idea struck me. If Mr. Chichester had indeed spent the last two years in the interior of Africa, how was it that he was not more sunburnt? His skin was as pink and white as a baby's. Surely there was something fishy there? Yet his manner and voice were so absolutely *it*. Too much so perhaps. Was he—or was he not—just a little like a *stage* clergyman?

I cast my mind back to the curates I had known at Little Hampsly. Some of them I had liked, some of them I had not, but certainly none of them had been quite like Mr. Chichester. They had been human—he was a glorified type.

I was debating all this when Sir Eustace Pedler passed down the deck. Just as he was abreast of Mr. Chichester, he stooped and picked up a piece of paper which he handed to him, remarking, "You've dropped something."

He passed on without stopping, and so probably did not notice Mr. Chichester's agitation. I did. Whatever it was he had dropped, its recovery agitated him considerably. He turned a sickly green, and crumpled up the sheet of paper into a ball. My suspicions were accentuated a hundred-fold.

He caught my eye, and hurried into explanations.

"A—a—fragment of a sermon I was composing," he said with a sickly smile.

"Indeed?" I rejoined politely.

A fragment of a sermon, indeed! No, Mr. Chichester—too weak for words!

He soon left me with a muttered excuse. I wished, oh, how I wished, that I had been the one to pick up that paper and not Sir Eustace Pedler! One thing was clear, Mr. Chichester could not be exempted from my list of suspects. I was inclined to put him top of the three.

After lunch, when I came up to the lounge for coffee, I noticed Sir Eustace and Pagett sitting with Mrs. Blair and Colonel Race. Mrs. Blair welcomed me with a smile, so I went over and joined them. They were talking about Italy.

"But it *is* misleading," Mrs. Blair insisted. "*Aqua calda* certainly *ought* to be cold water—not hot."

"You're not a Latin scholar," said Sir Eustace, smiling.

"Men are so superior about their Latin," said Mrs. Blair. "But all the same I notice that when you ask them to translate inscriptions in old churches they can never do it! They hem and haw, and get out of it somehow."

"Quite right," said Colonel Race. "I always do."

"But I love the Italians," continued Mrs. Blair. "They're so obliging—though even that has its embarrassing side. You ask them the way somewhere, and instead of saying 'first to the right, second to the left' or something that one could follow, they pour out a flood of well-meaning directions, and when you look bewildered they take you kindly by the arm and walk all the way there with you."

"Is that your experience in Florence, Pagett?" asked Sir Eustace, turning with a smile to his secretary.

For some reason the question seemed to disconcert Mr. Pagett. He stammered and flushed.

"Oh, quite so, yes—er quite so."

Then with a murmured excuse, he rose and left the table.

"I am beginning to suspect Guy Pagett of having committed some dark deed in Florence," remarked Sir Eustace, gazing after his secretary's retreating figure. "Whenever Florence or Italy is mentioned, he changes the subject, or bolts precipitately."

"Perhaps he murdered some one there," said Mrs. Blair hopefully. "He looks—I hope I'm not hurting your feelings, Sir Eustace—but he does look as though he might murder some one."

"Yes, pure Cinquecento! It amuses me sometimes—especially when one knows as well as I do how essentially law-abiding and respectable the poor fellow really is."

"He's been with you some time, hasn't he, Sir Eustace?" asked Colonel Race.

"Six years," said Sir Eustace, with a deep sigh.

"He must be quite invaluable to you," said Mrs. Blair.

"Oh, invaluable! Yes, quite invaluable." The poor man sounded even more depressed, as though the invaluableness of Mr. Pagett was a secret grief to him. Then he added more briskly: "But his face should really inspire you with confidence, my dear lady. No self-respecting murderer would ever consent to look like one. Crippen, now, I believe, was one of the pleasantest fellows imaginable."

"He was caught on a liner, wasn't he?" murmured Mrs. Blair.

There was a slight rattle behind us. I turned quickly. Mr. Chichester had dropped his coffee-cup.

Our party soon broke up; Mrs. Blair went below to sleep and I went out on deck. Colonel Race followed me.

"You're very elusive, Miss Beddingfeld. I looked for you everywhere last night at the dance."

"I went to bed early," I explained.

"Are you going to run away to-night too? Or are you going to dance with me?"

"I shall be very pleased to dance with you," I murmured shyly. "But Mrs. Blair——"

"Our friend, Mrs. Blair, doesn't care for dancing."

"And you do?"

"I care for dancing with you."

"Oh!" I said nervously.

I was a little afraid of Colonel Race. Nevertheless I was enjoying myself. This was better than discussing fossilized skulls with stuffy old professors! Colonel Race was really just my ideal of a stern silent Rhodesian. Possibly I might marry him! I hadn't been asked, it is true, but, as the Boy Scouts say, Be Prepared! And all women, without in the least meaning it, consider every man they meet as a possible husband for themselves or for their best friend.

I danced several times with him that evening. He danced well. When the dancing was over, and I was thinking of going to bed, he suggested a turn round the deck. We walked round three times and finally subsided into two deck-chairs. There was nobody else in sight.

We made desultory conversation for some time.

"Do you know, Miss Beddingfeld, I think that I once met your father? A very interesting man—on his own subject, and it's a subject that has a special fascination for me. In my humble way, I've done a bit in that line myself. Why, when I was in the Dordogne region——"

Our talk became technical. Colonel Race's boast was not an idle one. He knew a great deal. At the same time, he made one or two curious mistakes—slips of the tongue, I might almost have thought then. But he was quick to take his cue from me and to cover them up. Once he spoke of the Mousterian period as succeeding the Aurignacian—an absurd mistake for one who knew anything of the subject.

It was twelve o'clock when I went to my cabin. I was still puzzling over those queer discrepancies. Was it possible that he had "got the whole subject up" for the occasion—that really he knew nothing of archæology? I shook my head, vaguely dissatisfied with that solution.

Just as I was dropping off to sleep, I sat up with a sudden start as another idea flashed into my head. Had *he* been pumping *me*? Were those slight inaccuracies just tests—to see whether I really knew what I was talking about? In other words, he suspected me of not being genuinely Anne Beddingfeld.

Why?

(Extract from the diary of Sir Eustace Pedler)

There is something to be said for life on board ship. It is peaceful. My grey hairs fortunately exempt me from the indignities of bobbing for apples, running up and down the deck with potatoes and eggs, and the more painful sports of "Brother Bill" and Bolster Bar. What amusement people can find in these painful proceedings has always been a mystery to me. But there are many fools in the world. One praises God for their existence and keeps out of their way.

Fortunately I am an excellent sailor. Pagett, poor fellow, is not. He began turning green as soon as we were out of the Solent. I presume my other so-called secretary is also sea-sick. At any rate he has not yet made his appearance. But perhaps it is not sea-sickness, but high diplomacy. The great thing is that *I* have not been worried by him.

On the whole, the people on board are a mangy lot. Only two decent Bridge players and one decent-looking woman—Mrs. Clarence Blair. I've met her in town of course. She is one of the only women I know who can lay claim to a sense of humour. I enjoy talking to her, and should enjoy it more if it were not for a long-legged taciturn ass who has attached himself to her like a limpet. I cannot think that this Colonel Race really amuses her. He's good-looking in his way, but dull as ditch water. One of these strong silent men that lady novelists and young girls always rave over.

Guy Pagett struggled up on deck after we left Madeira and began babbling in a hollow voice about work. What the devil does any one want to work for on board ship? It is true that I promised my publishers my "Reminiscences" early in the summer, but what of it? Who really reads reminiscences? Old ladies in the suburbs. And what do my reminiscences amount to? I've knocked against a certain number of so-called famous people in my lifetime. With the assistance of Pagett, I invent insipid anecdotes about them. And, the truth of the matter is, Pagett is too honest for the job. He won't let me invent anecdotes about the people I might have met but haven't.

I tried kindness with him.

"You look a perfect wreck still, my dear chap," I said easily. "What you need is a deck-chair in the sun. No—not another word. The work must wait."

The next thing I knew he was worrying about an extra cabin. "There's no room to work in your cabin, Sir Eustace. It's full of trunks."

From his tone, you might have thought that trunks were blackbeetles, something that had no business to be there.

I explained to him that, though he might not be aware of the fact, it was usual to take a change of clothing with one when travelling. He gave the wan smile with which he always greets my attempts at humour, and then reverted to the business in hand.

"And we could hardly work in my little hole."

I know Pagett's "little holes"—he usually has the best cabin on the ship.

"I'm sorry the Captain didn't turn out for you this time," I said sarcastically. "Perhaps you'd like to dump some of your extra luggage in my cabin?"

Sarcasm is dangerous with a man like Pagett. He brightened up at once.

"Well, if I could get rid of the typewriter and the stationery trunk—"

The stationery trunk weighs several solid tons. It causes endless unpleasantness with the porters, and it is the aim of Pagett's life to foist it on me. It is a perpetual struggle between us. He seems to regard it as my special personal property. I, on the other hand, regard the charge of it as the only thing where a secretary is really useful.

"We'll get an extra cabin," I said hastily.

The thing seemed simple enough, but Pagett is a person who loves to make mysteries. He came to me the next day with a face like a Renaissance conspirator.

"You know you told me to get Cabin 17 for an office?"

"Well, what of it? Has the stationery trunk jammed in the doorway?"

"The doorways are the same size in all the cabins," replied Pagett seriously. "But I tell you, Sir Eustace, there's something very queer about that cabin."

Memories of reading *The Upper Berth* floated through my mind.

"If you mean that it's haunted," I said, "we're not going to sleep there, so I don't see that it matters. Ghosts don't affect typewriters."

Pagett said that it wasn't a ghost, and that, after all, he hadn't got Cabin 17. He told me a long, garbled story. Apparently he, and a Mr. Chichester, and a girl called Beddingfeld, had almost come to blows over the cabin. Needless to say, the girl had won, and Pagett was apparently feeling sore over the matter.

"Both Cabin 13 and 28 are better cabins," he re-

"Both 13 and 28 are better cabins," he reiterated. "But they wouldn't look at them."

"Well," I said, stifling a yawn, "for that matter, no more would you, my dear Pagett."

He gave me a reproachful look.

"You *told* me to get Cabin 17."

There is a touch of the "boy upon the burning deck" about Pagett.

"My dear fellow," I said testily, "I mentioned No. 17 because I happened to observe that it was vacant. But I didn't mean you to make a stand to the death about it— 13 or 28 would have done us equally well."

He looked hurt.

"There's something more, though," he insisted. "Miss Beddingfeld got the cabin, but this morning I saw Chichester coming out of it in a furtive sort of way."

I looked at him severely.

"If you're trying to get up a nasty scandal about Chichester, who is a missionary—though a perfectly poisonous person—and that attractive child, Anne Beddingfeld, I don't believe a word of it," I said coldly. "Anne Beddingfeld is an extremely nice girl—with particularly good legs. I should say she had far and away the best legs on board."

Pagett did not like my reference to Anne Beddingfeld's legs. He is the sort of man who never notices legs himself—or, if he does, would die sooner than say so. Also he thinks my appreciation of such things frivolous. I like annoying Pagett, so I continued maliciously:

"As you've made her acquaintance, you might ask her to dine at our table to-morrow night. It's the Fancy Dress dance. By the way, you'd better go down to the barber and select a fancy costume for me."

"Surely you will not go in fancy dress?" said Pagett, in tones of horror.

I could see that it was quite incompatible with his idea of my dignity. He looked shocked and pained. I had really no intention of donning fancy dress, but the complete discomfiture of Pagett was too tempting to be forborne.

"What do you mean?" I said. "Of course I shall wear fancy dress. So will you."

Pagett shuddered.

"So go down to the barber's and see about it," I finished.

"I don't think he'll have any out sizes," murmured Pagett, measuring my figure with his eye.

Without meaning it, Pagett can occasionally be extremely offensive.

"And order a table for six in the saloon," I said. "We'll have the Captain, the girl with the nice legs, Mrs. Blair—"

"You won't get Mrs. Blair without Colonel Race," Pagett interposed. "He's asked her to dine with him, I know."

Pagett always knows everything. I was justifiably annoyed.

"Who *is* Race?" I demanded, exasperated.

As I said before, Pagett always knows everything—or thinks he does. He looked mysterious again.

"They say he's a Secret Service chap, Sir Eustace. Rather a great gun too. But of course I don't know for certain."

"Isn't that like the Government?" I exclaimed. "Here's a man on board whose business it is to carry about secret documents, and they go giving them to a peaceful outsider, who only asks to be let alone."

Pagett looked even more mysterious. He came a pace nearer and dropped his voice.

"If you ask me, the whole thing is very queer, Sir Eustace. Look at that illness of mine before we started——"

"My dear fellow," I interrupted brutally, "that was a bilious attack. You're always having bilious attacks."

Pagett winced slightly.

"It wasn't the usual sort of bilious attack. This time——"

"For God's sake, don't go into the details of your condition, Pagett. I don't want to hear them."

"Very well, Sir Eustace. But my belief is that I was deliberately *poisoned!*"

"Ah!" I said. "You've been talking to Rayburn."

He did not deny it.

"At any rate, Sir Eustace, *he* thinks so—and he should be in a position to know."

"By the way, where is the chap?" I asked. "I've not set eyes on him since we came on board."

"He gives out that he's ill, and stays in his cabin, Sir Eustace." Pagett's voice dropped again. "But that's *camouflage*, I'm sure. So that he can watch better."

"Watch?"

"Over your safety, Sir Eustace. In case an attack should be made upon you."

"You're such a cheerful fellow, Pagett," I said. "I trust that your imagination runs away with you. If I were you I should go to the dance as a death's head or an executioner. It will suit your mournful style of beauty."

That shut him up for the time being. I went on deck. The Beddingfeld girl was deep in conversation with the missionary parson, Chichester. Women always flutter round parsons.

A man of my figure hates stooping, but I had the courtesy to pick up a bit of paper that was fluttering round the parson's feet.

I got no word of thanks for my pains. As a matter of fact, I couldn't help seeing what was written on the sheet of paper. There was just one sentence:

"Don't try to play a lone hand or it will be the worse for you."

That's a nice thing for a parson to have. Who is this fellow Chichester, I wonder? He *looks* mild as milk. But looks are deceptive. I shall ask Pagett about him. Pagett always knows everything.

I sank gracefully into my deck-chair by the side of Mrs. Blair, thereby interrupting her *tête-à-tête* with Race, and remarked that I didn't know what the clergy were coming to nowadays.

Then I asked her to dine with me on the night of the Fancy Dress dance. Somehow or other Race managed to get included in the invitation.

After lunch the Beddingfeld girl came and sat with us for coffee. I was right about her legs. They *are* the best on the ship. I shall certainly ask her to dinner as well.

I would very much like to know what mischief Pagett was up to in Florence. Whenever Italy is mentioned, he goes to pieces. If I did not know how intensely respectable he is—I should suspect him of some disreputable *amour* . . .

I wonder now! Even the most respectable men——It would cheer me up enormously if it was so.

Pagett—with a guilty secret! Splendid!

13

It has been a curious evening.

The only costume that fitted me in the barber's emporium was that of a Teddy Bear. I don't mind playing bears with some nice young girls on a winter's evening in England—but it's hardly an ideal costume for the equator. However, I created a good deal of merriment, and won first prize for "brought on board"—an absurd term for a costume hired for the evening. Still as nobody seemed to have the least idea whether they were made or brought, it didn't matter.

Mrs. Blair refused to dress up. Apparently she is at one with Pagett on the matter. Colonel Race followed her example. Anne Beddingfeld had concocted a gipsy costume for herself, and looked extraordinarily well. Pagett said he had a headache and didn't appear. To replace him I asked a quaint little fellow called Reeves. He's a prominent member of the South African Labour party. Horrible little man, but I want to keep in with him, as he gives me information that I need. I want to understand his Rand business from both sides.

Dancing was a hot affair. I danced twice with Anne Beddingfeld and she had to pretend she liked it. I danced once with Mrs. Blair, who didn't trouble to pretend, and victimized various other damsels whose appearance struck me favourably.

Then we went down to supper. I had ordered champagne; the steward suggested Clicquot 1911 as being the best they had on the boat and I fell in with his suggestion. I seemed to have hit on the one thing that would loosen Colonel Race's tongue. Far from being taciturn, the man became actually talkative. For a while this amused me, then it occurred to me that Colonel Race, and not myself, was becoming the life and soul of the party. He chaffed me at length about keeping a diary.

"It will reveal all your indiscretions one of these days, Pedler."

"My dear Race," I said, "I venture to suggest that I am not quite the fool you think me. I may commit indiscretions, but I don't write them down in black and white. After my death, my executors will know my opinion of a great many people, but I doubt if they will find anything to add or detract from their opinion of *me*. A diary is useful for recording the idiosyncrasies of other people—but not one's own."

"There is such a thing as unconscious self-revelation, though."

"In the eyes of the psycho-analyst, all things are vile," I replied sententiously.

"You must have had a very interesting life, Colonel Race?" said Miss Beddingfeld, gazing at him with wide, starry eyes.

That's how they do it, these girls! Othello charmed Desdemona by telling her stories, but, oh, didn't Desdemona charm Othello by the way she listened?

Anyway, the girl set Race off all right. He began to tell lion stories. A man who has shot lions in large quantities has an unfair advantage over other men. It seemed to me that it was time I, too, told a lion story. One of a more sprightly character.

"By the way," I remarked, "that reminds me of a rather exciting tale I heard. A friend of mine was out on a shooting trip somewhere in East Africa. One night he came out of his tent for some reason, and was startled by a low growl. He turned sharply and saw a lion crouching to spring. He had left his rifle in the tent. Quick as thought, he ducked, and the lion sprang right over his head. Annoyed at having missed him, the animal growled and prepared to spring again. Again he ducked, and again the lion sprang right over him. This happened a third time, but by now he was close to the entrance of the tent, and he darted in and seized his rifle. When he emerged, rifle in hand, the lion had disappeared. That puzzled him greatly. He crept round the back of the tent, where there was a little clearing. There, sure enough, was the lion, busily practising low jumps."

This was received with a roar of applause. I drank some champagne.

"On another occasion," I remarked, "this friend of mine had a second curious experience. He was trekking across country, and being anxious to arrive at his destination before the heat of the day he ordered his boys to inspan whilst it was still dark. They had some trouble in doing so, as the mules were very restive, but at last they managed it, and a start was made. The mules raced along like the wind, and when daylight came they saw why. In the darkness, the boys had inspanned a lion as the near wheeler."

This, too, was well received, a ripple of merriment going round the table, but I am not sure that the greatest tribute did not come from my friend, the Labour Member, who remained pale and serious.

"My God!" he said anxiously. "Who un'arnessed hem?"

"I must to go Rhodesia," said Mrs. Blair. "After what you have told us, Colonel Race, I simply must. It's a horrible journey though, five days in the train."

"You must join me on my private car," I said gallantly.

"Oh, Sir Eustace, how sweet of you, do you really mean it?"

"Do I mean it!" I exclaimed reproachfully, and drank another glass of champagne.

"Just about another week, and we shall be in South Africa," sighed Mrs. Blair.

"Ah, South Africa," I said sentimentally, and began to quote from a recent speech of mine at the Colonial Institute. "What has South Africa to show the world? What indeed? Her fruit and her farms, her wool and her wattles, her herds and her hides, her gold and her diamonds——"

I was hurrying on, because I knew that as soon as I paused Reeves would butt in and inform me that the hides were worthless because the animals hung themselves up on barbed wire or something of that sort, would crab everything else, and end up with the hardships of the miners on the Rand. And I was not in the mood to be abused as a Capitalist. However, the interruption came from another source at the magic word diamonds.

"Diamonds!" said Mrs. Blair ecstatically.

"Diamonds!" breathed Miss Beddingfeld.

They both addressed Colonel Race.

"I suppose you've been to Kimberley?"

I had been to Kimberley too, but I didn't manage to say so in time. Race was being inundated with questions. What were mines like? Was it true that the natives were kept shut up in compounds? And so on.

Race answered their questions and showed a good knowledge of his subject. He described the methods of housing the natives, the searches instituted, and the various precautions that De Beers took.

"Then it's practically impossible to steal any diamonds?" asked Mrs. Blair with as keen as air of disappointment as though she had been journeying there for the express purpose.

"Nothing's impossible, Mrs. Blair. Thefts do occur—like the case I told you of where the Kafir hid the stone in his wound."

"Yes, but on a large scale?"

"Once, in recent years. Just before the War in fact. You must remember the case, Pedler. You were in South Africa at the time?"

I nodded.

"Tell us," cried Miss Beddingfeld. "Oh, do tell us!"

Race smiled.

"Very well, you shall have the story. I suppose most of you have heard of Sir Laurence Eardsley, the great South African mining magnate? His mines were gold mines, but he comes into the story through his son. You may remember that just before the War rumours were afield of a new potential Kimberley hidden somewhere in the rocky floor of the British Guiana jungles. Two young explorers, so it was reported, had returned from that part of South America bringing with them a remarkable collection of rough diamonds, some of them of considerable size. Diamonds of small size had been found before in the neighbourhood of the Essequibo and Mazaruni rivers, but these two young men, John Eardsley and his friend Lucas, claimed to have discovered beds of great carbon deposits at the common head of two streams. The diamonds were of every colour, pink, blue, yellow, green, black, and the purest white. Eardsley and Lucas came to Kimberley where they were to submit their gems to inspection. At the same time a sensational robbery was found to have taken place at De Beers. When sending diamonds to England they are made up into a packet. This remains in the big safe, of which the two keys are held by two different men whilst a third man knows the combination. They are handed to the Bank, and the Bank sends them to England. Each package is worth, roughly, about £100,000.

"On this occasion, the Bank was struck by something a little unusual about the sealing of the packet. It was opened, and found to contain knobs of sugar!

"Exactly how suspicion came to fasten on John Eardsley I do not know. It was remembered that he had been very wild at Cambridge and that his father had paid his debts more than once. Anyhow, it soon got about that this story of South American diamond fields was all a fantasy. John Eardsley was arrested. In his possession was found a portion of the De Beer diamonds.

"But the case never came to court. Sir Laurence Eardsley paid over a sum equal to the missing diamonds and De Beers did not prosecute. Exactly how the robbery was committed has never been known. But the knowledge that his son was a thief broke the old man's heart. He had a stroke shortly afterwards. As for John, his Fate was in a way merciful. He enlisted, went to the War, fought there bravely, and was killed, thus wiping out the stain on his name. Sir Laurence himself had a third stroke and died about a month ago. He died intestate and his vast fortune passed to his next of kin, a man whom he hardly knew."

The Colonel paused. A babel of ejaculations and questions broke out. Something seemed to attract Miss Beddingfeld's attention, and she turned in her chair. At the little gasp she gave, I, too, turned.

My new secretary, Rayburn, was standing in the doorway. Under his tan, his face had the pallor of one who has seen a ghost. Evidently Race's story had moved him profoundly.

Suddenly conscious of our scrutiny, he turned abruptly and disappeared.

"Do you know who that is?" asked Anne Beddingfeld abruptly.

"That's my other secretary," I explained. "Mr. Rayburn. He's been seedy up to now."

She toyed with the bread by her plate.

"Has he been your secretary long?"

"Not very long," I said cautiously.

But caution is useless with a woman, the more you hold back, the more she presses forward. Anne Beddingfeld made no bones about it.

"How long?" she asked bluntly.

"Well—er—I engaged him just before I sailed. Old friend of mine recommended him."

She said nothing more, but relapsed into a thoughtful silence. I turned to Race with the feeling that it was my turn to display an interest in his story.

"Who is Sir Laurence's next of kin, Race? Do you know?"

"I should say so," he replied, with a smile. "I am!"

14

(Anne's Narrative Resumed)

It was on the night of the Fancy Dress dance that I decided that the time had come for me to confide in some one. So far I had played a lone hand and rather enjoyed it. Now suddenly everything was changed. I distrusted my own judgment and for the first time a feeling of loneliness and desolation crept over me.

I sat on the edge of my bunk, still in my gipsy dress, and considered the situation. I thought first of Colonel Race. He had seemed to like me. He would be kind, I was sure. And he was no fool. Yet, as I thought it over, I wavered. He was a man of commanding personality. He would take the whole matter out of my hands. And it was *my* mystery! There were other reasons, too, which I would hardly acknowledge to myself, but which made it inadvisable to confide in Colonel Race.

Then I thought of Mrs. Blair. She, too, had been kind to me. I did not delude myself into the belief that that really meant anything. It was probably a mere whim of the moment. All the same, I had it in my power to interest her. She was a woman who had experienced most of the ordinary sensations of life. I proposed to supply her with an extraordinary one! And I liked her; liked her ease of manner, her lack of sentimentality, her freedom from any form of affectation.

My mind was made up. I decided to seek her out then and there. She would hardly be in bed yet.

Then I remembered that I did not know the number of her cabin. My friend, the night stewardess, would probably know. I rang the bell. After some delay it was answered by a man. He gave me the information I wanted. Mrs. Blair's cabin was No. 71. He apologized for the delay in answering the bell, but explained that he had all the cabins to attend to.

"Where is the stewardess, then?" I asked.

"They all go off duty at ten o'clock."

"No—I mean the night stewardess."

"No stewardess on at night, miss."

"But—but a stewardess came the other night—about one o'clock."

"You must have been dreaming, miss. There's no stewardess on duty after ten."

He withdrew and I was left to digest this morsel of information. Who was the woman who had come to my cabin on the night of the 22nd? My face grew graver as I realized the cunning and audacity of my unknown antagonists. Then, pulling myself together, I left my own cabin and sought that of Mrs. Blair. I knocked at the door.

"Who's that?" called her voice from within.

"It's me—Anne Beddingfeld."

"Oh, come in, Gipsy girl."

I entered. A good deal of scattered clothing lay about, and Mrs. Blair herself was draped in one of the loveliest kimonos I had ever seen. It was all orange and gold and black and made my mouth water to look at it.

"Mrs. Blair," I said abruptly, "I want to tell you the story of my life—that is, if it isn't too late, and you won't be bored."

"Not a bit. I always hate going to bed," said Mrs. Blair, her face crinkling into smiles in the delightful way it had. "And I should love to hear the story of your life. You're a most unusual creature, Gipsy girl. Nobody else would think of bursting in on me at 1 A.M. to tell me the story of their life. Especially after snubbing my natural curiosity for weeks as you have done! I'm not accustomed to being snubbed. It's been quite a pleasing novelty. Sit down on the sofa and unburden your soul."

I told her the whole story. It took some time as I was conscientious over all the details. She gave a deep sigh when I had finished, but she did not say at all what I had expected her to say. Instead she looked at me, laughed a little and said:

"Do you know, Anne, you're a very unusual girl? Haven't you ever had qualms?"

"Qualms?" I asked, puzzled.

"Yes, qualms, qualms, qualms! Starting off alone with practically no money. What will you do when you find yourself in a strange country with all your money gone?"

"It's no good bothering about that until it comes. I've got plenty of money still. The twenty-five pounds that Mrs. Flemming gave me is practically intact, and then I won the sweeps yesterday. That's another fifteen pounds. Why, I've got *lots* of money. Forty pounds!"

"Lots of money! My God!" murmured Mrs. Blair. "*I* couldn't do it, Anne, and I've plenty of pluck in my own way. I couldn't start off gaily with a few pounds in my pocket and no idea as to what I was doing and where I was going."

"But that's the fun of it," I cried, thoroughly roused. "It gives one such a splendid feeling of adventure."

She looked at me, nodded once or twice, and then smiled.

"Lucky Anne! There aren't many people in the world who feel as you do."

"Well," I said impatiently, "what do you think of it all, Mrs. Blair?"

"I think it's the most thrilling thing I ever heard! Now, to begin with, you will stop calling me Mrs. Blair. Suzanne will be ever so much better. Is that agreed?"

"I should love it, Suzanne."

"Good girl. Now let's get down to business. You say that in Sir Eustace's secretary—not that long-faced Pagett, the other one—you recognized the man who was stabbed and came into your cabin for shelter?"

I nodded.

"That gives us two links connecting Sir Eustace with the tangle. The woman who was murdered in *his* house, and it's *his* secretary who gets stabbed at the mystic hour of one o'clock. I don't suspect Sir Eustace himself, but it can't be all coincidence. There's a connection somewhere even if he himself is unaware of it."

"Then there's the queer business of the stewardess," she continued thoughtfully. "What was she like?"

"I hardly noticed her. I was so excited and strung up—and a stewardess seemed such an anticlimax. But—yes—I did think her face was familiar. Of course it would be if I'd seen her about the ship."

"Her face seemed familiar to you," said Suzanne. "Sure she wasn't a man?"

"She was very tall," I admitted.

"Hum. Hardly Sir Eustace, I should think, nor Mr. Pagett——Wait!"

She caught up a scrap of paper and began drawing feverishly. She inspected the result with her head poised on one side.

"A very good likeness of the Rev. Edward Chichester. Now for the etceteras." She passed the paper over to me. "Is that your stewardess?"

"Why, yes," I cried. "Suzanne, how clever of you!"

She disdained the compliment with a light gesture.

"I've always had suspicions of that Chichester creature. Do you remember how he dropped his coffee-cup and turned a sickly green when we were discussing Crippen the other day?"

"And he tried to get Cabin 17!"

"Yes, it all fits in so far. But what does it all *mean?* What was really meant to happen at one o'clock in Cabin 17? It can't be the stabbing of the secretary. There would be no point in timing that for a special hour on a special day in a special place. No, it must have been some kind of appointment and he was on his way to keep it when they knifed him. But who was the appointment with? Certainly not with you. It might have been with Chichester. Or it might have been with Pagett."

"That seems unlikely," I objected, "they can see each other any time."

We both sat silent for a minute or two, then Suzanne started off on another tack.

"Could there have been anything hidden in the cabin?"

"That seems more probable," I agreed. "It would explain my things being ransacked the next morning. But there was nothing hidden there, I'm sure of it."

"The young man couldn't have slipped something into a drawer the night before?"

I shook my head.

"I should have seen him."

"Could it have been your precious piece of paper they were looking for?"

"It might have been, but it seems rather senseless. It was only a time and a date—and they were both past by then."

Suzanne nodded.

"That's so of course. No, it wasn't the paper. By the way, have you got it with you? I'd rather like to see it."

I had brought the paper with me as Exhibit A, and I handed it over to her. She scrutinized it, frowning.

"There's a dot after the 17. Why isn't there a dot after the 1 too?"

"There's a space," I pointed out.

"Yes, there's a space, but——"

Suddenly she rose and peered at the paper, holding it as close under the light as possible. There was a repressed excitement in her manner.

"Anne, that isn't a dot! That's a flaw in the paper! A flaw in the paper, you see? So you've got to ignore it, and just go by the spaces—the spaces!"

I had risen and was standing by her. I read out the figures as I now saw them.

"1 71 22."

"You see," said Suzanne, "it's the same, but not quite. It's one o'clock still, and the 22nd—but it's Cabin 71! *My* cabin, Anne!"

We stood staring at each other, so pleased with our new discovery and so rapt with excitement that you might have thought we had solved the whole mystery. Then I fell to earth with a bump.

"But, Suzanne, nothing happened here at one o'clock on the 22nd?"

Her face fell also. "No—it didn't."

Another idea struck me.

"This isn't your cabin, is it, Suzanne? I mean not the one you originally booked?"

"No, the purser changed me into it."

"I wonder if it was booked before sailing for some one—some one who didn't turn up. I suppose we could find out."

"We don't need to find out, Gipsy girl," cried Suzanne. "I know! The purser was telling me about it. The cabin was booked in the name of Mrs. Grey—but it seems that Mrs. Grey was merely a pseudonym for the famous Madame Nadina. She's a celebrated Russian dancer, you know. She's never appeared in London, but Paris has been quite mad about her. She had a terrific success there all through the War. A thoroughly bad lot, I believe, but most attractive. The purser expressed his regret that she wasn't on board in a most heartfelt fashion when he gave me her cabin, and then Colonel Race told me a lot about her. It seems there were very queer stories afloat in Paris. She was suspected of espionage, but they couldn't prove anything. I rather fancy Colonel Race was over there simply on that account. He's told me some very interesting things. There was a regular organized gang, not German in origin at all. In fact the head of it, a man always referred to as 'the Colonel' was thought to be an Englishman, but they never got any clue as to his identity. But there is no doubt that he controlled a considerable organization of international crooks. Robberies, espionages, assaults, he undertook them all—and usually provided an innocent scapegoat to pay the penalty. Diabolically clever, he must have been! This woman was supposed to be one of his agents, but they couldn't get hold of anything to go upon. Yes, Anne, we're on the right track. Nadina is just the woman to be mixed up in this business. The appointment on the morning of the 22nd was with her in this cabin. But where is she? Why didn't she sail?"

A light flashed upon me.

"She meant to sail," I said slowly.

"Then why didn't she?"

"*Because she was dead.* Suzanne, Nadina was the woman murdered at Marlow!"

My mind went back to the bare room in the empty house, and there swept over me again that indefinable sensation of menace and evil. With it came the memory of the falling pencil and the discovery of the roll of films. A roll of films—that struck a more recent note. Where had I heard of a roll of films? And why did I connect that thought with Mrs. Blair?

Suddenly I flew at her and almost shook her in my excitement.

"Your films! The ones that were passed to you through the ventilator? Wasn't that on the 22nd?"

"The ones I lost?"

"How do you know they were the same? Why would any one return them to you that way—in the middle of the night? It's a mad idea. No—they were a message, the films had been taken out of the yellow tin case, and something else put inside. Have you got it still?"

"I may have used it. No, here it is. I remember I tossed it into the rack at the side of the bunk."

She held it out to me.

It was an ordinary round tin cylinder, such as films are packed in for the tropics. I took it with trembling hand, but even as I did so my heart leapt. It was noticeably heavier than it should have been.

With shaking fingers I peeled off the strip of adhesive plaster that kept it air-tight. I pulled off the lid, and a stream of dull glassy pebbles rolled onto the bed.

"Pebbles," I said, keenly, disappointed.

"Pebbles?" cried Suzanne.

The ring in her voice excited me.

"Pebbles? No, Anne, not pebbles! *Diamonds!*"

Diamonds!

I stared, fascinated, at the glassy heap on the bunk. I picked up one which, but for the weight, might have been a fragment of broken bottle.

"Are you sure, Suzanne?"

"Oh, yes, my dear. I've seen rough diamonds too often to have any doubts. They're beauties too, Anne—and some of them are unique, I should say. There's a history behind these."

"The history we heard to-night," I cried.

"You mean——?"

"Colonel Race's story. It can't be a coincidence. He told it for a purpose."

"To see its effect, you mean?"

I nodded.

"Its effect on Sir Eustace?"

"Yes."

But, even as I said it, a doubt assailed me. Was it Sir Eustace who had been subjected to a test, or had the story been told for my benefit? I remembered the impression I had received on that former night of having been deliberately "pumped." For some reason or other, Colonel Race was suspicious. But where did he come in? What possible connection could he have with the affair?

"Who is Colonel Race?" I asked.

"That's rather a question," said Suzanne. "He's pretty well known as a big-game hunter, and, as you heard him say tonight, he was a distant cousin of Sir Laurence Eardsley. I've never actually met him until this trip. He journeys to and from Africa a good deal. There's a general idea that he does Secret Service work. I don't know whether it's true or not. He's certainly rather a mysterious creature."

"I suppose he came into a lot of money as Sir Laurence Eardsley's heir?"

"My dear Anne, he must be *rolling*. You know, he'd be a splendid match for you."

"I can't have a good go at him with you aboard the ship," I said, laughing. "Oh, these married women!"

"We do have a pull," murmured Suzanne complacently. "And everybody knows that I am absolutely devoted to Clarence—my husband, you know. It's so safe and pleasant to make love to a devoted wife."

"It must be very nice for Clarence to be married to someone like you."

"Well, I'm wearing to live with! Still, he can always escape to the Foreign Office, where he fixes his eyeglass in his eye, and goes to sleep in a big arm-chair. We might cable him to tell us all he knows about Race. I love sending cables. And they annoy Clarence so. He always says a letter would have done as well. I don't suppose he'd tell us anything, though. He is so frightfully discreet. That's what makes him so hard to live with for long on end. But let us go on with our matchmaking. I'm sure Colonel Race is very attracted to you, Anne. Give him a couple of glances from those wicked eyes of yours, and the deed is done. Every one gets engaged on board ship. There's nothing else to do."

"I don't want to get married."

"Don't you?" said Suzanne. "Why not? I love being married—even to Clarence!"

I disdained her flippancy.

"What I want to know is," I said with determination, "what has Colonel Race got to do with this? He's in it somewhere."

"You don't think it was mere chance, his telling that story?"

"No, I don't," I said decidedly. "He was watching us all narrowly. You remember, *some* of the diamonds were recovered, not all. Perhaps these are the missing ones— or perhaps——"

"Perhaps what?"

I did not answer directly.

"I should like to know," I said, "what became of the other young man. Not Eardsley but—what was his name?—Lucas!"

"We're getting some light on the thing, anyway. It's the diamonds all these people are after. It must have been to obtain possession of the diamonds that 'The Man in the Brown Suit' killed Nadina."

"He didn't kill her," I said sharply.

"Of course he killed her. Who else could have done so?"

"I don't know. But I'm sure he didn't kill her."

"He went into the house three minutes after her and came out as white as a sheet."

"Because he found her dead."

"But nobody else went in."

"Then the murderer was in the house already, or else he got in some other way. There's no need for him to pass the lodge, he could have climbed over the wall."

Suzanne glanced at me sharply.

"'The Man in the Brown Suit,'" she mused. "Who was he, I wonder? Anyway, he was identical with the 'doctor' in the Tube. He would have had time to remove his make-up and follow the woman to Marlow. She and Carton were to have met there, they both had an order to view the same house, and if they took such elaborate precautions to make their meeting appear accidental they must have suspected they were being followed. All the same, Carton did *not* know that his shadower was the 'Man in the Brown Suit.' When he recognized him, the shock was so great that he lost his head completely and stepped back onto the line. That all seems pretty clear, don't you think so, Anne?"

I did not reply.

"Yes, that's how it was. He took the paper from the dead man, and in his hurry to get away he dropped it. Then he followed the woman to Marlow. What did he do when he left there, when he had killed her—or, according to you, found her dead. Where did he go?"

Still I said nothing.

"I wonder, now," said Suzanne musingly. "Is it possible that he induced Sir Eustace Pedler to bring him on board as his secretary? It would be a unique chance of getting safely out of England, and dodging the hue and cry. But how did he square Sir Eustace? It looks as though he had some hold over him."

"Or over Pagett," I suggested in spite of myself.

"You don't seem to like Pagett, Anne. Sir Eustace says he's a most capable and hard-working young man. And, really, he may be for all we know against him. Well, to continue my surmises. Rayburn is the 'Man in the Brown Suit.' He had read the paper he dropped. Therefore, misled by the dot as you were, he attempts to reach Cabin 17 at one o'clock on the 22nd, having previously tried to get possession of the cabin through Pagett. On the way there somebody knifes him——"

"Who?" I interpolated.

"Chichester. Yes, it all fits in. Cable to Lord Nasby that you have found 'The Man in the Brown Suit,' and your fortune's made, Anne!"

"There are several things you've overlooked."

"What things? Rayburn's got a scar, I know—but a scar can be faked easily enough. He's the right height and build. What's the description of a head with which you pulverized them at Scotland Yard?"

I trembled. Suzanne was a well-educated, well-read woman, but I prayed that she might not be conversant with technical terms of anthropology.

"Dolichocephalic," I said lightly.

Suzanne looked doubtful.

"Was that it?"

"Yes. Long-headed, you know. A head whose width is less than 75 per cent. of its length," I explained fluently.

There was a pause. I was just beginning to breathe freely when Suzanne said suddenly:

"What's the opposite?"

"What do you mean—the opposite?"

"Well, there must be an opposite. What do you call the heads whose breadth is more than 15 per cent. of their length."

"Brachycephalic," I murmured unwillingly.

"That's it. I thought that was what you said."

"Did I? It was a slip of the tongue. I meant dolichocephalic," I said with all the assurance I could muster.

Suzanne looked at me searchingly. Then she laughed.

"You lie very well, Gipsy girl. But it will save time and trouble now if you tell me all about it."

"There's nothing to tell," I said unwillingly.

"Isn't there?" said Suzanne gently.

"I suppose I shall have to tell you," I said slowly. "I'm not ashamed of it. You can't be ashamed of something that just—happens to you. That's what he did. He was detestable—rude and ungrateful—but that I think I understand. It's like a dog that's been chained up—or badly treated—it'll bite anybody. That's what he was like—bitter and snarling. I don't know why I care—but I do. I care horribly. Just seeing him has turned my whole life upside-down. I love him. I want him. I'll walk all over Africa barefoot till I find him, and I'll make him care for me. I'd die for him. I'd work for him, slave for him, steal for him, even beg or borrow for him! There—now you know!"

Suzanne looked at me for a long time.

"You're very un-English, Gipsy girl," she said at last. "There's not a scrap of the sentimental about you. I've never met any one who was at once so practical and so passionate. I shall never care for any one like that— mercifully for me—and yet—and yet I envy you, Gipsy girl. It's something to be able to care. Most people can't. But what a mercy for your little doctor man that you didn't marry him. He doesn't sound at all the sort of individual who would enjoy keeping high explosive in the house! So there's to be no cabling to Lord Nasby?"

I shook my head.

"And yet you believe him to be innocent?"

"I also believe that innocent people can be hanged."

"Hm! yes. But, Anne, dear, you can face facts, face them now. In spite of all you say, he may have murdered this woman."

"No," I said. "He didn't."

"That's sentiment."

"No, it isn't. He might have killed her. He may even have followed her there with that idea in his mind. But he wouldn't take a bit of black cord and strangle her with it. If he'd done it, he would have strangled her with his bare hands."

Suzanne gave a little shiver. Her eyes narrowed appreciately.

"Hm! Anne, I am beginning to see why you find this young man of yours so attractive!"

16

I got an opportunity of tackling Colonel Race on the following morning. The auction of the sweep had just been concluded, and we walked up and down the deck together.

"How's the gipsy this morning? Longing for land and her caravan?"

I shook my head.

"Now that the sea is behaving so nicely, I feel I should like to stay on it for ever and ever."

"What enthusiasm!"

We leant together over the rail. It was a glassy calm. The sea looked as though it had been oiled. There were great patches of colour on it, blue, pale green, emerald, purple and deep orange, like a cubist picture. There was an occasional flash of silver that showed the flying fish. The air was moist and warm, almost sticky. Its breath was like a perfumed caress.

"That was a very interesting story you told us last night," I said, breaking the silence.

"Which one?"

"The one about the diamonds."

"I believe women are always interested in diamonds."

"Of course we are. By the way, what became of the other young man? You said there were two of them."

"Young Lucas? Well, of course, they couldn't prosecute one without the other, so he went scot-free too."

"And what happened to him—eventually, I mean. Does any one know?"

Colonel Race was looking straight ahead of him out to sea. His face was as devoid of expression as a mask, but I had an idea that he did not like my questions. Nevertheless, he replied readily enough:

"He went to the War and acquitted himself bravely. He was reported Missing and Wounded—believed killed."

That told me what I wanted to know. I asked no more. But more than ever I wondered how much Colonel Race knew. The part he was playing in all this puzzled me.

One other thing I did. That was to interview the night steward. With a little financial encouragement, I soon got him to talk.

"The lady wasn't frightened, was she, miss? It seemed a harmless sort of joke. A bet, or so I understood."

I got it all out of him, little by little. On the voyage from Cape Town to England one of the passengers had handed him a roll of films with instructions that they were to be dropped onto the bunk in Cabin 71 at 1 A.M. on January 22nd on the outward journey. A lady would be occupying the cabin, and the affair was described as a bet. I gathered that the steward had been liberally paid for his part in the transaction. The lady's name had not been mentioned. Of course, as Mrs. Blair went straight into Cabin 71, interviewing the purser as soon as she got on board, it never occurred to the steward that she was not the lady in question. The name of the passenger who had arranged the transaction with Carton, and his description tallied exactly with that of the man killed on the Tube.

So one mystery, at all events, was cleared up, and the diamonds were obviously the key to the whole situation.

Those last days on the *Kilmorden* seemed to pass very quickly. As we drew nearer and nearer to Cape Town, I was forced to consider carefully my future plans. There were so many people I wanted to keep an eye on. Mr. Chichester, Sir Eustace and his secretary, and—yes, Colonel Race! What was I to do about it? Naturally it was Chichester who had first claim on my attention. Indeed, I was on the point of reluctantly dismissing Sir Eustace and Mr. Pagett from their position of suspicious characters, when a chance conversation awakened fresh doubts in my mind.

I had not forgotten Mr. Pagett's incomprehensible emotion at the mention of Florence. On the last evening on board we were all sitting on deck and Sir Eustace addressed a perfectly innocent question to his secretary. I forget exactly what it was, something to do with railway delays in Italy, but at once I noticed that Mr. Pagett was displaying the same uneasiness which had caught my attention before. When Sir Eustace claimed Mrs. Blair for a dance, I quickly moved into the chair next to the secretary. I was determined to get to the bottom of the matter.

"I have always longed to go to Italy," I said. "And especially to Florence. Didn't you enjoy it very much there?"

"Indeed I did, Miss Beddingfeld. If you will excuse me, there is some correspondence of Sir Eustace's that——"

I took hold of him firmly by his coat sleeve.

"Oh, you mustn't run away!" I cried with the skittish accent of an elderly dowager. "I'm sure Sir Eustace wouldn't like you to leave me alone with no one to talk to. You never seem to want to talk about Florence. Oh, Mr. Pagett, I believe you have a guilty secret!"

I still had my hand on his arm, and I could feel the sudden start he gave.

"Not at all, Miss Beddingfeld, not at all," he said earnestly. "I should be only too delighted to tell you all about it, but there really are some cables——"

"Oh, Mr. Pagett, what a thin pretence. I shall tell Sir Eustace——"

I got no further. He gave another jump. The man's nerves seemed in a shocking state.

"What is it you want to know?"

The resigned martyrdom of his tone made me smile inwardly.

"Oh, everything! The pictures, the olive trees——"

I paused, rather at a loss myself.

"I suppose you speak Italian?" I resumed.

"Not a word, unfortunately. But of course, with hall porters and—er—guides."

"Exactly," I hastened to reply. "And which was your favourite picture?"

"Oh, er—the Madonna—er—Raphael, you know."

"Dear old Florence," I murmured sentimentally. "So picturesque on the banks of the Arno. A beautiful river. And the Duomo, you remember the Duomo?"

"Of course, of course."

"Another beautiful river, is it not?" I hazarded. "Almost more beautiful than the Arno?"

"Decidedly so, I should say."

Emboldened by the success of my little trap, I proceeded further. But there was little room for doubt. Mr. Pagett delivered himself into my hands with every word he uttered. The man had never been in Florence in his life.

But, if not in Florence, where had he been? In England? Actually in England at the time of the Mill House Mystery? I decided on a bold step.

"The curious thing is," I said, "that I fancied I had seen you before somewhere. But I must be mistaken— since you were in Florence at the time. And yet——"

I studied him frankly. There was a hunted look in his eyes. He passed his tongue over his dry lips.

"Where—er—where——"

"—did I think I had seen you?" I finished for him. "At Marlow. You know Marlow? Why, of course, how stupid of me, Sir Eustace has a house there!"

But with an incoherent muttered excuse, my victim rose and fled.

That night I invaded Suzanne's cabin, alight with excitement.

"You see, Suzanne," I urged, as I finished my tale, "he was in England, in Marlow, at the time of the murder. Are you so sure that 'The Man in the Brown Suit' is guilty?"

"I'm sure of one thing," said Suzanne, twinkling unexpectedly.

"What's that?"

"That 'The Man in the Brown Suit' is better looking than poor Mr. Pagett. No, Anne, don't get cross. I was only teasing. Sit down here. Joking apart, I think you've made a very important discovery. Up till now, we've considered Pagett as having an alibi. Now we know he hasn't."

"Exactly," I said. "We must keep an eye on him."

"As well as everybody else," she said ruefully. "Well, that's one of the things I wanted to talk to you about. That—and finance. No, don't stick your nose in the air. I know you are absurdly proud and independent, but you've got to listen to horse sense over this. We're partners—I wouldn't offer you a penny because I liked you, or because you're a friendless girl—what I want is a thrill, and I'm prepared to pay for it. We're going into this together regardless of expense. To begin with you'll come with me to the Mount Nelson Hotel at my expense, and we'll plan out our campaign."

We argued the point. In the end I gave in. But I didn't like it. I wanted to do the thing on my own.

"That's settled," said Suzanne at last, getting up and stretching herself with a big yawn. "I'm exhausted with my own eloquence. Now then, let us discuss our victims. Mr. Chichester is going on to Durban. Sir Eustace is going to the Mount Nelson Hotel in Cape Town and then up to Rhodesia. He's going to have a private car on the railway, and in a moment of expansion, after his fourth glass of champagne the other night, he offered me a place in it. I dare say he didn't really mean it, but, all the same, he can't very well back out if I hold him to it."

"Good," I approved. "You keep an eye on Sir Eustace and Pagett, and I take on Chichester. But what about Colonel Race?"

Suzanne looked at me queerly.

"Anne, you can't possibly suspect——"

"I do. I suspect everybody. I'm in the mood when one looks round for the most unlikely person."

"Colonel Race is going to Rhodesia too," said Suzanne thoughtfully. "If we could arrange for Sir Eustace to invite him also—"

"You can manage it. You can manage anything."

"I love butter," purred Suzanne.

We parted on the understanding that Suzanne should employ her talents to the best advantage.

I felt too excited to go to bed immediately. It was my last night on board. Early to-morrow morning we should be in Table Bay.

I slipped up on deck. The breeze was fresh and cool. The boat was rolling a little in the choppy sea. The decks were dark and deserted. It was after midnight.

I leaned over the rail, watching the phosphorescent trail of foam. Ahead of us lay Africa, we were rushing towards it through the dark water. I felt alone in a wonderful world. Wrapped in a strange peace, I stood there, taking no heed of time, lost in a dream.

And suddenly I had a curious intimate premonition of danger. I had heard nothing, but I swung round instinctively. A shadowy form had crept up behind me. As I turned, it sprang. One hand gripped my throat, stifling any cry I might have uttered. I fought desperately, but I had no chance. I was half choking from the grip on my throat, but I bit and clung and scratched in the most approved feminine fashion. The man was handicapped by having to keep me from crying out. If he had succeeded in reaching me unawares it would have been easy enough for him to sling me overboard with a sudden heave. The sharks would have taken care of the rest.

Struggle as I would, I felt myself weakening. My assailant felt it too. He put out all his strength. And then, running on swift noiseless feet, another shadow joined in. With one blow of his fist, he sent my opponent crashing headlong to the deck. Released, I fell back against the rail, sick and trembling.

My rescuer turned to me with a quick movement.

"You're hurt!"

There was something savage in his tone—a menace against the person who had dared to hurt me. Even before he spoke I had recognized him. It was my man—the man with the scar.

But that one moment in which his attention had been diverted to me had been enough for the fallen enemy. Quick as a flash he had risen to his feet and taken to his heels down the deck. With an oath Rayburn sprang after him.

I always hate being out of things. I joined the chase—a bad third. Round the deck we went to the starboard side of the ship. There by the saloon door lay the man in a crumpled heap. Rayburn was bending over him.

"Did you hit him again?" I called breathlessly.

"There was no need," he replied grimly. "I found him collapsed by the door. Or else he couldn't get it open and is shamming. We'll soon see about that. And we'll see who he is too."

With a beating heart I drew near. I had realized at once that my assailant was a bigger man than Chichester. Anyway, Chichester was a flabby creature who might use a knife at a pinch, but who would have little strength in his bare hands.

Rayburn struck a match. We both uttered an ejaculation. The man was Guy Pagett.

Rayburn appeared absolutely stupefied by the discovery.

"Pagett," he murmured. "My God, Pagett."

I felt a slight sense of superiority.

"You seem surprised."

"I am," he said heavily. "I never suspected——" He wheeled suddenly round on me. "And you? You're not? You recognized him, I suppose, when he attacked you?"

"No, I didn't. All the same, I'm not so very surprised."

He stared at me suspiciously.

"Where do you come in, I wonder? And how much do you know?"

I smiled.

"A good deal, Mr.—er—Lucas!"

He caught my arm, the unconscious strength of his grip made me wince.

"Where did you get that name?" he asked hoarsely.

"Isn't it yours?" I demanded sweetly. "Or do you prefer to be called 'The Man in the Brown Suit'?"

That did stagger him. He released my arm and fell back a pace or two.

"Are you a girl or a witch?" he breathed.

"I'm a friend." I advanced a step towards him. "I offered you my help once—I offer it again. Will you have it?"

The fierceness of his answer took me aback.

"No. I'll have no truck with you or with any woman. Do your damnedest."

As before, my own temper began to rise.

"Perhaps," I said, "you don't realize how much in my power you are? A word from me to the Captain——"

"Say it," he sneered. Then advancing with a quick step: "And whilst we're realizing things, my girl, do you realize that you're in *my* power this minute? I could take you by the throat like this." With a swift gesture he suited the action to the word. I felt his two hands clasp my throat and press—ever so little. "Like this—and squeeze the life out of you! And then—like our unconscious friend here, but with more success—fling your dead body to the sharks. What do you say to that?"

I said nothing. I laughed. And yet I knew that the danger was real. Just as that moment he hated me. But I knew that I loved the danger, loved the feeling of his hands on my throat. That I would not have exchanged that moment for any other moment in my life. . . .

With a short laugh he released me.

"What's your name?" he asked abruptly.

"Anne Beddingfeld."

"Does nothing frighten you, Anne Beddingfeld?"

"Oh, yes," I said, with an assumption of coolness I was far from feeling. "Wasps, sarcastic women, very young men, cockroaches, and superior shop assistants."

He gave the same short laugh as before. Then he stirred the unconscious form of Pagett with his feet.

"What shall we do with this junk? Throw it overboard?" he asked carelessly.

"If you like," I answered with equal calm.

"I admire your whole-hearted, blood-thirsty instincts, Miss Beddingfeld. But we will leave him to recover at his leisure. He is not seriously hurt."

"You shrink from a second murder, I see," I said sweetly.

"A second murder?"

He looked genuinely puzzled.

"The woman at Marlow," I reminded him, watching the effect of my words closely.

An ugly brooding expression settled down on his face. He seemed to have forgotten my presence.

"I might have killed her," he said. "Sometimes I believe that I meant to kill her. . . ."

A wild rush of feeling, hatred of the dead woman, surged through me. *I* could have killed her that moment, had she stood before me. . . . For he must have loved her once—he must—he must—to have felt like that!

I regained control of myself and spoke in my normal voice:

"We seem to have said all there is to be said—except good night."

"Good night and good-bye, Miss Beddingfeld."

"Au revoir, Mr. Lucas."

Again he flinched at the name. He came nearer.

"Why do you say that—au revoir, I mean?"

"Because I have a fancy that we shall meet again."

"Not if I can help it!"

Emphatic as his tone was, it did not offend me. On the contrary I hugged myself with secret satisfaction. I am not quite a fool.

"All the same," I said gravely, "I think we shall."

"Why?"

I shook my head, unable to explain the feeling that had actuated my words.

"I never wish to see you again," he said suddenly and violently.

It was really a very rude thing to say, but I only laughed softly and slipped away into the darkness.

I heard him start after me, and then pause, and a word floated down the deck. I think it was "witch"!

17

(Extract from the diary of Sir Eustace Pedler)

MOUNT NELSON HOTEL,
CAPE TOWN.

It is really the greatest relief to get off the *Kilmorden*. The whole time that I was on board I was conscious of being surrounded by a network of intrigue. To put the lid on everything, Guy Pagett must needs engage in a drunken brawl the last night. It is all very well to explain it away, but that is what it actually amounts to. What else would you think if a man comes to you with a lump the size of an egg on the side of his head and an eye coloured all the tints of the rainbow?

Of course Pagett would insist on trying to be mysterious about the whole thing. According to him, you would think his black eye was the direct result of his devotion to my interests. His story was extraordinarily vague and rambling, and it was a long time before I could make head or tail of it.

To begin with, it appears he caught sight of a man behaving suspiciously. Those are Pagett's words. He has taken them straight from the pages of a German Spy Story. What he means by a man behaving suspiciously he doesn't know himself. I said so to him.

"He was slinking along in a very furtive manner, and it was the middle of the night, Sir Eustace."

"Well, what were you doing yourself? Why weren't you in bed and asleep like a good Christian?" I demanded irritably.

"I had been coding those cables of yours, Sir Eustace, and typing the diary up to date."

Trust Pagett to be always in the right and a martyr over it!

"Well?"

"I just thought I would have a look around before turning in, Sir Eustace. The man was coming down the passage from your cabin. I thought at once there was something wrong by the way he looked about him. He slunk up the stairs by the saloon. I followed him."

"My dear Pagett," I said, "why shouldn't the poor chap go on deck without having his footsteps dogged? Lots of people even sleep on deck—very uncomfortable, I've always thought. The sailors wash you down with the rest of the deck at five in the morning." I shuddered at the idea.

"Anyway," I continued, "if you went worrying some poor devil who was suffering from insomnia, I don't wonder he landed you one."

Pagett looked patient.

"If you would hear me out, Sir Eustace. I was convinced the man had been prowling about near your cabin where he had no business to be. The only two cabins down that passage are yours and Colonel Race's."

"Race," I said, lighting a cigar carefully, "can look after himself without your assistance, Pagett." I added as an afterthought: "So can I."

Pagett came nearer and breathed heavily as he always does before imparting a secret.

"You see, Sir Eustace, I fancied—and now indeed I am sure—it was Rayburn."

"Rayburn?"

"Yes, Sir Eustace."

I shook my head.

"Rayburn has far too much sense to attempt to wake me up in the middle of the night."

"Quite so, Sir Eustace. I think it was Colonel Race he went to see. A secret meeting—for orders!"

"Don't hiss at me, Pagett," I said, drawing back a little, "and do control your breathing. Your idea is absurd. Why should they want to have a secret meeting in the middle of the night? If they'd anything to say to each other, they could hobnob over beef-tea in a perfectly casual and natural manner."

I could see that Pagett was not in the least convinced.

"*Something* was going on last night, Sir Eustace," he urged, "or why should Rayburn assault me so brutally."

"You're quite sure it was Rayburn?"

Pagett appeared to be perfectly convinced of that. It was the only part of the story that he wasn't vague about.

"There's something very queer about all this," he said. "To begin with, where *is* Rayburn?"

It's perfectly true that we haven't seen the fellow since we came on shore. He did not come up to the hotel with us. I decline to believe that he is afraid of Pagett, however.

Altogether the whole thing is very annoying. One of my secretaries has vanished into the blue, and the other looks like a disreputable prize-fighter. I can't take him about with me in his present condition. I shall be the laughing-stock of Cape Town. I have an appointment later in the day to deliver old Milray's *billet-doux*, but I shall not take Pagett with me. Confound the fellow and his prowling ways.

Altogether I am decidedly out of temper. I had poisonous breakfast with poisonous people. Dutch waitresses with thick ankles who took half an hour to bring me a bad bit of fish. And this farce of getting up at 5 A.M. on arrival at the port to see a blinking doctor and hold your hands above your head simply makes me tired.

LATER.

A very serious thing has occurred. I went to my appointment with the Prime Minister, taking Milray's sealed letter. It didn't look as though it had been tampered with, but inside was a blank sheet of paper!

Now, I suppose, I'm in the devil of a mess. Why I ever let that bleating old fool Milray embroil me in the matter I can't think.

Pagett is a famous Job's comforter. He displays a certain gloomy satisfaction that maddens me. Also, he has taken advantage of my perturbation to saddle me with the stationery trunk. Unless he is careful, the next funeral he attends will be his own.

However, in the end I had to listen to him.

"Supposing, Sir Eustace, that Rayburn had overheard a word or two of your conversation with Mr. Milray in the street? Remember, you had no written authority from Mr. Milray. You accepted Rayburn on his own valuation."

"You think Rayburn is a crook, then?" I said slowly.

Pagett did. How far his views were influenced by resentment over his black eye I didn't know. He made out a pretty fair case against Rayburn. And the disappearance of the latter told against him. My idea was to do nothing in the matter. A man who has permitted himself to be made a thorough fool of is not anxious to broadcast the fact.

But Pagett, his energy unimpaired by his recent mis-
fortunes, was all for vigorous measures. He had his way
of course. He bustled out to the police station, sent innumerable cables, and brought a herd of English and
Dutch officials to drink whiskies and sodas at my expense.

We got Milray's answer that evening. He knew nothing of my late secretary! There was only one spot of
comfort to be extracted from the situation.

"At any rate," I said to Pagett, "you weren't poisoned.
You had one of your ordinary bilious attacks."

I saw him wince. It was my only score.

LATER.

Pagett is in his element. His brain positively scintillates
with bright ideas. He will have it now that Rayburn is
none other than the famous "Man in the Brown Suit." I
dare say he is right. He usually is. But all this is getting
unpleasant. The sooner I get off to Rhodesia the better.
I have explained to Pagett that he is not to accompany
me.

"You see, my dear fellow," I said, "you must remain
here on the spot. You might be required to identify Rayburn any minute. And, besides, I have my dignity as an
English Member of Parliament to think of. I can't go
about with a secretary who has apparently recently been
indulging in a vulgar street-brawl."

Pagett winced. He is such a respectable fellow that
his appearance is pain and tribulation to him.

"But what will you do about your correspondence and
the notes for your speeches, Sir Eustace?"

"I shall manage," I said airily.

"Your private car is to be attached to the eleven-
o'clock train to-morrow, Wednesday morning," Pagett

continued. "I have made all arrangements. Is Mrs. Blair taking a maid with her?"

"Mrs. Blair?" I gasped.

"She tells me you offered her a place."

So I did, now I come to think of it. On the night of the Fancy Dress ball. I even urged her to come. But I never thought she would! Delightful as she is, I do not know that I want Mrs. Blair's society all the way to Rhodesia and back. Women require such a lot of attention. And they are confoundedly in the way sometimes.

"Have I asked any one else?" I said nervously. One does these things in moments of expansion.

"Mrs. Blair seemed to think you had asked Colonel Race as well."

I groaned.

"I must have been very drunk if I asked Race. Very drunk indeed. Take my advice, Pagett, and let your black eye be a warning to you, don't go on the bust again."

"As you know, I am a teetotaller, Sir Eustace."

"Much wiser to take the pledge if you have a weakness that way. I haven't asked any one else, have I, Pagett?"

"Not that I know of, Sir Eustace."

I heaved a sigh of relief.

"There's Miss Beddingfeld," I said thoughtfully. "She wants to get to Rhodesia to dig up bones, I believe. I've a good mind to offer her a temporary job as a secretary. She can typewrite, I know, for she told me so."

To my surprise, Pagett opposed the idea vehemently. He does not like Anne Beddingfeld. Ever since the night of the black eye, he has displayed uncontrollable emotion whenever she is mentioned. Pagett is full of mysteries nowadays.

Just to annoy him, I shall ask the girl. As I said before, she has extremely nice legs.

18

(Anne's Narrative Resumed)

I don't suppose that as long as I live I shall forget my first sight of Table Mountain. I got up frightfully early and went out on deck. I went right up to the boat deck which I believe is a heinous offence, but I decided to dare something in the cause of solitude. We were just steaming into Table Bay. There were fleecy white clouds hovering above Table Mountain, and nestling on the slopes below, right down to the sea, was the sleeping town, gilded and bewitched by the morning sunlight.

It made me catch my breath and have that curious hungry pain inside that seizes one sometimes when one comes across something that's extra beautiful. I'm not very good at expressing these things, but I knew well enough that I had found, if only for a fleeting moment, the thing that I had been looking for ever since I left Little Hampsly. Something new, something hitherto undreamed of, something that satisfied my aching hunger for romance.

Perfectly silently, or so it seemed to me, the *Kilmorden* glided nearer and nearer. It was still very like a dream. Like all dreamers, however, I could not let my dream alone. We poor humans are so anxious not to miss anything.

"This is South Africa," I kept saying to myself industriously, "South Africa, South Africa. You are seeing the world. This is the world. You are seeing it. Think of it, Anne Beddingfeld, you pudding-head. You're seeing the world."

I had thought that I had the boat deck to myself, but now I observed another figure leaning over the rail, absorbed as I had been in the rapidly approaching city. Even before he turned his head I knew who it was. The scene of last night seemed unreal and melodramatic in the peaceful morning sunlight. What must he have thought of me? It made me hot to realize the things that I had said. And I hadn't meant them—or had I?

I turned my head resolutely away and stared hard at Table Mountain. If Rayburn had come up here to be alone, I, at least, need not disturb him by advertising my presence.

But to my intense surprise I heard a light footfall on the deck behind me, and then his voice, pleasant and normal:

"Miss Beddingfeld."

"Yes."

I turned.

"I want to apologize to you. I behaved like a perfect boor last night."

"It—it was a peculiar night," I said hastily.

It was not a very lucid remark, but it was absolutely the only thing I could think of.

"Will you forgive me?"

I held out my hand without a word. He took it.

"There's something else I want to say." His gravity deepened. "Miss Beddingfeld, you may not know it, but you are mixed up in a rather dangerous business."

"I gathered as much," I said.

"No, you don't. You can't possibly know. I want to warn you. Leave the whole thing alone. It can't concern you really. Don't let your curiosity lead you to tamper with other people's business. No, please don't get angry again. I'm not speaking of myself. You've no idea of what you might come up against—these men will stop at nothing. They are absolutely ruthless. Already you're in danger—look at last night. They fancy you know something. Your only chance is to persuade them that they're mistaken. But be careful, always be on the look out for danger, and, look here, if at any time you should fall into their hands, don't try and be clever—tell the whole truth, it will be your only chance."

"You make my flesh creep, Mr. Rayburn," I said, with some truth. "Why do you take the trouble to warn me?"

He did not answer for some minutes, then he said in a low voice:

"It may be the last thing I can do for you. Once on shore I shall be all right—but I may not get on shore."

"What?" I cried.

"You see, I'm afraid you're not the only person on board who knows that I am 'The Man in the Brown Suit.' "

"If you think that I told——" I said hotly.

He reassured me with a smile.

"I don't doubt you, Miss Beddingfeld. If I ever said I did, I lied. No, but there's one person on board who's known all along. He's only got to speak—and my number's up. All the same, I'm taking a sporting chance that he won't speak."

"Why?"

"Because he's a man who likes playing a lone hand. And when the police have got me I should be of no further use to him. Free, I might be! Well, an hour will show."

He laughed rather mockingly, but I saw his face harden. If he had gambled with Fate, he was a good gambler. He could lose and smile.

"In any case," he said lightly, "I don't suppose we shall meet again."

"No," I said slowly. "I suppose not."

"So—good-bye."

"Good-bye."

He gripped my hand hard, just for a minute his curious light eyes seemed to burn into mine, then he turned abruptly and left me. I heard his footsteps ringing along the deck. They echoed and re-echoed. I felt that I should hear them always. Footsteps—going out of my life.

I can admit frankly that I did not enjoy the next two hours. Not till I stood on the wharf, having finished with most of the ridiculous formalities that bureaucracies require, did I breathe freely once more. No arrest had been made, and I realized that it was a heavenly day, and that I was extremely hungry. I joined Suzanne. In any case, I was staying the night with her at the hotel. The boat did not go on to Port Elizabeth and Durban until the following morning. We got into a taxi and drove to the Mount Nelson.

It was all heavenly. The sun, the air, the flowers! When I thought of Little Hampsly in January, the mud knee-deep, and the sure-to-be-falling rain I hugged myself with delight. Suzanne was not nearly so enthusiastic. She has travelled a great deal of course. Besides, she is not the type that gets excited before breakfast. She snubbed me severely when I let out an enthusiastic yelp at the sight of a giant blue convolvulus.

By the way, I should like to make it clear here and now that this story will not be a story on South Africa. I guarantee no genuine local colour—you know the sort

of thing—half a dozen words in italics on every page. I
admire it very much, but I can't do it. In South Sea
Islands, of course, you make an immediate reference to
bêche-de-mer. I don't know what *bêche-de-mer* is, I
never have known, I probably never shall know. I've
guessed once or twice and guessed wrong. In South Africa I know you at once begin to talk about a *stoep*—I
do know what a *stoep* is—it's the thing round a house
and you sit on it. In various other parts of the would you
call it a veranda, a piazza, and a ha-ha. Then again, there
are pawpaws. I had often read of pawpaws. I discovered
at once what they were, because I had one plumped
down in front of me for breakfast. I thought at first that
it was a melon gone bad. The Dutch waitress enlightened
me, and persuaded me to use lemon juice and sugar and
try again. I had always vaguely associated it with a *hula-
hula*, which, I believe, though I may be wrong, is a kind
of straw skirt that Hawaiian girls dance in. No, I think
I am wrong—that is a *lava-lava*.

At any rate, all these things are very cheering after
England. I can't help thinking that it would brighten our
cold Island life if one could have a breakfast of *bacon-
bacon*, and then go out clad in a *jumper-jumper* to pay
the books.

Suzanne was a little tamer after breakfast. They had
given me a room next to hers with a lovely view right
out over Table Bay. I looked at the view whilst Suzanne
hunted for some special face-cream. When she had
found it and started an immediate application, she became capable of listening to me.

"Did you see Sir Eustace?" I asked. "He was march-
ing out of the breakfast room as we went in. He'd had
some bad fish or something and was just telling the head
waiter what he thought about it, and he bounced a peach
on the floor to show how hard it was—only it wasn't

quite as hard as he thought and it squashed."

Suzanne smiled.

"Sir Eustace doesn't like getting up early any more than I do. But, Anne, did you see Mr. Pagett? I ran against him in the passage. He's got a black eye. What can he have been doing?"

"Only trying to push me overboard," I replied nonchalantly.

It was a distinct score for me. Suzanne left her face half anointed and pressed for details. I gave them to her.

"It all gets more and more mysterious," she cried. "I thought I was going to have the soft job sticking to Sir Eustace, and that you would have all the fun with the Rev. Edward Chichester, but now I'm not so sure. I hope Pagett won't push me off the train some dark night."

"I think you're still above suspicion, Suzanne. But, if the worst happens, I'll wire Clarence."

"That reminds me—give me a cable form. Let me see now, what shall I say. 'Implicated in the most thrilling mystery please send me a thousand pounds at once Suzanne.' "

I took the form from her, and pointed out that she could eliminate a "the," an "a," and possibly, if she didn't care about being polite, a "please." Suzanne, however, appears to be perfectly reckless in money matters. Instead of attending to my economical suggestions, she added three words more: "enjoying myself hugely."

Suzanne was engaged to lunch with friends of hers, who came to the hotel about eleven o'clock to fetch her. I was left to my own devices. I went down through the grounds of the hotel, crossed the tram-lines and followed a cool shady avenue right down till I came to the main street. I strolled about, seeing the sights, enjoying the sunlight and the black-faced sellers of flowers and fruits. I also discovered a place where they had the most delicious ice-cream sodas. Finally, I bought a sixpenny basket of peaches and retraced my steps to the hotel.

To my surprise and pleasure I found a note awaiting me. It was from the curator of the Museum. He had read of my arrival on the *Kilmorden*, in which I was described as the daughter of the late Professor Beddingfeld. He had known my father slightly and had had a great admiration for him. He went on to say that his wife would be delighted if I would come out and have tea with them that afternoon at their Villa at Muizenberg. He gave me instructions for getting there.

It was pleasant to think that poor Papa was still remembered and highly thought of. I foresaw that I would have to be personally escorted round the Museum before I left Cape Town, but I risked that. To most people it would have been a treat—but one can have too much of a good thing if one is brought up on it, morning, noon and night.

I put on my best hat (one of Suzanne's cast-offs) and my least crumpled white linen and started off after lunch. I caught a fast train to Muizenberg and got there in about half an hour. It was a nice trip. We wound slowly round the base of Table Mountain, and some of the flowers were lovely. My geography being weak, I had never fully realized that Cape Town is on a peninsula, consequently I was rather surprised on getting out of the train to find myself facing the sea once more. There was some perfectly entrancing bathing going on. The people had short curved boards and came floating in on the waves. It was far too early to go to tea. I made for the bathing pavilion, and when they said would I have a surf board, I said "Yes, please." Surfing looks perfectly easy. *It isn't.* I say no more. I got very angry and fairly hurled my plank from me. Nevertheless, I determined to return on the first possible opportunity and have another go. I would not be beaten. Quite by mistake I then got a good run on my board, and came out delirious with happiness. Surfing is like that. You are either vigorously cursing or else you are idiotically pleased with yourself.

I found the Villa Medgee after some little difficulty. It was right up on the side of the moutain, isolated from the other cottages and villas. I rang the bell, and a smiling Kafir boy answered it.

"Mrs. Raffini?" I inquired.

He ushered me in, preceded me down the passage and flung open a door. Just as I was about to pass in, I hesitated. I felt a sudden misgiving. I stepped over the threshold and the door swung sharply to behind me.

A man rose from his seat behind a table and came forward with outstretched hand.

"So glad we have persuaded you to visit us, Miss Beddingfeld," he said.

He was a tall man, obviously a Dutchman, with a flaming orange beard. He did not look in the least like the curator of a museum. In fact, I realized in a flash that I had made a fool of myself.

I was in the hands of the enemy.

19

It reminded me forcibly of Episode III in "The Perils of Pamela." How often had I not sat in the sixpenny seats, eating a twopenny bar of milk chocolate, and yearning for similar things to happen to me. Well, they had happened with a vengeance. And somehow it was not nearly so amusing as I had imagined. It's all very well on the screen—you have the comfortable knowledge that there's bound to be an Episode IV. But in real life there was absolutely no guarantee that Anna the Adventuress might not terminate abruptly at the end of any Episode.

Yes, I was in a tight place. All the things that Rayburn had said that morning came back to me with unpleasant distinctness. Tell the truth, he had said. Well, I could always do that, but was it going to help me? To begin with, would my story be believed? Would they consider it likely or possible that I had started off on this mad escapade simply on the strength of a scrap of paper smelling of moth balls? It sounded to me a wildly incredible tale. In that moment of cold sanity I cursed myself for a melodramatic idiot, and yearned for the peaceful boredom of Little Hampsly.

All this passed through my mind in less time than it takes to tell. My first instinctive movement was to step backwards and feel for the handle of the door. My captor merely grinned.

"Here you are and here you stay," he remarked facetiously.

I did my best to put a bold face upon the matter.

"I was invited to come here by the curator of the Cape Town Museum. If I have made a mistake——"

"A mistake? Oh, yes, a big mistake!"

He laughed coarsely.

"What right have you to detain me? I shall inform the police——"

"Yap, yap, yap—like a little toy dog." He laughed.

I sat down on a chair.

"I can only conclude that you are a dangerous lunatic," I said coldly.

"Indeed?"

"I should like to point out to you that my friends are perfectly aware where I have gone, and that if I have not returned by this evening, they will come in search of me. You understand?"

"So your friends know where you are, do they? Which of them?"

Thus challenged, I did a lightning calculation of chances. Should I mention Sir Eustace? He was a well-known man, and his name might carry weight. But if they were in touch with Pagett, they might know I was lying. Better not risk Sir Eustace.

"Mrs. Blair for one," I said lightly. "A friend of mine with whom I am staying."

"I think not," said my captor, slyly shaking his orange head. "You have not seen her since eleven this morning. And you received our note bidding you come here, at lunch-time."

His words showed me how closely my movements had been followed, but I was not going to give in without a fight.

"You are very clever," I said. "Perhaps you have heard of that useful invention, the telephone? Mrs. Blair called me up on it when I was resting in my room after lunch. I told her then where I was going this afternoon."

To my great satisfaction, I saw a shade of uneasiness pass over his face. Clearly he had overlooked the possibility that Suzanne might have telephoned to me. I wished she really had done so!

"Enough of this," he said harshly, rising.

"What are you going to do with me?" I asked, still endeavouring to appear composed.

"Put you where you can do no harm in case your friends come after you."

For a moment my blood ran cold, but his next words reassured me.

"To-morrow you'll have some questions to answer, and after you've answered them we shall know what to do with you. And I can tell you, young lady, we've more ways than one of making obstinate little fools talk."

It was not cheering, but it was at least a respite. I had until to-morrow. This man was clearly an underling obeying the orders of a superior. Could that superior by any chance be Pagett?

He called and two Kafirs appeared. I was taken upstairs. Despite my struggles, I was gagged and then bound hand and foot. The room into which they had taken me was a kind of attic right under the roof. It was dusty and showed little signs of having been occupied. The Dutchman made a mock bow and withdrew, closing the door behind him.

I was quite helpless. Turn and twist as I would, I could not loosen my hands in the slightest degree, and the gag prevented me from crying out. If, by any possible chance, any one did come to the house, I could do nothing to attract their attention. Down below I heard the sound of a door shutting. Evidently the Dutchman was going out.

It was maddening not to be able to do anything. I strained again at my bonds, but the knots held. I desisted at last, and either fainted or fell asleep. When I awoke I was in pain all over. It was quite dark now, and I judged that the night must be well advanced, for the moon was high in the heavens and shining down through the dusty skylight. The gag was half choking me and the stiffness and pain were unendurable.

It was then that my eyes fell on a bit of broken glass lying in the corner. A moonbeam slanted right down on it, and its glistening had caught my attention. As I looked at it, an idea came into my head.

My arms and legs were helpless, but surely I could still *roll*. Slowly and awkwardly, I set myself in motion. It was not easy. Besides being extremely painful, since I could not guard my face with my arms, it was also exceedingly difficult to keep any particular direction.

I tended to roll in every direction except the one I wanted to go. In the end, however, I came right up against my objective. It almost touched my bound hands.

Even then it was not easy. It took an infinity of time before I could wriggle the glass into such a position, wedged against the wall, that it would rub up and down on my bonds. It was a long heart-rending process, and I almost despaired, but in the end I succeeded in sawing through the cords that bound my wrists. The rest was a matter of time. Once I had restored circulation to my hands by rubbing the wrists vigorously, I was able to undo the gag. One or two full breaths did a lot for me.

Very soon I had undone the last knot, though even then it was some time before I could stand on my feet, but at last I stood erect, swinging my arms to and fro to restore the circulation, and wishing above all things that I could get hold of something to eat.

I waited about a quarter of an hour, to be quite sure of my recovered strength. Then I tiptoed noiselessly to the door. As I had hoped, it was not locked, only latched. I unlatched it and peeped cautiously out.

Everything was still. The moonlight came in through a window and showed me the dusty uncarpeted staircase. Cautiously I crept down it. Still no sound—but as I stood on the landing below, a faint murmur of voices reached me. I stopped dead and stood there for some time. A clock on the wall registered the fact that it was after midnight.

I was fully aware of the risks I might run if I descended lower, but my curiosity was too much for me. With infinite precautions I prepared to explore. I crept softly down the last flight of stairs and stood in the square hall. I looked round me—and then caught my breath with a gasp. A Kafir boy was sitting by the hall door. He had not seen me, indeed I soon realized by his breathing that he was fast asleep.

Should I retreat, or should I go on? The voices came from the room I had been shown into on arrival. One of them was that of my Dutch friend, the other I could not for the moment recognize, though it seemed vaguely familiar.

In the end I decided that it was clearly my duty to hear all I could. I must risk the Kafir boy waking up. I crossed the hall noiselessly and knelt by the study door. For a moment or two I could hear no better. The voices were louder, but I could not distinguish what they said.

I applied my eye to the keyhole instead of my ear. As I had guessed, one of the speakers was the big Dutchman. The other man was sitting outside my circumscribed range of vision.

Suddenly he rose to get himself a drink. His back, black clad and decorous, came into view. Even before he turned round I knew who he was.

Mr. Chichester!

Now I began to make out the words.

"All the same, it is dangerous. Suppose her friends come after her?"

It was the big man speaking. Chichester answered him. He had dropped his clerical voice entirely. No wonder I had not recognized it.

"All bluff. They haven't an idea where she is."

"She spoke very positively."

"I dare say. I've looked into the matter, and we've nothing to fear. Anyway, it's the 'Colonel's' orders. You don't want to go against them, I suppose?"

The Dutchman ejaculated something in his own language. I judged it to be a hasty disclaimer.

"But why knock her on the head?" he growled. "It would be simple. The boat is all ready. She could be taken out to sea?"

"Yes," said Chichester meditatively. "That is what I should do. She knows too much, that is certain. But the 'Colonel' is a man who likes to play a lone hand—though no one else must do so." Something in his own words seemed to awaken a memory that annoyed him. "He wants information of some kind from this girl."

He had paused before the information, and the Dutchman was quick to catch him up.

"Information?"

"Something of the kind."

"Diamonds," I said to myself.

"And now," continued Chichester, "give me the lists."

For a long time their conversation was quite incomprehensible to me. It seemed to deal with large quantities of vegetables. Dates were mentioned, prices, and various names of places which I did not know. It was quite half an hour before they had finished their checking and counting.

"Good," said Chichester, and there was a sound as though he pushed back his chair. "I will take these with me for the 'Colonel' to see."

"When do you leave?"

"Ten o'clock to-morrow morning will do."

"Do you want to see the girl before you go?"

"No. There are strict orders that no one is to see her until the 'Colonel' comes. Is she all right?"

"I looked in on her when I came in for dinner. She was asleep, I think. What about food?"

"A little starvation will do no harm. The 'Colonel' will be here some time to-morrow. She will answer questions better if she is hungry. No one had better go near her till then. Is she securely tied up?"

The Dutchman laughed.

"What do you think?"

They both laughed. So did I, under my breath. Then, as the sounds seemed to betoken that they were about to come out of the room, I beat a hasty retreat. I was just in time. As I reached the head of the stairs, I heard the door of the room open, and at the same time the Kafir stirred and moved. My retreat by the way of the hall door was not to be thought of. I retired prudently to the attic, gathered my bonds round me and lay down again on the floor, in case they should take it into their heads to come and look at me.

They did not do so, however. After about an hour, I crept down the stairs, but the Kafir by the door was awake and humming softly to himself. I was anxious to get out of the house, but I did not quite see how to manage it.

In the end I was forced to retreat to the attic again.
The Kafir was clearly on guard for the night. I remained
here patiently all through the sounds of early morning
preparation. The men breakfasted in the hall, I could
hear their voices distinctly floating up the stairs. I was
getting thoroughly unnerved. How on earth was I to get
out of the house?

I counselled myself to be patient. A rash move might
spoil everything. After breakfast came the sounds of
Chichester departing. To my intense relief, the Dutchman accompanied him.

I waited breathlessly. Breakfast was being cleared
away, the work of the house was being done. At last,
the various activities seemed to die down. I slipped out
from my lair once more. Very carefully I crept down the
stairs. The hall was empty. Like a flash I was across it,
had unlatched the door, and was outside in the sunshine.
I ran down the drive like one possessed.

Once outside, I resumed a normal walk. People stared
at me curiously, and I do not wonder. My face and
clothes must have been covered in dust from rolling
about in the attic. At last I came to a garage. I went in.

"I have met with an accident," I explained. "I want a
car to take me to Cape Town at once. I must catch the
boat to Durban."

I had not long to wait. Ten minutes later I was speed-
ing along in the direction of Cape Town. I must know
if Chichester was on the boat. Whether to sail on her
myself or not, I could not determine, but in the end I
decided to do so. Chichester would not know that I had
seen him in the Villa at Muizenberg. He would doubtless
lay further traps for me, but I was forewarned. And he
was the man I was after, the man who was seeking the
diamonds on behalf of the mysterious "Colonel."

Alas, for my plans! As I arrived at the docks, the *Kilmorden Castle* was steaming out to sea. And I had no means of knowing whether Chichester had sailed on her or not!

20

I drove to the hotel. There was no one in the lounge that I knew. I ran upstairs and tapped on Suzanne's door. Her voice bade me "come in." When she saw who it was she literally fell on my neck.

"Anne, dear, where have you been? I've been worried to death about you. What have you been doing?"

"Having adventures," I replied. "Episode III of 'The Perils of Pamela.' "

I told her the whole story. She gave vent to a deep sigh when I finished.

"Why do these things always happen to you?" she demanded plaintively. "Why does no one gag me and bind me hand and foot?"

"You wouldn't like it if they did," I assured her. "To tell you the truth, I'm not nearly so keen on having adventures myself as I was. A little of that sort of thing goes a long way."

Suzanne seemed unconvinced. An hour or two of gagging and binding would have changed her views quickly enough. Suzanne likes thrills, but she hates being uncomfortable.

"And what are we all doing now?" she asked.

"I don't quite know," I said thoughtfully. "You still go to Rhodesia, of course, to keep an eye on Pagett——"

"And you?"

That was just my difficulty. Had Chichester gone on the *Kilmorden*, or had he not? Did he mean to carry out his original plan of going to Durban? The hour of his leaving Muizenberg seemed to point to an affirmative answer to both questions. In that case, I might go to Durban by train. I fancied that I should get there before the boat. On the other hand, if the news of my escape were wired to Chichester, and also the information that I had left Cape Town for Durban, nothing was simpler for him than to leave the boat at either Port Elizabeth or East London and so give me the slip completely.

It was rather a knotty problem.

"We'll inquire about trains to Durban anyway," I said.

"And it's not too late for morning tea," said Suzanne. "We'll have it in the lounge."

The Durban train left at 8.15 that evening, so they told me at the office. For the moment I postponed decision and joined Suzanne for somewhat belated "eleven-o'clock tea."

"Do you feel that you would really recognize Chichester again—in any other disguise, I mean?" asked Suzanne.

I shook my head ruefully.

"I certainly didn't recognize him as the stewardess, and never should have but for your drawing."

"The man's a professional actor, I'm sure of it," said Suzanne thoughtfully. "His make-up is perfectly marvellous. He might come off the boat as a navvy or something, and you'd never spot him."

"You're very cheering," I said.

At that minute, Colonel Race stepped in through the window and came and joined us.

"What is Sir Eustace doing?" asked Suzanne. "I haven't seen him about to-day."

Rather an odd expression passed over the Colonel's face.

"He's got a little trouble of his own to attend to which is keeping him busy."

"Tell us about it."

"I mustn't tell tales out of school."

"Tell us something—even if you have to invent it for our special benefit."

"Well, what would you say to the famous 'Man in the Brown Suit' having made the voyage with us?"

"*What?*"

I felt the colour die out of my face and then surge back again. Fortunately Colonel Race was not looking at me.

"It's a fact, I believe. Every port watched for him and he bamboozled Pedler into bringing him out as his secretary!"

"Not Mr. Pagett?"

"Oh, not Pagett—the other fellow. Rayburn, he called himself."

"Have they arrested him?" asked Suzanne. Under the table she gave my hand a reassuring squeeze. I waited breathlessly for an answer.

"He seems to have disappeared into thin air."

"How does Sir Eustace take it?"

"Regards it as a personal insult offered him by Fate."

An opportunity of hearing Sir Eustace's views on the matter presented itself later in the day. We were awakened from a refreshing afternoon nap by a page-boy with a note. In touching terms it requested the pleasure of our company at tea in his sitting-room.

The poor man was indeed in a pitiable state. He poured out his troubles to us, encouraged by Suzanne's sympathetic murmurs. (She does that sort of thing very well.)

"First a perfectly strange woman has the impertinence to get herself murdered in my house—on purpose to annoy me, I believe. Why my house? Why, of all the houses in Great Britain, choose the Mill House? What harm had I ever done the woman that she must needs get herself murdered there?"

Suzanne made one of her sympathetic noises again and Sir Eustace proceeded in a still more aggrieved tone.

"And, if that's not enough, the fellow who murdered her has the impudence, the colossal impudence, to attach himself to me as my secretary. My secretary, if you please! I'm tired of secretaries, I won't have any more secretaries. Either they're concealed murderers or else they're drunken brawlers. Have you seen Pagett's black eye? But of course you have. How can I go about with a secretary like that? And his face is such a nasty shade of yellow too—just the colour that doesn't go with a black eye. I've done with secretaries—unless I have a girl. A nice girl, with liquid eyes, who'll hold my hand when I'm feeling cross. What about you, Miss Anne. Will you take on the job?"

"How often shall I have to hold your hand?" I asked, laughing.

"All day long," replied Sir Eustace gallantly.

"I shan't get much typing done at that rate," I reminded him.

"That doesn't matter. All this work is Pagett's idea. He works me to death. I'm looking forward to leaving him behind in Cape Town."

"He is staying behind?"

"Yes, he'll enjoy himself thoroughly sleuthing about after Rayburn. That's the sort of thing suits Pagett down to the ground. He adores intrigues. But I'm quite serious in my offer. Will you come? Mrs. Blair here is a competent chaperon, and you can have a half-holiday every now and then to dig for bones."

"Thank you very much, Sir Eustace," I said cautiously, "but I think I'm leaving for Durban to-night."

"Now don't be an obstinate girl. Remember, there are lots of lions in Rhodesia. You'll like lions. All girls do."

"Will they be practising low jumps?" I asked, laughing. "No, thank you very much, but I must go to Durban."

Sir Eustace looked at me, sighed deeply, then opened the door of the adjoining room and called to Pagett.

"If you've quite finished your afternoon sleep, my dear fellow, perhaps you'd do a little work for change."

Guy Pagett appeared in the doorway. He bowed to us both, starting slightly at the sight of me, and replied in a melancholy voice:

"I have been typing that memorandum all this afternoon, Sir Eustace."

"Well, stop typing it then. Go down to the Trade Commissioner's Office, or the Board of Agriculture, or the Chamber of Mines, or one of these places, and ask them to lend me some kind of a woman to take to Rhodesia. She must have liquid eyes and not object to my holding her hand."

"Yes, Sir Eustace. I will ask for a competent shorthand-typist."

"Pagett's a malicious fellow," said Sir Eustace, after the secretary had departed. "I'd be prepared to bet that he'll pick out some slab-faced creature on purpose to annoy me. She must have nice feet too—I forgot to mention that."

I clutched Suzanne excitedly by the hand and almost dragged her along to her room.

"Now, Suzanne," I said, "we've got to make plans—and make them quickly. Pagett is staying behind here—you heard that?"

"Yes. I suppose that means that I shan't be allowed to go to Rhodesia—which is very annoying, because I *want* to go to Rhodesia. How tiresome."

"Cheer up," I said. "You're going all right. I don't see how you could back out at the last moment without its appearing frightfully suspicious. And, besides, Pagett might suddenly be summoned by Sir Eustace, and it would be far harder for you to attach yourself to him for the journey up."

"It would hardly be respectable," said Suzanne, dimpling. "I should have to pretend a fatal passion for him as an excuse."

"On the other hand, if you were there when he arrived, it would all be perfectly simple and natural. Besides, I don't think we ought to lose sight of the other two entirely."

"Oh, Anne, you surely can't suspect Colonel Race or Sir Eustace?"

"I suspect everybody," I said darkly, "and if you've read any detective stories, Suzanne, you must know that it's always the most unlikely person who's the villain. Lots of criminals have been cheerful fat men like Sir Eustace."

"Colonel Race isn't particularly fat—or particularly cheerful either."

"Sometimes they're lean and saturnine," I retorted. "I don't say I seriously suspect either of them, but, after all, the woman was murdered in Sir Eustace's house——"

"Yes, yes, we needn't go over all that again. I'll watch him for you, Anne, and if he gets any fatter and any more cheerful, I'll send you a telegram at once. 'Sir E. swelling. Highly suspicious. Come at once.'"

"Really, Suzanne," I cried, "you seem to think all this is a game!"

"I know I do," said Suzanne, unabashed. "It seems like that. It's your fault, Anne. I've got imbued with your 'Let's have an adventure' spirit. It doesn't seem a bit real. Dear me, if Clarence knew that I was running about Africa tracking dangerous criminals, he'd have a fit."

"Why don't you cable him about it?" I asked sarcastically.

Suzanne's sense of humour always fails her when it comes to sending cables. She considered my suggestion in perfectly good faith.

"I might. It would have to be a very long one." Her eyes brightened at the thought. "But I think it's better not. Husbands always want to interfere with perfectly harmless amusements."

"Well," I said, summing up the situation, "you will keep an eye on Sir Eustace and Colonel Race——"

"I know why I've got to watch Sir Eustace," interrupted Suzanne, "because of his figure and his humorous conversation. But I think it's carrying it rather far to suspect Colonel Race, I do indeed: Why, he's something to do with the Secret Service. Do you know, Anne, I believe the best thing we could do would be to confide in him and tell him the whole story."

I objected vigorously to this unsporting proposal. I recognized in it the disastrous effects of matrimony. How often have I not heard a perfectly intelligent female say, in the tone of one clinching an argument, "*Edgar* says——" And all the time you are perfectly aware that Edgar is a perfect fool. Suzanne, by reason of her married state, was yearning to lean upon some man or other.

However, she promised faithfully that she would not breathe a word to Colonel Race, and we went on with our plan-making.

"It's quite clear that I must stay here and watch Pagett, and this is the best way to do it. I must pretend to leave for Durban this evening, taking my luggage down and so on, but really I shall go to some small hotel in the town. I can alter my appearance a little—wear a fair toupee and one of those thick white lace veils, and I shall have a much better chance of seeing what he's really at if he thinks I'm safely out of the way."

Suzanne approved this plan heartily. We made due and ostentatious preparations, inquiring once more about the departure of the train at the office and packing my luggage.

We dined together in the restaurant. Colonel Race did not appear, but Sir Eustace and Pagett were at their table in the window. Pagett left the table half-way through the meal, which annoyed me, as I had planned to say good-bye to him. However, doubtless Sir Eustace would do as well. I went over to him when I had finished.

"Good-bye, Sir Eustace," I said. "I'm off to-night to Durban."

Sir Eustace sighed heavily.

"So I heard. You wouldn't like me to come with you, would you?"

"I should love it."

"Nice girl. Sure you won't change your mind and come and look for lions in Rhodesia?"

"Quite sure."

"He must be a very handsome fellow," said Sir Eustace plaintively. "Some young whipper-snapper in Durban, I suppose, who puts my mature charms completely in the shade. By the way, Pagett's going down in the car in a minute or two. He could take you to the station."

"Oh, no, thank you," I said hastily. "Mrs. Blair and I have got our own taxi ordered."

To go down with Guy Pagett was the last thing I wanted! Sir Eustace looked at me attentively.

"I don't believe you like Pagett. I don't blame you. Of all the officious, interfering asses—going about with the air of a martyr, and doing everything he can to annoy and upset me!"

"What has he done now?" I inquired with some curiosity.

"He's got hold of a secretary for me. You never saw such a woman! Forty, if she's a day, wears pince-nez and sensible boots and an air of brisk efficiency that will be the death of me. A regular slab-faced woman."

"Won't she hold your hand?"

"I devoutly hope not!" exclaimed Sir Eustace. "That would be the last straw. Well, good-bye, liquid eyes. If I shoot a lion I shan't give you the skin—after the base way you've deserted me."

He squeezed my hand warmly and we parted. Suzanne was waiting for me in the hall. She was to come down to see me off.

"Let's start at once," I said hastily, and motioned to the man to get a taxi.

Then a voice behind me made me start:

"Excuse me, Miss Beddingfeld, but I'm just going down in a car. I can drop you and Mrs. Blair at the station."

"Oh, thank you," I said hastily. "But there's no need to trouble you. I——"

"No trouble at all, I assure you. Put the luggage in, porter."

I was helpless. I might have protested further, but a slight warning nudge from Suzanne urged me to be on my guard.

"Thank you, Mr. Pagett," I said coldly.

We all got into the car. As we raced down the road into the town, I racked my brains for something to say. In the end Pagett himself broke the silence.

"I have secured a very capable secretary for Sir Eustace," he observed. "Miss Pettigrew."

"He wasn't exactly raving about her just now," I remarked.

Pagett looked at me coldly.

"She is a proficient shorthand-typist," he said repressively.

We pulled up in front of the station. Here surely he would leave us. I turned with outstretched hand—but no.

"I'll come and see you off. It's just eight o'clock, your train goes in a quarter of an hour."

He gave efficient directions to porters. I stood helpless, not daring to look at Suzanne. The man suspected. He was determined to make sure that I did go by the train. And what could I do? Nothing. I saw myself, in a quarter of an hour's time, steaming out of the station with Pagett planted on the platform waving me adieu. He had turned the tables on me adroitly. His manner towards me had changed, moreover. It was full of an uneasy geniality which sat ill upon him, and which nauseated me. The man was an oily hypocrite. First he tried to murder me, and now he paid me compliments! Did he imagine for one minute that I hadn't recognized him that night on the boat? No, it was a pose, a pose which he forced me to acquiesce in, his tongue in his cheek all the while.

Helpless as a sheep, I moved along under his expert directions. My luggage was piled in my sleeping compartment—I had a two-berth one to myself. It was twelve minutes past eight. In three minutes the train would start.

But Pagett had reckoned without Suzanne.

"It will be a terribly hot journey, Anne," she said suddenly. "Especially going through the Karoo to-morrow. You've got some eau-du-Cologne or lavender water with you, haven't you?"

My cue was plain.

"Oh, dear," I cried. "I left my eau-de-Cologne on the dressing-table at the hotel."

Suzanne's habit of command served her well. She turned imperiously to Pagett.

"Mr. Pagett. Quick. You've just time. There's a chemist almost opposite the train. Anne must have some eau-de-Cologne."

He hesitated, but Suzanne's imperative manner was too much for him. She is a born autocrat. He went. Suzanne followed him with her eyes till he disappeared.

"Quick, Anne, get out the other side—in case he hasn't really gone, but is watching us from the end of the platform. Never mind your luggage. You can telegraph about that tomorrow. Oh, if only the train starts on time!"

I opened the gate on the opposite side to the platform and climbed down. Nobody was observing me. I could just see Suzanne standing where I had left her, looking up at the train and apparently chatting to me at the window. A whistle blew, the train began to draw out. Then I heard feet racing furiously up the platform. I withdrew to the shadow of a friendly bookstall and watched.

Suzanne turned from waving her handkerchief to the retreating train.

"Too late, Mr. Pagett," she said cheerfully. "She's gone. Is that the eau-de-Cologne? What a pity we didn't think of it sooner!"

They passed not far from me on their way out of the station. Guy Pagett was extremely hot. He had evidently run all the way to the chemist and back.

"Shall I get you a taxi, Mrs. Blair?"

Suzanne did not fail in her rôle.

"Yes, please. Can't I give you a lift back? Have you much to do for Sir Eustace? Dear me, I wish Anne Beddingfeld was coming with us to-morrow. I don't like the idea of a young girl like that travelling off to Durban all by herself. But she was set upon it. Some little attraction there, I fancy——"

They passed out of ear-shot. Clever Suzanne. She had saved me.

I allowed a minute or two to elapse and then I too made my way out of the station, almost colliding as I did so with a man—an unpleasant-looking man with a nose disproportionately big for his face.

21

I had no further difficulty in carrying out my plans. I found a small hotel in a back street, got a room there, paid a deposit as I had no luggage with me, and went placidly to bed.

On the following morning I was up early and went out into town to purchase a modest wardrobe. My idea was to do nothing until after the departure of the eleven-o'clock train to Rhodesia with most of the party on board. Pagett was not likely to indulge in any nefarious activities until he had got rid of them. Accordingly I took a tram out of the town and proceeded to enjoy a country walk. It was comparatively cool, and I was glad to stretch my legs after the long voyage and my close confinement at Muizenberg.

A lot hinges on small things. My shoe-lace came untied, and I stopped to do it up. The road had just turned a corner, and as I was bending over the offending shoe a man came right round and almost walked into me. He lifted his hat, murmuring an apology, and went on. It struck me at the time that his face was vaguely familiar, but at the moment I thought no more of it. I looked at my wrist-watch. The time was getting on. I turned my feet in the direction of Cape Town.

There was a tram on the point of going and I had to run for it. I heard other footsteps running behind me. I swung myself on and so did the other runner. I recognized him at once. It was the man who had passed me on the road when my shoe came untied, and in a flash I knew why his face was familiar. It was the small man with the big nose whom I had run into on leaving the station the night before.

The coincidence was rather startling. Could it be possible that the man was deliberately following me? I resolved to test that as promptly as possible. I rang the bell and got off at the next stop. The man did not get off. I withdrew into the shadow of a shop doorway and watched. He alighted at the next stop and walked back in my direction.

The case was clear enough. I was being followed. I had crowed too soon. My victory over Guy Pagett took on another aspect. I hailed the next tram and, as I expected, my shadower also got on. I gave myself up to some very serious thinking.

It was perfectly apparent that I had stumbled on a bigger thing than I knew. The murder in the house at Marlow was not an isolated incident committed by a solitary individual. I was up against a gang, and, thanks to Colonel Race's revelations to Suzanne, and what I had overheard at the house at Muizenberg, I was beginning to understand some of its manifold activities. Systematized crime, organized by the man known to his followers as the "Colonel"! I remembered some of the talk I had heard on board ship, of the strike on the Rand and the causes underlying it—and the belief that some secret organization was at work fomenting the agitation. That was the "Colonel's" work, his emissaries were acting according to plan. He took no part in these things himself, I had always heard, as he limited himself to directing and organizing. The brain-work—not the dangerous labour—for him. But still it well might be that he himself was on the spot, directing affairs from an apparently impeccable position.

That, then, was the meaning of Colonel Race's presence on the *Kilmorden Castle*. He was out after the arch-criminal. Everything fitted in with that assumption. He was some one high up in the Secret Service whose business it was to lay the "Colonel" by the heels.

I nodded to myself—things were becoming very clear to me. What of my part in the affair? Where did I come in? Was it only diamonds they were after? I shook my head. Great as the value of the diamonds might be, they hardly accounted for the desperate attempts which had been made to get me out of the way. No, I stood for more than that. In some way, unknown to myself, I was a menace, a danger! Some knowledge that I had, or that they thought I had, made them anxious to remove me at all costs—and that knowledge was bound up somehow with the diamonds. There was one person, I felt sure, who could enlighten me—if he would! The Man in the Brown Suit—Harry Rayburn. He knew the other half of the story. But he had vanished into the darkness, he was a hunted creature flying from pursuit. In all probability he and I would never meet again. . . .

I brought myself back with a jerk to the actualities of the moment. It was no good thinking sentimentally of Harry Rayburn. He had displayed the greatest antipathy to me from the first. Or, at least——There I was again—dreaming! The real problem was what to do—*now!*

I, priding myself upon my rôle of watcher, had become the watched. And I was afraid! For the first time I began to lose my nerve. I was the little bit of grit that was impeding the smooth working of the great machine—and I fancied that the machine would have a short way with little bits of grit. Once Harry Rayburn had saved me, once I had saved myself—but I felt suddenly that the odds were heavily against me. My enemies were all around me in every direction, and they were closing in. If I continued to play a lone hand I was doomed.

I rallied myself with an effort. After all, what could they do? I was in a civilized city—with policemen every few yards. I would be wary in the future. They should not trap me again as they had done in Muizenberg.

As I reached this point in my meditations, the train arrived at Adderly Street. I got out. Undecided what to do, I walked slowly up the left-hand side of the street. I did not trouble to look if my watcher was behind me. I knew he was. I walked into Cartwright's and ordered two coffee ice-cream sodas—to steady my nerves. A man, I suppose, would have had a stiff peg; but girls derive a lot of comfort from ice-cream sodas. I applied myself to the end of the straw with gusto. The cool liquid went trickling down my throat in the most agreeable manner. I pushed the first glass aside empty.

I was sitting on one of the little high stools in front of the counter. Out of the tail of my eye, I saw my tracker come in and sit down unostentatiously at a little table near the door. I finished the second coffee soda and demanded a maple one. I can drink practically an unlimited amount of ice-cream sodas.

Suddenly the man by the door got up and went out. That surprised me. If he was going to wait outside, why not wait outside from the beginning. I slipped down from my stool and went cautiously to the door. I drew back quickly into the shadow. The man was talking to Guy Pagett.

If I had ever had any doubts, that would have settled it. Pagett had his watch out and was looking at it. They exchanged a few brief words, and then the secretary swung on down the street towards the station. Evidently he had given his orders. But what were they?

Suddenly my heart leapt into my mouth. The man who had followed me crossed to the middle of the road and spoke to a policeman. He spoke at some length, gesticulating towards Cartwright's and evidently explaining something. I saw the plan at once. I was to be arrested on some charge or other—pocket-picking, perhaps. It would be easy enough for the gang to put through a simple little matter like that. Of what good to protest my innocence? They would have seen to every detail. Long ago they had brought a charge of robbing De Beers against Harry Rayburn, and he had not been able to disprove it, though I had little doubt but that he had been absolutely blameless. What chance had I against such a "frame up" as the "Colonel" could devise?

I glanced up at the clock almost mechanically, and immediately another aspect of the case struck me. I saw the point of Guy Pagett's looking at his watch. It was just on eleven, and at eleven the mail train left for Rhodesia bearing with it the influential friends who might otherwise come to my rescue. That was the reason of my immunity up to now. From last night till eleven this morning I had been safe, but now the net was closing in upon me.

I hurriedly open my bag and paid for my drinks, and as I did so, my heart seemed to stand still, *for inside it was a man's wallet stuffed with notes!* It must have been deftly introduced into my handbag as I left the tram.

Promptly I lost my head. I hurried out of Cartwright's. The little man with the big nose and the policeman were just crossing the road. They saw me, and the little man designated me excitedly to the policeman. I took to my heels and ran. I judged him to be a slow policeman. I should get a start. But I had no plan, even then. I just ran for my life down Adderly Street. People began to stare. I felt that in another minute some one would stop me.

An idea flashed into my head.

"The station?" I asked, in a breathless gasp.

"Just down on the right."

I sped on. It is permissible to run for a train. I turned into the station, but as I did so I heard footsteps close behind me. The little man with the big nose was a champion sprinter. I foresaw that I should be stopped before I got to the platform I was in search of. I looked up to the clock—one minute to eleven. I might just do it if my plan succeeded.

I had entered the station by the main entrance in Adderly Street. I now darted out again through the side exit. Directly opposite me was the side entrance to the post office, the main entrance to which is in Adderly Street.

As I expected, my pursuer, instead of following me in, ran down the street to cut me off when I emerged by the main entrance, or to warn the policeman to do so.

In an instant I slipped across the street again and back into the station. I ran like a lunatic. It was just eleven. The long train was moving as I appeared on the platform. A porter tried to stop me, but I wriggled myself out of his grasp and sprang upon the footboard. I mounted the two steps and opened the gate. I was safe! The train was gathering way.

We passed a man standing by himself at the end of the platform. I waved to him.

"Good-bye, Mr. Pagett," I shouted.

Never have I seen a man more taken aback. He looked as though he had seen a ghost.

In a minute or two I was having trouble with the conductor. But I took a lofty tone.

"I am Sir Eustace Pedler's secretary," I said haughtily. "Please take me to his private car."

Suzanne and Colonel Race were standing on the rear observation platform. They both uttered an exclamation of utter surprise at seeing me.

"Hullo, Miss Anne," cried Colonel Race, "where have you turned up from? I thought you'd gone to Durban. What an unexpected person you are."

Suzanne said nothing, but her eyes asked a hundred questions.

"I must report myself to my chief," I said demurely. "Where is he?"

"He's in the office—middle compartment—dictating at an incredible rate to the unfortunate Miss Pettigrew."

"This enthusiasm for work is something new," I commented.

"H'm!" said Colonel Race. "His idea is, I think, to give her sufficient work to chain her to her typewriter in her own compartment for the rest of the day."

I laughed. Then, followed by the other two, I sought out Sir Eustace. He was striding up and down the circumscribed space, hurling a flood of words at the unfortunate secretary whom I now saw for the first time. A tall, square woman in drab clothing, with pince-nez and an efficient air. I judged that she was finding it difficult to keep pace with Sir Eustace, for her pencil was flying along, and she was frowning horribly.

I stepped into the compartment.

"Come aboard, sir," I said saucily.

Sir Eustace paused dead in the middle of a complicated sentence on the labour situation and stared at me. Miss Pettigrew must be a nervous creature, in spite of her efficient air, for she jumped as though she had been shot.

"God bless my soul!" ejaculated Sir Eustace. "What about the young man in Durban?"

"I prefer you," I said softly.

"Darling," said Sir Eustace. "You can start holding my hand at once."

Miss Pettigrew coughed, and Sir Eustace hastily withdrew his hand.

"Ah, yes," he said. "Let me see, where were we? Yes. Tylman Roos, in his speech at——What's the matter? Why aren't you taking it down?"

"I think," said Colonel Race gently, "that Miss Pettigrew has broken her pencil."

He took it from her and sharpened it. Sir Eustace stared, and so did I. There was something in Colonel Race's tone that I did not quite understand.

(Extract from the diary of Sir Eustace Pedler)

I am inclined to abandon my Reminiscences. Instead I shall write a short article entitled "Secretaries I have had." As regards secretaries, I seem to have fallen under a blight. At one minute I have no secretaries, at another I have too many. At the present minute I am journeying to Rhodesia with a pack of women. Race goes off with the two best-looking, of course, and leaves me with the dud. That is what always happens to me—and, after all, this is *my* private car, not Race's.

Also Anne Beddingfeld is accompanying me to Rhodesia on the pretext of being my temporary secretary. But all this afternoon she has been out on the observation platform with Race exclaiming at the beauty of the Hex River Pass. It is true that I told her her principal duty would be to hold my hand. But she isn't even doing that. Perhaps she is afraid of Miss Pettigrew. I don't blame her if so. There is nothing attractive about Miss Pettigrew—she is a repellent female with large feet, more like a man than a woman.

There is something very mysterious about Anne Beddingfeld. She jumped on board the train at the last minute, puffing like a steam-engine for all the world as though she'd been running a race—and yet Pagett told me that he'd seen her off to Durban last night! Either

Pagett has been drinking again or else the girl must have an astral body.

And she never explains. Nobody ever explains. Yes, "Secretaries I have had." No. 1, a murderer fleeing from justice. No. 2, a secret drinker who carries on disreputable intrigues in Italy. No. 3, a beautiful girl who possesses the useful faculty of being in two places at once. No. 4, Miss Pettigrew, who, I have no doubt, is really a particularly dangerous crook in disguise! Probably one of Pagett's Italian friends that he has palmed off on me. I shouldn't wonder if the world found some day that it had been grossly deceived by Pagett. On the whole, I think Rayburn was the best of the bunch. He never worried me or got in my way. Guy Pagett has had the impertinence to have the stationery trunk put in here. None of us can move without falling over it.

I went out on the observation platform just now, expecting my appearance to be greeted with hails of delight. Both the women were listening spellbound to one of Race's travellers' tales. I shall label this car—not "Sir Eustace Pedler and Party," but "Colonel Race and Harem."

Then Mrs. Blair must needs begin taking silly photographs. Every time we went round a particularly appalling curve, as we climbed higher and higher, she snapped at the engine.

"You see the point," she cried delightedly. "It must be some curve if you can photograph the front part of the train from the back, and with the mountain background it will look awfully dangerous."

I pointed out to her that no one could possibly tell it had been taken from the back of the train. She looked at me pityingly.

"I shall write underneath it: 'Taken from the train. Engine going round a curve.' "

"You could write that under any snapshot of a train," I said. Women never think of these simple things.

"I'm glad we've come up here in daylight," cried Anne Beddingfeld. "I shouldn't have seen this if I'd gone last night to Durban, should I?"

"No," said Colonel Race, smiling. "You'd have waked up to-morrow morning to find yourself in the Karoo, a hot, dusty desert of stones and rocks."

"I'm glad I changed my mind," said Anne, sighing contentedly, and looking round.

It was rather a wonderful sight. The great mountains laboured ever steadily upwards.

"Is this the best train in the day to Rhodesia?" asked Anne Beddingfeld.

"In the day?" laughed Race. "Why, my dear Miss Anne, there are only three trains a week. Mondays, Wednesdays and Saturdays. Do you realize that you don't arrive at the Falls until Saturday next?"

"How well we shall know each other by that time," said Mrs. Blair maliciously. "How long are you going to stay at the Falls, Sir Eustace?"

"That depends," I said cautiously.

"On what?"

"On how things go at Johannesburg. My original idea was to stay a couple of days or so at the Falls—which I've never seen, though this is my third visit to Africa—and then go on to Jo'burg and study the conditions of things on the Rand. At home, you know, I pose as being an authority on South African politics. But from all I hear, Jo'burg will be a particularly unpleasant place to visit in about a week's time. I don't want to study conditions in the midst of a raging revolution."

Race smiled in a rather superior manner.

"I think your fears are exaggerated, Sir Eustace. There will be no great danger in Jo'burg."

The women immediately looked at him in the "What a brave hero you are" manner. It annoyed me intensely. I am every bit as brave as Race—but I lack the figure. These long, lean, brown men have it all their own way.

"I suppose you'll be there," I said coldly.

"Very possibly. We might travel together."

"I'm not sure that I shan't stay on at the Falls a bit," I answered non-committally. Why is Race so anxious that I should go to Jo'burg? He's got his eye on Anne, I believe. "What are your plans, Miss Anne?"

"That depends," she replied demurely, copying me.

"I thought you were my secretary," I objected.

"Oh, but I've been cut out. You've been holding Miss Pettigrew's hand all the afternoon."

"Whatever I've been doing, I can swear I've not been doing that," I assured her.

THURSDAY NIGHT.

We have just left Kimberley. Race was made to tell the story of the diamond robbery all over again. Why are women so excited by anything to do with diamonds?

At last Anne Beddingfeld has shed her veil of mystery. It seems that she's a newspaper correspondent. She sent an immense cable from De Aar this morning. To judge by the jabbering that went on nearly all night in Mrs. Blair's cabin, she must have been reading aloud all her special articles for years to come.

It seems that all along she's been on the track of "The Man in the Brown Suit." Apparently she didn't spot him on the *Kilmorden*—in fact, she hardly had the chance, but she's now very busy cabling home: "How I journeyed out with the Murderer," and inventing highly fictitious stories of "What he said to me," etc. I know how these things are done. I do them myself, in my Reminiscences when Pagett will let me. And of course one of Nasby's efficient staff will brighten up the details still more, so that when it appears in the *Daily Budget* Rayburn won't recognize himself.

The girl's clever, though. All on her own, apparently, she's ferreted out the identity of the woman who was killed in my house. She was a Russian dancer called Nadina. I asked Anne Beddingfeld if she was sure of this. She replied that it was merely a deduction—quite in the Sherlock Holmes manner. However, I gather that she had cabled it home to Nasby as a proved fact. Women have these intuitions—I've no doubt that Anne Beddingfeld is perfectly right in her guess—but to call it a deduction is absurd.

How she ever got on the staff of the *Daily Budget* is more than I can imagine. But she is the kind of young woman who does these things. Impossible to withstand her. She is full of coaxing ways that mask an invincible determination. Look how she has got into my private car!

I am beginning to have an inkling why. Race said something about the police suspecting that Rayburn would make for Rhodesia. He might just have got off by Monday's train. They telegraphed all along the line, I presume, and no one of his description was found, but that says little. He's an astute young man and he knows Africa. He's probably exquisitely disguised as an old Kafir woman—and the simple police continue to look for a handsome young man with a scar, dressed in the height of European fashion. I never did quite swallow that scar.

Anyway, Anne Beddingfeld is on his track. She wants the glory of discovering him for herself and the *Daily Budget*. Young women are very cold-blooded nowadays. I hinted to her that it was an unwomanly action. She laughed at me. She assured me that did she run him to earth her fortune was made. Race doesn't like it, either, I can see. Perhaps Rayburn is on this train. If so, we may all be murdered in our beds. I said so to Mrs. Blair—but she seemed quite to welcome the idea, and remarked that if I were murdered it would be really a terrific scoop for Anne! A scoop for Anne indeed!

To-morrow we shall be going through Bechuanaland. The dust will be atrocious. Also at every station, little Kafir children come and sell you quaint wooden animals that they carve themselves. Also mealie bowls and baskets. I am rather afraid that Mrs. Blair may run amok. There is a primitive charm about these toys that I feel will appeal to her.

FRIDAY EVENING.

As I feared. Mrs. Blair and Anne have bought forty-nine wooden animals!

23

(Anne's Narrative Resumed)

I thoroughly enjoyed the journey up to Rhodesia. There was something new and exciting to see every day. First the wonderful scenery of the Hex river valley, then the desolate grandeur of the Karoo, and finally that wonderful straight stretch of line in Bechuanaland, and the perfectly adorable toys the natives brought to sell. Suzanne and I were nearly left behind at each station—if you could call them stations. It seemed to me that the train just stopped whenever it felt like it, and no sooner had it done so than a horde of natives materialized out of the empty landscape, holding up mealie bowls and sugar canes and fur karosses and adorable carved wooden animals. Suzanne began at once to make a collection of the latter. I imitated her example—most of them cost a "tiki" (threepence) and each was different. There were giraffes and tigers and snakes and a melancholy looking eland and absurd little black warriors. We enjoyed ourselves enormously.

Sir Eustace tried to restrain us—but in vain. I still think it was a miracle we were not left behind at some oasis of the line. South African trains don't hoot or get excited when they are going to start off again. They just glide quietly away, and you look up from your bargaining and run for your life.

Suzanne's amazement at seeing me climb upon the train at Cape Town can be imagined. We held an exhaustive survey of the situation on the first evening out. We talked half the night.

It had become clear to me that defensive tactics must be adopted as well as aggressive ones. Travelling with Sir Eustace Pedler and his party, I was fairly safe. Both he and Colonel Race were powerful protectors, and I judged that my enemies would not wish to stir up a hornet's nest about *my* ears. Also, as long as I was near Sir Eustace, I was more or less in touch with Guy Pagett—and Guy Pagett was the heart of the mystery. I asked Suzanne whether in her opinion it was possible that Pagett himself was the mysterious "Colonel." His subordinate position was, of course, against the assumption, but it had struck me once or twice that, for all his autocratic ways, Sir Eustace was really very much influenced by his secretary. He was an easy-going man, and one whom an adroit secretary might be able to twist round his little finger. The comparative obscurity of his position might in reality be useful to him, since he would be anxious to be well out of the limelight.

Suzanne, however, negatived these ideas very strongly. She refused to believe that Guy Pagett was the ruling spirit. The real head—the "Colonel"—was somewhere in the background and had probably been already in Africa at the time of our arrival.

I agreed that there was much to be said for her view, but I was not entirely satisfied. For in each suspicious instance Pagett had been shown as the directing genius. It was true that his personality seemed to lack the assurance and decision that one would expect from a master criminal—but after all, according to Colonel Race, it was brain work only that this mysterious leader supplied, and creative genius is often allied to a weak and timorous physical constitution.

"There speaks the Professor's daughter," interrupted Suzanne, when I had got to this point in my argument.

"It's true, all the same. On the other hand, Pagett may be the Grand Vizier, so to speak, of the All Highest." I was silent for a minute or two, and then went on musingly: "I wish I knew how Sir Eustace made his money!"

"Suspecting him again?"

"Suzanne, I've got into that state that I can't help suspecting anybody! I don't really suspect him—but, after all, he *is* Pagett's employer, and he *did* own the Mill House."

"I've always heard that he made his money in some way he isn't anxious to talk about," said Suzanne thoughtfully. "But that doesn't necessarily mean crime—it might be tin-tacks or hair restorer!"

I agreed ruefully.

"I suppose," said Suzanne doubtfully, "that we're not barking up the wrong tree? Being led completely astray, I mean, by assuming Pagett's complicity? Supposing that, after all, he is a perfectly honest man?"

I considered that for a minute or two, then I shook my head.

"I can't believe that."

"After all, he has his explanations for everything."

"Y—es, but they're not very convincing. For instance, the night he tried to throw me overboard on the *Kilmorden*, he says he followed Rayburn up on deck and Rayburn turned and knocked me down. Now we know that's not true."

"No," said Suzanne unwillingly. "But we only heard the story at secondhand from Sir Eustace. If we'd heard it direct from Pagett himself, it might have been different. You know how people always get a story a little wrong when they repeat it."

I turned the thing over in my mind.

"No," I said at last, "I don't see any way out. Pagett's guilty. You can't get away from the fact that he tried to throw me overboard, and everything else fits in. Why are you so persistent in this new idea of yours?"

"Because of his face?"

"His face? But——"

"Yes, I know what you're going to say. It's a sinister face. That's just it. No man with a face like that could be really sinister. It must be a colossal joke on the part of Nature."

I did not believe much in Suzanne's argument. I know a lot about Nature in past ages. If she's got a sense of humour, she doesn't show it much. Suzanne is just the sort of person who would clothe Nature with all her own attributes.

We passed on to discuss our immediate plans. It was clear to me that I must have some kind of standing. I couldn't go on avoiding explanations for ever. The solution of all my difficulties lay ready to my hand, though I didn't think of it for some time. The *Daily Budget!* My silence or my speech could no longer affect Harry Rayburn. He was marked down as "The Man in the Brown Suit" through no fault of mine. I could help him best by seeming to be against him. The "Colonel" and his gang must have no suspicion that there existed any friendly feeling between me and the man they had elected to be the scapegoat of the murder at Marlow. As far as I knew, the woman killed was still unidentified. I would cable to Lord Nasby, suggesting that she was no other than the famous Russian dancer "Nadina" who had been delighting Paris for so long. It seemed incredible to me that she had not been identified already—but when I learnt more of the case long afterwards I saw how natural it really was.

Nadina had never been to England during her successful career in Paris. She was unknown to London audiences. The pictures in the papers of the Marlow victim were so blurred and unrecognizable that it is small wonder no one identified them. And, on the other hand, Nadina had kept her intention of visiting England a profound secret from every one. The day after the murder a letter had been received by her manager purporting to be from the dancer, in which she said that she was returning to Russia on urgent private affairs and that he must deal with her broken contract as best he could.

All this, of course, I only learned afterwards. With Suzanne's full approval, I sent a long cable from De Aar. It arrived at a psychological moment (this again, of course, I learnt afterwards). The *Daily Budget* was hard up for a sensation. My guess was verified and proved to be correct and the *Daily Budget* had the scoop of its lifetime. "Victim of the Mill House Murder identified by our special reporter." And so on. "Our reporter makes voyage with the murderer. 'The Man in the Brown Suit.' What he is really like."

The main facts were, of course, cabled to the South African papers, but I only read my own lengthy articles at a much later date! I received approval and full instructions by cable at Bulawayo. I was on the staff of the *Daily Budget*, and I had a private word of congratulation from Lord Nasby himself. I was definitely accredited to hunt down the murderer, and I, and only I, knew that the murderer was not Harry Rayburn! But let the world think that it was he—best so for the present.

We arrived at Bulawayo early on Saturday morning. I was disappointed in the place. It was very hot, and I hated the hotel. Also Sir Eustace was what I can only describe as thoroughly sulky. I think it was all our wooden animals that annoyed him—especially the big giraffe. It was a colossal giraffe with an impossible neck, a mild eye and a dejected tail. It had character. It had charm. A controversy was already arising as to whom it belonged—me or Suzanne. We had each contributed a tiki to its purchase. Suzanne advanced the claims of seniority and the married state, I stuck to the position that I had been the first to behold its beauty.

In the meantime, I must admit, it occupied a good deal of this three-dimensional space of ours. To carry forty-nine wooden animals, all of awkward shape, and all of extremely brittle wood, is somewhat of a problem. Two porters were laden with a bunch of animals each—and one promptly dropped a ravishing group of ostriches and broke their heads off. Warned by this, Suzanne and I carried all we could, Colonel Race helped, and I pressed the big giraffe into Sir Eustace's arms. Even the correct Miss Pettigrew did not escape, a large hippopotamus and two black warriors fell to her share. I had a feeling Miss Pettigrew didn't like me. Perhaps she fancied I was a bold hussy. Anyway, she avoided me as much as she could. And the funny thing was, her face seemed vaguely familiar to me, though I couldn't quite place it.

We reposed ourselves most of the morning, and in the afternoon we drove out to the Matoppos to see Rhodes's grave. That is to say, we were to have done so, but at the last moment Sir Eustace backed out. He was very nearly in as bad a temper as the morning we arrived at Cape Town—when he bounced the peaches on the floor and they squashed! Evidently arriving early in the morning at places is bad for his temperament. He cursed the porters, he cursed the waiters at breakfast, he cursed the whole hotel management, he would doubtless have liked to curse Miss Pettigrew who hovered around with her pencil and pad, but I don't think even Sir Eustace would have dared to curse Miss Pettigrew. She's just like the efficient secretary in a book. I only rescued our dear giraffe just in time. I feel Sir Eustace would have liked to dash him to the ground.

To return to our expedition, after Sir Eustace had backed out, Miss Pettigrew said she would remain at home in case he might want her. And at the very last minute Suzanne sent down a message to say she had a headache. So Colonel Race and I drove off alone.

He is a strange man. One doesn't notice it so much in a crowd. But, when one is alone with him, the sense of his personality seems really almost overpowering. He becomes more taciturn, and yet his silence seems to say more than speech might do.

It was so that day that we drove to the Matoppos through the soft yellow brown scrub. Everything seemed strangely silent—except our car which I should think was the first Ford ever made by man! The upholstery of it was torn to ribbons and, though I know nothing about engines, even I could guess that all was not as it should be in its interior.

By and by the character of the country changed. Great boulders appeared, piled up into fantastic shapes. I felt suddenly that I had got into a primitive era. Just for a moment Neanderthal men seemed quite as real to me as they had to Papa. I turned to Colonel Race.

"There must have been giants once," I said dreamily. "And their children were just like children are to-day—they played with handfuls of pebbles, piling them up and knocking them down, and the more cleverly they balanced them, the better pleased they were. If I were to give a name to this place I should call it 'The Country of Giant Children.'"

"Perhaps you're nearer the mark than you know," said Colonel Race gravely. "Simple, primitive, big—that is Africa."

I nodded appreciatively.

"You love it, don't you?" I asked.

"Yes. But to live in it long—well, it makes one what you would call cruel. One comes to hold life and death very lightly."

"Yes," I said, thinking of Harry Rayburn. He had been like that too. "But not cruel to weak things?"

"Opinions differ as to what are and are not 'weak things,' Miss Anne."

There was a note of seriousness in his voice which almost startled me. I felt that I knew very little really of this man at my side.

"I meant children and dogs, I think."

"I can truthfully say I've never been cruel to children or dogs. So you don't class women as 'weak things'?"

I considered.

"No, I don't think I do—though they are, I suppose. That is, they are nowadays. But Papa always said that in the beginning men and women roamed the world together, equal in strength—like lions and tigers——"

"And giraffes?" interpolated Colonel Race slyly.

I laughed. Every one makes fun of that giraffe.

"And giraffes. They were nomadic, you see. It wasn't till they settled down in communities, and women did one kind of thing and men another that women got weak. And of course, underneath, one is still the same—one *feels* the same, I mean, and that is why women worship physical strength in men—it's what they once had and have lost."

"Almost ancestor worship, in fact?"

"Something of the kind."

"And you really think that's true? That women worship strength, I mean?"

"I think it's quite true—if one's honest. You think you admire moral qualities, but when you fall in love, you revert to the primitive where the physical is all that counts. But I don't think that's the end—if you lived in primitive conditions it would be all right, but you don't—and so, in the end, the other thing wins after all. It's the things that are apparently conquered that always do win, isn't it? They win in the only way that counts. Like what the Bible says about losing your soul and finding it."

"In the end," said Colonel Race thoughtfully, "you fall in love—and you fall out of it, is that what you mean?"

"Not exactly, but you can put it that way if you like."

"But I don't think you've ever fallen out of love, Miss Anne?"

"No, I haven't," I admitted frankly.

"Or fallen in love, either?"

I did not answer.

The car drew up at our destination and brought the conversation to a close. We got out and began the slow ascent to the World's View. Not for the first time, I felt a slight discomfort in Colonel Race's company. He veiled his thoughts so well behind those impenetrable black eyes. He frightened me a little. He had always frightened me. I never knew where I stood with him.

We climbed in silence till we reached the spot where Rhodes lies guarded by giant boulders. A strange eerie place, far from the haunts of men, that sings a ceaseless pæan of rugged beauty.

We sat there for some time in silence. Then descended once more, but diverging slightly from the path. Sometimes it was a rough scramble and once we came to a sharp slope or rock that was almost sheer.

Colonel Race went first, then turned to help me.

"Better lift you," he said suddenly, and swung me off my feet with a quick gesture.

I felt the strength of him as he set me down and released his clasp. A man of iron, with muscles like taut steel. And again, I felt afraid, especially as he did not move aside, but stood directly in front of me, staring into my face.

"What are you really doing here, Anne Beddingfeld?" he said abruptly.

"I'm a gipsy seeing the world."

"Yes, that's true enough. The newspaper correspondent is only a pretext. You've not the soul of the journalist. You're out for your own hand—snatching at life. But that's not all."

What was he going to make me tell him? I was afraid—afraid. I looked him full in the face. My eyes can't keep secrets like his, but they can carry the war into the enemy's country.

"What are *you* really doing here, Colonel Race?" I asked deliberately.

For a moment I thought he wasn't going to answer. He was clearly taken aback, though. At last he spoke, and his words seemed to afford him a grim amusement.

"Pursuing ambition," he said. "Just that—pursuing ambition. You will remember, Miss Beddingfeld, that 'by that sin fell the angels,' etc."

"They say," I said slowly, "that you are really connected with the Government—that you are in the Secret Service. Is that true?"

Was it my fancy, or did he hesitate for a fraction of a second before he answered?

"I can assure you, Miss Beddingfeld, that I am out here strictly as a private individual travelling for my own pleasure."

Thinking the answer over later, it struck me as slightly ambiguous. Perhaps he meant it to be so.

We rejoined the car in silence. Half-way back to Bulawayo we stopped for tea at a somewhat primitive structure at the side of the road. The proprietor was digging in the garden and seemed annoyed at being disturbed. After an interminable wait he brought us some stale cakes and some lukewarm tea. Then he disappeared to his garden again.

No sooner had he departed than we were surrounded by cats. Six of them all miaowing piteously at once. The racket was deafening. I offered them some pieces of cake. They devoured them ravenously. I poured all the milk there was into a saucer and they fought each other to get it.

"Oh," I cried indignantly, "they're starved! It's wicked. Please, please, order some more milk and another plate of cake."

Colonel Race departed silently to do my bidding. The cats had begun miaowing again. He returned with a big jug of milk and the cats finished it all.

I got up with determination on my face.

"I'm going to take those cats home with us—I shan'
leave them here."

"My dear child, don't be absurd. You can't carry si
cats as well as fifty wooden animals round with you."

"Never mind the wooden animals. These cats ar
alive. I shall take them back with me."

"You will do nothing of the kind." I looked at hin
resentfully, but he went on: "You think me cruel—bu
one can't go through life sentimentalizing over thes
things. It's no good standing out—I shan't allow you t
take them. It's a primitive country, you know, and I'n
stronger than you."

I always know when I am beaten. I went down to th
car with tears in my eyes.

"They're probably short of food just to-day," he ex
plained consolingly. "That man's wife has gone int
Bulawayo for stores. So it will be all right. And anyway
you know, the world's full of starving cats."

"Don't—don't," I said fiercely.

"I'm teaching you to realize life as it is. I'm teachin
you to be hard and ruthless—like I am. That's the secre
of strength—and the secret of success."

"I'd sooner be dead than hard," I said passionately.

We got into the car and started off. I pulled mysel
together again slowly. Suddenly, to my intense astonish
ment, he took my hand in his.

"Anne," he said gently, "I want you. Will you marr
me?"

I was utterly taken aback.

"Oh, no," I stammered. "I can't."

"Why not?"

"I don't care for you in that way. I've never though
of you like that."

"I see. Is that the only reason?"

I had to be honest. I owed it him.

"No," I said, "it is not. You see—I—care for some one else."

"I see," he said again. "And was that true at the beginning—when I first saw you—on the *Kilmorden*?"

"No," I whispered. "It was—since then."

"I see," he said for the third time, but this time there was a purposeful ring in his voice that made me turn and look at him. His face was grimmer than I had ever seen it.

"What—what do you mean?" I faltered.

He looked at me, inscrutable, dominating.

"Only—that I know now what I have to do."

His words sent a shiver through me. There was a determination behind them that I did not understand—and it frightened me.

We neither of us said any more until we got back to the hotel. I went straight up to Suzanne. She was lying on her bed reading, and did not look in the least as though she had a headache.

"Here reposes the perfect gooseberry," she remarked. "*Alias* the tactful chaperone. Why, Anne dear, what's the matter?"

For I had burst into a flood of tears.

I told her about the cats—I felt it wasn't fair to tell her about Colonel Race. But Suzanne is very sharp. I think she saw that there was something more behind.

"You haven't caught a chill, have you, Anne? Sounds absurd even to suggest such things in this heat, but you keep on shivering."

"It's nothing," I said. "Nerves—or some one walking over my grave. I keep feeling something dreadful's going to happen."

"Don't be silly," said Suzanne, with decision. "Let's talk of something interesting. Anne, about those diamonds——"

"What about them?"

"I'm not sure they're safe with me. It was all righ
before, no one could think they'd be amongst my things
But now that every one knows we're such friends, you
and I, I'll be under suspicion too."

"Nobody knows they're in a roll of films, though,"
argued. "It's a splendid hiding-place and I really don'
think we could better it."

She agreed doubtfully, but said we would discuss i
again when we got to the Falls.

Our train went at nine o'clock. Sir Eustace's tempe
was still far from good, and Miss Pettigrew looked sub
dued. Colonel Race was completely himself. I felt tha
I had dreamed the whole conversation on the way back

I slept heavily that night on my hard bunk, strugglin
with ill-defined, menacing dreams. I awoke with a head
ache and went out on the observation platform of th
car. It was fresh and lovely, and everywhere, as far a
one could see, were the undulating wooded hills. I love
it—loved it more than any place I had ever seen.
wished then that I could have a little hut somewhere i
the heart of the scrub and live there always—always. . .

Just before half-past two, Colonel Race called me ou
from the "office" and pointed to a bouquet-shaped whit
mist that hovered over one portion of the bush.

"The spray from the Falls," he said. "We are nearl
there."

I was still wrapped in that strange dream feeling c
exaltation that had succeeded my troubled night. Ver
strongly implanted in me was the feeling that I had com
home. . . . Home! And yet I had never been here before–
or had I in dreams?

We walked from the train to the hotel, a big whit
building closely wired against mosquitoes. There wer
no roads, no houses. We went out on the *stoep* and

uttered a gasp. There, half a mile away, facing us, were the Falls. I've never seen anything so grand and beautiful—I never shall.

"Anne, you're fey," said Suzanne, as we sat down to lunch. "I've never seen you like this before."

She stared at me curiously.

"Am I?" I laughed, but I felt that my laugh was unnatural. "It's just that I love it all."

"It's more than that."

A little frown creased her brow—one of apprehension.

Yes, I was happy, but beyond that I had the curious feeling that I was waiting for something—something that would happen soon. I was excited—restless.

After tea we strolled out, got on the trolley and were pushed by smiling blacks down the little tracks of rails to the bridge.

It was a marvellous sight, the great chasm and the rushing waters below, and the veil of mist and spray in front of us that parted every now and then for one brief minute to show the cataract of water and then closed up again in its impenetrable mystery. That, to my mind, has always been the fascination of the Falls—their elusive quality. You always think you're going to see—and you never do.

We crossed the bridge and walked slowly on by the path that was marked out with white stone on either side and led round the brink of the gorge. Finally we arrived in a big clearing where on the left a path led downwards towards the chasm.

"The palm gully," explained Colonel Race. "Shall we go down? Or shall we leave it until to-morrow? It will take some time, and it's a good climb up again."

"We'll leave it until to-morrow," said Sir Eustace with decision. He isn't at all fond of strenuous physical exercise, I have noticed.

He led the way back. As we went, we passed a fine native stalking along. Behind him came a woman who seemed to have the entire household belongings piled upon her head! The collection included a frying pan!

"I never have my camera when I want it," groaned Suzanne.

"That's an opportunity that will occur often enough, Mrs. Blair," said Colonel Race. "So don't lament."

We arrived back on the bridge.

"Shall we go into the rainbow forest?" he continued. "Or are you afraid of getting wet?"

Suzanne and I accompanied him. Sir Eustace went back to the hotel. I was rather disappointed in the rainbow forest. There weren't nearly enough rainbows, and we got soaked to the skin, but every now and then we got a glimpse of the Falls opposite and realized how enormously wide they are. Oh, dear, dear Falls, how I love and worship you and always shall!

We got back to the hotel just in time to change for dinner. Sir Eustace seems to have taken a positive antipathy to Colonel Race. Suzanne and I rallied him gently, but didn't get much satisfaction.

After dinner, he retired to his sitting-room, dragging Miss Pettigrew with him. Suzanne and I talked for a while with Colonel Race, and then she declared, with an immense yawn, that she was going to bed. I didn't want to be left alone with him, so I got up too and went to my room.

But I was far too excited to go to sleep. I did not even undress. I lay back in a chair and gave myself up to dreaming. And all the time I was conscious of something coming nearer and nearer. . . .

There was a knock at the door and I started. I got up and went to it. A little black boy held out a note. It was addressed to me in a handwriting I did not know. I took t and came back into the room. I stood there holding it. At last I opened it. It was very short:

"I must see you. I dare not come to the hotel. Will you come to the clearing by the palm gully? In memory of Cabin 17 please come. The man you knew as Harry Rayburn."

My heart beat to suffocation. He was here then! Oh, I had known it—I had known it all along! I had felt him near me. All unwittingly I had come to his place of retreat.

I wound a scarf round my head and stole to the door. I must be careful. He was hunted down. No one must see me meet him. I stole alone to Suzanne's room. She was fast asleep. I could hear her breathing evenly.

Sir Eustace? I paused outside the door of his sitting-room. Yes, he was dictating to Miss Pettigrew, I could hear her monotonous voice repeating. "I therefore venture to suggest, that in tackling this problem of coloured labour——" She paused for him to continue, and I heard him grunt something angrily.

I stole on again. Colonel Race's room was empty. I did not see him in the lounge. And he was the man I feared most! Still, I could waste no more time. I slipped quickly out of the hotel and took the path to the bridge.

I crossed it and stood there waiting in the shadow. If any one had followed me, I should see them crossing the bridge. But the minutes passed, and no one came. I had not been followed. I turned and took the path to the clearing. I took six paces or so and then stopped. Something had rustled behind me. It could not be any one who had followed me from the hotel. It was some one who was already here, waiting.

And immediately, without rhyme or reason, but with the sureness of instinct, I knew that it was I myself who was threatened. It was the same feeling as I had had on the *Kilmorden* that night—a sure instinct warning me of danger.

I looked sharply over my shoulder. Silence. I moved on a pace or two. Again I heard that rustle. Still walking, I looked over my shoulder again. A man's figure came out of the shadow. He saw that I saw him, and jumped forward, hard on my track.

It was too dark to recognize anybody. All I could see was that he was tall, and a European, not a native. I took to my heels and ran. I heard him pounding behind. I ran quicker, keeping my eyes fixed on the white stones that showed me where to step, for there was no moon that night.

And suddenly my foot felt nothingness. I heard the man behind me laugh, an evil, sinister laugh. It rang in my ears, as I fell headlong—down—down—down to destruction far beneath.

25

I came to myself slowly and painfully. I was conscious of an aching head and a shooting pain down my left arm when I tried to move, and everything seemed dream-like and unreal. Nightmare visions floated before me. I felt myself falling—falling again. Once Harry Rayburn's face seemed to come to me out of the mist. Almost I imagined it real. Then it floated away again, mocking me. Once, I remember, some one put a cup to my lips and I drank. A black face grinned into mine—a devil's face, I thought it, and screamed out. Then dreams again—long troubled dreams in which I vainly sought Harry Rayburn to warn him—warn him—what of? I did not know myself. But there was some danger—some great danger—and I alone could save him. Then darkness again, merciful darkness, and real sleep.

I woke at last myself again. The long nightmare was over. I remembered perfectly everything that had happened, my hurried flight from the hotel to meet Harry, the man in the shadows and that last terrible moment of falling. . . .

By some miracle or other I had not been killed. I was bruised and aching and very weak, but I was alive. But where was I? Moving my head with difficulty I looked round me. I was in a small room with rough wooden walls. On them were hung skins of animals and various tusks of ivory. I was lying on a kind of rough couch, also covered with skins, and my left arm was bandaged up and felt stiff and uncomfortable. At first I thought I was alone, and then I saw a man's figure sitting between me and the light, his head turned toward the window. He was so still that he might have been carved out of wood. Something in the close-cropped black head was familiar to me, but I did not dare to let my imagination run astray. Suddenly he turned, and I caught my breath. It was Harry Rayburn. Harry Rayburn in the flesh.

He rose and came over to me.

"Feeling better?" he said a trifle awkwardly.

I could not answer. The tears were running down my face. I was weak still, but I held his hand in both of mine. If only I could die like this, whilst he stood there looking down on me with that new look in his eyes.

"Don't cry, Anne. Please don't cry. You're safe now. No one shall hurt you."

He went and fetched a cup and brought it to me.

"Drink some of this milk."

I drank obediently. He went on talking in a low coaxing tone such as he might have used to a child.

"Don't ask any more questions now. Go to sleep again. You'll be stronger by and by. I'll go away if you like."

"No," I said urgently. "No, no."

"Then I'll stay."

He brought a small stool over beside me and sat there. He laid his hand over mine, and, soothed and comforted, I dropped off to sleep once more.

It must have been evening then, but when I woke again, the sun was high in the heavens. I was alone in the hut, but as I stirred an old native woman came running in. She was hideous as sin, but she grinned at me encouragingly. She brought me water in a basin and helped me wash my face and hands. Then she brought

ne a large bowl of soup, and I finished it every drop! I
asked her several questions, but she only grinned and
nodded and chattered away in a guttural language, so I
gathered she knew no English.

Suddenly she stood up and drew back respectfully as
Harry Rayburn entered. He gave her a nod of dismissal
and she went out leaving us alone. He smiled at me.

"Really better to-day!"

"Yes, indeed, but very bewildered still. Where am I?"

"You're on a small island on the Zambesi about four
miles up from the Falls."

"Do—do my friends know I'm here?"

He shook his head.

"I must send word to them."

"That is as you like of course, but if I were you I
should wait until you are a little stronger."

"Why?"

He did not answer immediately, so I went on.

"How long have I been here?"

"Nearly a month."

"Oh!" I cried. "I must send word to Suzanne. She'll
be terribly anxious."

"Who is Suzanne?"

"Mrs. Blair. I was with her and Sir Eustace and Colonel Race at the hotel—but you knew that surely?"

He shook his head.

"I know nothing, except that I found you, caught in
the fork of a tree, unconscious and with a badly
wrenched arm."

"Where was the tree?"

"Overhanging the ravine. But for your clothes catch-
ing on the branches, you would infallibly have been
dashed to pieces."

I shuddered. Then a thought struck me.

"You say you didn't know I was there. What about the note then?"

"What note?"

"The note you sent me, asking me to meet you in the clearing."

He stared at me.

"I sent no note."

I felt myself flushing up to the roots of my hair. Fortunately he did not seem to notice.

"How did you come to be on the spot in such a marvellous manner?" I asked in as nonchalant a manner as I could assume. "And what are you doing in this part of the world, anyway?"

"I live here," he said simply.

"On this island?"

"Yes, I came here after the War. Sometimes I take parties from the hotel out in my boat, but it costs me very little to live, and mostly I do as I please."

"You live here all alone?"

"I am not pining for society, I assure you," he replied coldly.

"I am sorry to have inflicted mine upon you," I retorted, "but I seem to have had very little to say in the matter."

To my surprise his eyes twinkled a little.

"None whatever. I slung you across my shoulder like a sack of coal and carried you to my boat. Quite like a primitive man of the Stone Age."

"But for a different reason," I put in.

He flushed this time, a deep burning blush. The tan of his face was suffused.

"But you haven't told me how you came to be wandering about so conveniently for me?" I said hastily, to cover his confusion.

"I couldn't sleep. I was restless—disturbed—had the feeling something was going to happen. In the end I took the boat and came ashore and tramped down towards the Falls. I was just at the head of the palm gully when I heard you scream."

"Why didn't you get help from the hotel instead of carting me all the way here?" I asked.

He flushed again.

"I suppose it seems an unpardonable liberty to you— but I don't think that even now you realize your danger! You think I should have informed your friends? No, I swore to myself that I'd take better care of you than any one else could. Not a soul comes to this island. I got old Batani, whom I cured of a fever once, to come and look after you. She's loyal. She'll never say a word. I could keep you here for months and no one would ever know."

I could keep you here for months and no one would ever know! How some words please one!

"You did quite right," I said quietly. "And I shall not send word to any one. A day or so more anxiety doesn't make much difference. It's not as though they were my own people. They're only acquaintances really—even Suzanne. And whoever wrote that note must have known—a great deal. It was not the work of an outsider."

I managed to mention the note this time without blushing at all.

"If you would be guided by me——" he said, hesitating.

"I don't expect I shall be," I answered candidly. "But there's no harm in hearing."

"Do you always do what you like, Miss Beddingfeld?"

"Usually," I replied cautiously. To any one else I would have said "Always."

"I pity your husband," he said unexpectedly.

"You needn't," I retorted. "I shouldn't dream of marrying any one unless I was madly in love with them. And of course there is really nothing a woman enjoys so much as doing all the things she doesn't like for the sake of some one she *does* like. And the more self-willed she is, the more she likes it."

"I'm afraid I disagree with you. The boot is on the other leg as a rule." He spoke with a slight sneer.

"Exactly," I cried eagerly. "And that's why there are so many unhappy marriages. It's all the fault of the men. Either they give way to their women—and then the women despise them, or else they are utterly selfish, insist on their own way and never say 'thank you.' Successful husbands make their wives do just what they want, and then make a frightful fuss of them for doing it. Women like to be mastered, but they hate not to have their sacrifices appreciated. On the other hand, men don't really appreciate women who are nice to them all the time. When I am married, I shall be a devil most of the time, but every now and then, when my husband least expects it, I shall show him what a perfect angel I can be!"

Harry laughed outright.

"What a cat and dog life you will lead."

"Lovers always fight," I assured him. "Because they don't understand each other. And by the time they do understand each other they aren't in love any more."

"Does the reverse hold true? Are people who fight each other always lovers?"

"I—I don't know," I said, momentarily confused.

He turned away to the fireplace.

"Like some more soup?" he asked in a casual tone.

"Yes, please. I'm so hungry that I could eat a hippopotamus."

"That's good."

He busied himself with the fire; I watched.

"When I can get off the couch, I'll cook for you," I promised.

"I don't suppose you know anything about cooking."

"I can warm up things out of tins as well as you can," I retorted, pointing to a row of tins on the mantelpiece.

"Touché," he said, and laughed.

His whole face changed when he laughed. It became boyish, happy—a different personality.

I enjoyed my soup. As I ate it I reminded him that he had not, after all, tendered me his advice.

"Ah, yes, what I was going to say was this. If I were you I would stay quietly *perdu* here until you are quite strong again. Your enemies will believe you dead. They will hardly be surprised at not finding the body. It would have been dashed to pieces on the rocks and carried down with the torrent."

I shivered.

"Once you are completely restored to health, you can journey quietly on to Beria and get a boat to take you back to England."

"That would be very tame," I objected scornfully.

"There speaks a foolish schoolgirl."

"I'm not a foolish schoolgirl," I cried indignantly. "I'm a woman."

"God help me, so you are," he muttered, and went abruptly out.

My recovery was rapid. The two injuries I had sustained were a knock on the head and a badly wrenched arm. The latter was the most serious and, to begin with, my rescuer had believed it to be actually broken. A careful examination, however, convinced him that it was not so, and although it was very painful I was recovering the use of it quite quickly.

It was a strange time. We were cut off from the world, alone together as Adam and Eve might have been—but with what a difference! Old Batani hovered about counting no more than a dog might have done. I insisted on doing the cooking, or as much of it as I could manage with one arm. Harry was out a good part of the time, but we spent long hours together lying out in the shade of the palms, talking and quarrelling—discussing everything under high heaven, quarrelling and making it up again. We bickered a good deal, but there grew up between us a real and lasting comradeship such as I could never have believed possible. That—and something else.

The time was drawing near, I knew it, when I should be well enough to leave and I realized it with a heavy heart. Was he going to let me go? Without a word? Without a sign? He had fits of silence, long moody intervals, moments when he would spring up and tramp off by himself. One evening the crisis came. We had finished our simple meal and were sitting in the doorway of the hut. The sun was sinking.

Hairpins were necessities of life with which Harry had not been able to provide me, and my hair, straight and black, hung to my knees. I sat, my chin on my hands, lost in meditation. I felt rather than saw Harry looking at me.

"You look like a witch, Anne," he said at last, and there was something in his voice that had never been there before.

He reached out his hand and touched my hair. I shivered. Suddenly he sprang up with an oath.

"You must leave here to-morrow, do you hear?" he cried. "I—I can't bear any more. I'm only a man after all. You must go, Anne. You must. You're not a fool. You know yourself that this can't go on."

"I suppose not," I said slowly. "But—it's been happy, hasn't it?"

"Happy? It's been hell!"

"As bad as that!"

"What do you torment me for? Why are you mocking at me? Why do you say that—laughing into your hair?"

"I wasn't laughing. And I'm not mocking. If you want me to go, I'll go. But if you want me to stay—I'll stay."

"Not that!" he cried vehemently. "Not that. Don't tempt me, Anne. Do you realize what I am? A criminal twice over. A man hunted down. They know me here as Harry Parker—they think I've been away on a trek up country, but any day they may put two and two together—and then the blow will fall. You're so young, Anne, and so beautiful—with the kind of beauty that sends men mad. All the world's before you—love, life, everything. Mine's behind me—scorched, spoiled, with a taste of bitter ashes."

"If you don't want me——"

"You know I want you. You know that I'd give my soul to pick you up in my arms and keep you here, hidden away from the world, for ever and ever. And you're tempting me, Anne. You, with your long witch's hair, and your eyes that are golden and brown and green and never stop laughing even when your mouth is grave. But I'll save you from yourself and from me. You shall go to-night. You shall go to Beira—"

"I'm not going to Beira," I interrupted.

"You are. You shall go to Beira if I have to take you there myself and throw you on to the boat. What do you think I'm made of? Do you think I'll wake up night after night, fearing they've got you? One can't go on counting on miracles happening. You must go back to England, Anne—and—and marry and be happy."

"With a steady man who'll give me a good home!"

"Better that than—utter disaster."

"And what of you?"

His face grew grim and set.

"I've got my work ready to hand. Don't ask what it is. You can guess, I dare say. But I'll tell you this—I'll clear my name, or die in the attempt, and I'll choke the life out of the damned scoundrel who did his best to murder you the other night."

"We must be fair," I said. "He didn't actually push me over."

"He'd no need to. His plan was cleverer than that. I went up to the path afterwards. Everything looked all right, but by the marks on the ground I saw that the stones which outline the path had been taken up and put down again in a slightly different place. There are tall bushes growing just over the edge. He'd balanced the outside stones on them, so that you'd think you were still on the path when in reality you were stepping into nothingness. God help him if I lay my hands upon him!"

He paused a minute and then said in a totally different tone:

"We've never spoken of these things, Anne, have we? But the time's come. I want you to hear the whole story—from the beginning."

"If it hurts you to go over the past, don't tell me," I said in a low voice.

"But I want you to know. I never thought I should speak of that part of my life to any one. Funny, isn't it, the tricks Fate plays?"

He was silent for a minute or two. The sun had set, and the velvety darkness of the African night was enveloping us like a mantle.

"Some of it I know," I said gently.

"What do you know?"

"I know that your real name is Harry Lucas."

Still he hesitated—not looking at me, but staring straight out in front of him. I had no clue as to what was passing in his mind, but at last he jerked his head forward as though acquiescing in some unspoken decision of his own and began his story.

26

"You are right. My real name is Harry Lucas. My father was a retired soldier who came out to farm in Rhodesia. He died when I was in my second year at Cambridge."

"Were you fond of him?" I asked suddenly.

"I—don't know."

Then he flushed and went on with sudden vehemence:

"Why do I say that? I *did* love my father. We said bitter things to each other the last time I saw him, and we had many rows over my wildness and my debts, but I cared for the old man. I know how much now—when it's too late," he continued more quietly. "It was at Cambridge that I met the other fellow—"

"Young Eardsley?"

"Yes—young Eardsley. His father, as you know, was one of South Africa's most prominent men. We drifted together at once, my friend and I. We had our love of South Africa in common and we both had a taste for the untrodden places of the world. After he left Cambridge, Eardsley had a final quarrel with his father. The old man had paid his debts twice, he refused to do so again. There was a bitter scene between them. Sir Laurence declared himself at the end of his patience—he would do no more for his son. He must stand on his own legs for a while. The result was, as you know, that those two young men went off to South America together, prospecting for diamonds. I'm not going into that now, but we had a wonderful time out there. Hardships in plenty, you understand, but it was a good life—a hand-to-mouth scramble for existence far from the beaten track—and, my God! that's the place to know a friend. There was a bond forged between us two out there that only death could have broken. Well, as Colonel Race told you, our efforts were crowned with success. We found a second Kimberley in the heart of the British Guiana jungles. I can't tell you our elation. It wasn't so much the actual value in money of the find—you see, Eardsley was used to money, and he knew that when his father died he would be a millionaire, and Lucas had always been poor and was used to it. No, it was the sheer delight of discovery."

He paused, and then added, almost apologetically:

"You don't mind my telling it this way, do you? As though I wasn't in it at all. It seems like that now when I look back and see those two boys. I almost forget that one of them was—Harry Rayburn."

"Tell it any way you like," I said, as he went on:

"We came to Kimberley—very cock-a-hoop over our find. We brought a magnificent selection of diamonds with us to submit to the experts. And then—in the hotel at Kimberley—we met her——"

I stiffened a little, and the hand that rested on the doorpost clenched itself involuntarily.

"Anita Grünberg—that was her name. She was an actress. Quite young and very beautiful. She was South African born, but her mother was a Hungarian, I believe. There was some sort of mystery about her, and that, of course, heightened her attraction for two boys home from the wilds. She must have had an easy task. We both fell for her right away, and we both took it hard. It was the first shadow that had ever come between us— but even then it didn't weaken our friendship. Each of us, I honestly believe, was willing to stand aside for the other to go in and win. But that wasn't her game. Sometimes, afterwards, I wondered why it hadn't been, for Sir Laurence Eardsley's son was quite a *parti*. But the truth of it was that she was married—to a sorter in De Beers'—though nobody knew of it. She pretended enormous interests in our discovery, and we told her all about it and even showed her the diamonds. Delilah—that's what she should have been called—and she played her part well!

"The De Beers robbery was discovered, and like a thunderclap the police came down upon us. They seized our diamonds. We only laughed at first—the whole thing was so absurd. And then the diamonds were produced in court—and without question they were the stones stolen from De Beers'. Anita Grünberg had disappeared. She had effected the substitution neatly enough, and our story that these were not the stones originally in our possession was laughed to scorn.

"Sir Laurence Eardsley had enormous influence. He succeeded in getting the case dismissed—but it left two young men ruined and disgraced to face the world with the stigma of thief attached to their names, and it pretty well broke the old fellow's heart. He had one bitter interview with his son in which he heaped upon him every reproach imaginable. He had done what he could to save the family name, but from that day on his son was his son no longer. He cast him off utterly. And the boy, like the proud young fool that he was, remained silent, disdaining to protest his innocence in the face of his father's disbelief. He came out furious from the interview—his friend was waiting for him. A week later war was declared. The two friends enlisted together. You know what happened. The best pal a man ever had was killed, partly through his own mad recklessness in rushing into unnecessary danger. He died with his name tarnished. . . .

"I swear to you, Anne, that it was mainly on his account that I was so bitter against that woman. It had gone deeper with him than me. I had been madly in love with her for the moment—I even think that I frightened her sometimes—but with him it was a quieter and deeper feeling. She had been the very centre of his universe—and her betrayal of him tore up the very roots of life. The blow stunned him and left him paralyzed."

Harry paused. After a minute or two he went on:

"As you know, I was reported 'Missing, presumed killed.' I never troubled to correct the mistake. I took the name of Parker and came to this island, which I knew of old. At the beginning of the War, I had had ambitious hopes of proving my innocence, but now all that spirit seemed dead. All I felt was, 'What's the good?' My pal was dead, neither he nor I had any living relations who would care. I was supposed to be dead too, let it remain at that. I led a peaceful existence here, neither happy nor unhappy—numbed of all feeling. I see now, though I did not realize it at the time, that that was partly the effect of the War.

"And then one day something occurred to wake me right up again. I was taking a party of people in my boat on a trip up the river, and I was standing at the landing-stage, helping them in, when one of the men uttered a startled exclamation. It focused my attention on him. He was a small, thin man with a beard, and he was staring at me for all he was worth as though I was a ghost. So powerful was his emotion that it awakened my curiosity. I made inquiries about him at the hotel and learned that his name was Carton, that he came from Kimberley, and that he was a diamond-sorter employed by De Beers'. In a minute all the old sense of wrong surged over me again. I left the island and went to Kimberley.

"I could find out little more about him, however. In the end, I decided that I must force an interview. I took my revolver with me. In the brief glimpse I had had of him, I had realized that he was a physical coward. No sooner were we face to face than I recognized that he was afraid of me. I soon forced him to tell me all he knew. He had engineered part of the robbery and Anita Grünberg was his wife. He had once caught sight of both of us when we were dining with her at the hotel, and, having read that I was killed, my appearance in the flesh at the Falls had startled him badly. He and Anita had married quite young, but she had soon drifted away from him. She had got in with a bad lot, he told me—and it was then for the first time that I heard of the 'Colonel.' Carton himself had never been mixed up in anything except this one affair—so he solemnly assured me, and I was inclined to believe him. He was emphatically not of the stuff of which successful criminals are made.

"I still had the feeling that he was keeping back something. As a test, I threatened to shoot him there and then, declaring that I cared very little what became of me now. In a frenzy of terror he poured out a further story. It seems that Anita Grünberg did not quite trust the 'Colonel.' Whilst pretending to hand over to him the stones she had taken from the hotel, she kept back some in her own possession. Carton advised her, with his technical knowledge, which to keep. If, at any time, these stones were produced, they were of such colour and quality as to be readily identifiable, and the experts' at De Beers' would admit at once that these stones had never passed through their hands. In this way my story of a substitution would be supported, my name would be cleared, and suspicion would be diverted to the proper quarter. I gathered that, contrary to his usual practice, the 'Colonel' himself had been concerned in this affair, therefore Anita felt satisfied that she had a real hold over him, should she need it. Carton now proposed that I should make a bargain with Anita Grünberg, or Nadina, as she now called herself. For a sufficient sum of money he thought that she would be willing to give up the diamonds and betray her former employer. He would cable to her immediately.

"I was still suspicious of Carton. He was a man whom it was easy enough to frighten, but who, in his fright, would tell so many lies that to sift the truth out from them would be no easy job. I went back to the hotel and waited. By the following evening I judged that he would have received the reply to his cable. I called round at his house and was told that Mr. Carton was away, but would be returning on the morrow. Instantly I became suspicious. In the nick of time I found out that he was in reality sailing for England on the *Kilmorden Castle*, which left Cape Town in two day's time. I had just time to journey down and catch the same boat.

"I had no intention of alarming Carton by revealing my presence on board. I had done a good deal of acting in my time at Cambridge, and it was comparatively easy for me to transform myself into a grave bearded gentleman of middle age. I avoided Carton carefully on board the boat, keeping to my own cabin as far as possible under the presence of illness.

"I had no difficulty in trailing him when we got to London. He went straight to a hotel and did not go out until the following day. He left the hotel shortly before one o'clock. I was behind him. He went straight to a house-agent in Knightsbridge. There he asked for particulars of houses to let on the river.

"I was at the next table also inquiring about houses. Then suddenly in walked Anita Grünberg, Nadina—

whatever you like to call her. Superb, insolent, and almost as beautiful as ever. God! how I hated her. There she was, the woman who had ruined my life—and who had also ruined a better life than mine. At that minute I could have put my hands round her neck and squeezed the life out of her inch by inch! Just for a minute or two I saw red. I hardly took in what the agent was saying. It was her voice that I heard next, high and clear, with an exaggerated foreign accent: 'The Mill House, Marlow. The property of Sir Eustace Pedler. That sounds as though it might suit me. At any rate, I will go and see it.'

"The man wrote her an order, and she walked out again in her regal insolent manner. Not by word or a sign had she recognized Carton, yet I was sure that their meeting there was a preconceived plan. Then I started to jump to conclusions. Not knowing that Sir Eustace was at Cannes, I thought that this house-hunting business was a mere pretext for meeting him in the Mill House. I knew that he had been in South Africa at the time of the robbery, and never having seen him I immediately leaped to the conclusion that he himself was the mysterious 'Colonel' of whom I had heard so much.

"I followed my two suspects along Knightsbridge. Nadina went into the Hyde Park Hotel. I quickened my pace and went in also. She walked straight into the restaurant, and I decided that I would not risk her recognizing me at the moment, but would continue to follow Carton. I was in great hopes that he was going to get the diamonds, and that by suddenly appearing and making myself known to him when he least expected it I might startle the truth out of him. I followed him down into the Tube station at Hyde Park Corner. He was standing by himself at the end of the platform. There was some girl standing near, but no one else. I decided that

I would accost him then and there. You know what happened. In the sudden shock of seeing a man whom he imagined far away in South Africa, he lost his head and stepped back upon the line. He was always a coward. Under the pretext of being a doctor, I managed to search his pockets. There was a wallet with some notes in it and one or two unimportant letters, there was a roll of films—which I must have dropped somewhere later—and there was a piece of paper with an appointment made on it for the 22nd on the *Kilmorden Castle*. In my haste to get away before any one detained me, I dropped that also, but fortunately I remembered the figures.

"I hurried to the nearest cloak-room and hastily removed my make-up. I did not want to be laid by the heels for picking a dead man's pocket. Then I retraced my steps to the Hyde Park Hotel. Nadina was still having lunch. I needn't describe in detail how I followed her down to Marlow. She went into the house, and I spoke to the woman at the lodge, pretending that I was with her. Then I, too, went in."

He stopped. There was a tense silence.

"You will believe me, Anne, won't you? I swear before God that what I am going to say is true. I went into the house after her with something like murder in my heart—and she was dead! I found her in that first-floor room—God! It was horrible. Dead—and I was not more than three minutes behind her. And there was no sign of any one else in the house! Of course I realized at once the terrible position I was in. By one master-stroke the blackmailed had rid himself of the blackmailer, and at the same time had provided a victim to whom the crime would be ascribed. The hand of the 'Colonel' was very plain. For the second time I was to be his victim. Fool that I had been to walk into the trap so easily.

"I hardly know what I did next. I managed to go out of the place looking fairly normal, but I knew that it could not be long before the crime was discovered and a description of my appearance telegraphed all over the country.

"I lay low for some days, not daring to make a move. In the end chance came to my aid. I overheard a conversation between two middle-aged gentlemen in the street, one of whom proved to be Sir Eustace Pedler. I at once conceived the idea of attaching myself to him as his secretary. The fragment of conversation I had overheard gave me my clue. I was now no longer so sure that Sir Eustace Pedler was the 'Colonel.' His house might have been appointed as a rendezvous by accident, or for some obscure motive that I had not fathomed."

"Do you know," I interrupted, "that Guy Pagett was in Marlow at the date of the murder?"

"That settles it then. I thought he was at Cannes with Sir Eustace."

"He was supposed to be in Florence—but he certainly never went *there*. I'm pretty certain he was really in Marlow, but of course I can't prove it."

"And to think I never suspected Pagett for a minute until the night he tried to throw you overboard. The man's a marvellous actor."

"Yes, isn't he?"

"That explains why the Mill House was chosen. Pagett could probably get in and out of it unobserved. Of course he made no objection to my accompanying Sir Eustace across in the boat. He didn't want me laid by the heels immediately. You see, evidently Nadina didn't bring the jewels with her to the rendezvous as they had counted on her doing. I fancy that Carton really had them and concealed them somewhere on the *Kilmorden Castle*—that's where he came in. They hoped that I might have some clue as to where they were hidden. As long as the 'Colonel' did not recover the diamonds, he was still in danger—hence his anxiety to get them at all costs. Where the devil Carton hid them—if he did hide them, I don't know."

"That's another story," I quoted. "*My* story. And I'm going to tell it to you now."

27

Harry listened attentively whilst I recounted all the events that I have narrated in these pages. The thing that bewildered and astonished him most was to find that all along the diamonds had been in my possession—or rather in Suzanne's. That was a fact he had never suspected. Of course, after hearing his story, I realized the point of Carton's little arrangement—or rather Nadina's, since I had no doubt that it was her brain which had conceived the plan. No surprise tactics executed against her or her husband could result in the seizure of the diamonds. The secret was locked in her own brain, and the "Colonel" was not likely to guess that they had been entrusted to the keeping of an ocean steward!

Harry's vindication from the old charge of theft seemed assured. It was the other, graver charge that paralyzed all our activities. For, as things stood, he could not come out in the open to prove his case.

The one thing we came back to, again and again, was the identity of the "Colonel." Was he, or was he not, Guy Pagett?

"I should say he was but for one thing," said Harry. "It seems pretty much of a certainty that it was Pagett who murdered Anita Grünberg at Marlow—and that certainly lends colour to the supposition that he is actually the 'Colonel,' since Anita's business was not of the nature to be discussed with a subordinate. No—the only thing that militates against that theory is the attempt to put you out of the way on the night of your arrival here. You saw Pagett left behind at Cape Town—by no possible means could he have arrived here before the following Wednesday. He is unlikely to have any emissaries in this part of the world, and all his plans were laid to deal with you in Cape Town. He might, of course, have cabled instructions to some lieutenant of his in Johannesburg, who could have joined the Rhodesian train at Mafeking, but his instructions would have had to be particularly definite to allow of that note being written."

We sat silent for a moment, then Harry went on slowly:

"You say that Mrs. Blair was asleep when you left the hotel and that you heard Sir Eustace dictating to Miss Pettigrew? Where was Colonel Race?"

"I could not find him anywhere."

"Had he any reason to believe that—you and I might be friendly with each other?"

"He might have had," I answered thoughtfully, remembering our conversation on the way back from the Matoppos. "He's a very powerful personality," I continued, "but not at all my idea of the 'Colonel.' And, anyway, such an idea would be absurd. He's in the Secret Service."

"How do we know that he is? It's the easiest thing in the world to throw out a hint of that kind. No one contradicts it, and the rumour spreads until every one believes it as gospel truth. It provides an excuse for all sorts of doubtful things. Anne, do you like Race?"

"I do—and I don't. He repels me and at the same time fascinates me; but I know one thing, I'm always a little afraid of him."

"He was in South Africa, you know, at the time of the Kimberley robbery," said Harry slowly.

"But it was he who told Suzanne all about the 'Colonel' and how he had been in Paris trying to get on his track."

"*Camouflage*—of a particularly clever kind."

"But where does Pagett come in? Is he in Race's pay?"

"Perhaps," said Harry slowly, "he doesn't come in at all."

"What?"

"Think back, Anne. Did you ever hear Pagett's own account of that night on the *Kilmorden*?"

"Yes—through Sir Eustace."

I repeated it. Harry listened closely.

"He saw a man coming from the direction of Sir Eustace's cabin and followed him up on deck. Is that what he says? Now, who had the cabin opposite to Sir Eustace? Colonel Race. Supposing Colonel Race crept up on deck, and, foiled in his attack on you, fled round the deck and met Pagett just coming through the saloon door. He knocks him down and springs inside, closing the door. We dash round and find Pagett lying there. How's that?"

"You forget that he declares positively it was you who knocked him down."

"Well, suppose that just as he regains consciousness he sees me disappearing in the distance? Wouldn't he take it for granted that I was his assailant? Especially as he thought all along it was I he was following?"

"It's possible, yes," I said slowly. "But it alters all our ideas. And there are other things."

"Most of them are open to explanation. The man who followed you in Cape Town spoke to Pagett, and Pagett looked at his watch. The man might have merely asked him the time."

"It was just a coincidence, you mean?"

"Not exactly. There's a method in all this, connecting Pagett with the affair. Why was the Mill House chosen for the murder? Was it because Pagett had been in Kimberley when the diamonds were stolen? Would *he* have been made the scapegoat if I had not appeared so providentially upon the scene?"

"Then you think he may be entirely innocent?"

"It looks like it, but, if so, we've got to find out what he was doing in Marlow. If he's got a reasonable explanation of that, we're on the right track."

He got up.

"It's past midnight. Turn in, Anne, and get some sleep. Just before dawn I'll take you over in the boat. You must catch the train at Livingstone. I've got a friend there who will keep you hidden away until the train starts. You go to Bulawayo and catch the Beira train there. I can find out from my friend in Livingstone what's going on at the hotel and where your friends are now."

"Beira," I said meditatively.

"Yes, Anne, it's Beira for you. This is man's work. Leave it to me."

We had had a momentary respite from emotion whilst we talked the situation out, but it was on us again now. We did not even look at each other.

"Very well," I said, and passed into the hut.

I lay down on the skin-covered couch, but I didn't sleep, and outside I could hear Harry Rayburn pacing up and down, up and down through the long dark hours. At last he called me:

"Come, Anne, it's time to go."

I got up and came out obediently. It was still quite dark, but I knew that dawn was not far off.

"We'll take the canoe, not the motor-boat——" Harry began, when suddenly he stopped dead and held up his hand.

"Hush! What's that?"

I listened, but could hear nothing. His ears were sharper than mine, however, the ears of a man who has lived long in the wilderness. Presently I heard it too— the faint splash of paddles in the water coming from the direction of the right bank of the river and rapidly approaching our little landing-stage.

We strained our eyes in the darkness, and could make out a dark blur on the surface of the water. It was a boat. Then there was a momentary spurt of flame. Some one had struck a match. By its light I recognized one figure, the red-bearded Dutchman of the villa at Muizenberg. The others were natives.

"Quick—back to the hut."

Harry swept me back with him. He took down a couple of rifles and a revolver from the wall.

"Can you load a rifle?"

"I never have. Show me how."

I grasped his instructions well enough. We closed the door and Harry stood by the window which overlooked the landing-stage. The boat was just about to run alongside it.

"Who's that?" called out Harry in a ringing voice.

Any doubt we might have had as to our visitors' intentions was swiftly resolved. A hail of bullets splattered round us. Fortunately neither of us was hit. Harry raised the rifle. It spat murderously, and again and again. I heard two groans and a splash.

"That's given 'em something to think about," he muttered grimly, as he reached for the second rifle. "Stand well back, Anne, for God's sake. And load quickly."

More bullets. One just grazed Harry's cheek. His answering fire was more deadly than theirs. I had the rifle reloaded when he turned for it. He caught me close with his left arm and kissed me once savagely before he turned to the windows again. Suddenly he uttered a shout.

"They're going—had enough of it. They're a good mark out there on the water, and they can't see how many of us there are. They're routed for the moment— but they'll come back. We'll have to get ready for them." He flung down the rifle and turned to me.

"Anne! You beauty! You wonder! You little queen! As brave as a lion. Black-haired witch!"

He caught me in his arms. He kissed my hair, my eyes, my mouth.

"And now to business," he said, suddenly releasing me. "Get out those tins of paraffin."

I did as I was told. He was busy inside the hut. Presently I saw him on the roof of the hut, crawling along with something in his arms. He rejoined me in a minute or two.

"Go down to the boat. We'll have to carry it across the island to the other side."

He picked up the paraffin as I disappeared.

"They're coming back," I called softly. I had seen the blur moving out from the opposite shore.

He ran down to me.

"Just in time. Why—where the hell's the boat?"

Both had been cut adrift. Harry whistled softly.

"We're in a tight place, honey. Mind?"

"Not with you."

"Ah, but dying together's not much fun. We'll do better than that. See—they've got two boat-loads this time. Going to land at two different points. Now for my little scenic effect."

Almost as he spoke a long flame shot up from the hut. Its light illuminated two crouching figures huddled together on the roof.

"My old clothes—stuffed with rags—but they won't tumble to it for some time. Come, Anne, we've got to try desperate means."

Hand in hand, we raced across the island. Only a narrow channel of water divided it from the shore on that side.

"We've got to swim for it. Can you swim at all, Anne? Not that it matters. I can get you across. It's the wrong side for a boat—too many rocks, but the right side for swimming, and the right side for Livingstone."

"I can swim a little—farther than that. What's the danger, Harry?" For I had seen the grim look on his face. "Sharks?"

"No, you little goose. Sharks live in the sea. But you're sharp, Anne. Crocs, that's the trouble."

"Crocodiles?"

"Yes, don't think of them—or say your prayers, whichever you feel inclined."

We plunged in. My prayers must have been efficacious, for we reached the shore without adventure, and drew ourselves up wet and dripping on the bank.

"Now for Livingstone. It's rough going, I'm afraid, and wet clothes won't make it any better. But it's got to be done."

That walk was a nightmare. My wet skirts flapped round my legs, and my stockings were soon torn off by the thorns. Finally, I stopped, utterly exhausted. Harry came back to me.

"Hold up, honey. I'll carry you for a bit."

That was the way I came into Livingstone, slung across his shoulder like a sack of coals. How he did it for all that way, I don't know. The first faint light of dawn was just breaking. Harry's friend was a young man of twenty odd who kept a store of native curios. His name was Ned—perhaps he had another, but I never heard it. He didn't seem in the least surprised to see Harry walk in, dripping wet, holding an equally dripping female by the hand. Men are very wonderful.

He gave us food to eat, and hot coffee, and got our clothes dried for us whilst we rolled ourselves in Manchester blankets of gaudy hue. In the tiny back room of the hut we were safe from observation whilst he departed to make judicious inquiries as to what had become of Sir Eustace's party, and whether any of them were still at the hotel.

It was then that I informed Harry that nothing would induce me to go to Beira. I never meant to, anyway, but now all reason for such proceedings had vanished. The point of the plan had been that my enemies believed me dead. Now that they knew I wasn't dead, my going to Beira would do no good whatever. They could easily follow me there and murder me quietly. I should have no one to protect me. It was finally arranged that I should join Suzanne, wherever she was, and devote all my energies to taking care of myself. On no account was I to seek adventures or endeavour to checkmate the "Colonel."

I was to remain quietly with her and await instructions from Harry. The diamonds were to be deposited in the Bank at Kimberley under the name of Parker.

"There's one thing," I said thoughtfully, "we ought to have a code of some kind. We don't want to be hoodwinked again by messages purporting to come from one to the other."

"That's easy enough. Any message that comes *genuinely* from me will have the word 'and' crossed out in it."

"Without trade-mark, none genuine," I murmured. "What about wires?"

"Any wires from me will be signed 'Andy.' "

"Train will be in before long, Harry," said Ned, putting his head in and withdrawing it immediately.

I stood up.

"And shall I marry a nice steady man if I find one?" I asked demurely.

Harry came close to me.

"My God! Anne, if you ever marry any one else but me, I'll wring his neck. And as for you——"

"Yes," I said, pleasurably excited.

"I shall carry you away and beat you black and blue!"

"What a delightful husband I have chosen," I said satirically. "And doesn't he change his mind overnight!"

28

(Extract from the diary of Sir Eustace Pedler)

As I remarked once before, I am essentially a man of peace. I yearn for a quiet life—and that's just the one thing I don't seem able to have. I am always in the middle of storms and alarms. The relief of getting away from Pagett with his incessant nosing out of intrigues was enormous, and Miss Pettigrew is certainly a useful creature. Although there is nothing of the houri about her, one or two of her accomplishments are invaluable. It is true that I had a touch of liver at Bulawayo and behaved like a bear in consequence, but I had had a disturbed night in the train. At 3 A.M. an exquisitely dressed young man looking like a musical-comedy hero of the Wild West entered my compartment and asked where I was going. Disregarding my first murmur of "Tea—and for God's sake don't put sugar in it," he repeated his question, laying stress on the fact that he was not a waiter but an Immigration officer. I finally succeeded in satisfying him that I was suffering from no infectious disease, that I was visiting Rhodesia from the purest of motives, and further gratified him with my full Christian names and my place of birth. I then endeavoured to snatch a little sleep, but some officious ass aroused me at 5.30 with a cup of liquid sugar which he called tea. I don't think I threw it at him, but I know that that was what I wanted to do. He brought me unsugared tea, stone cold, at 6, and I then fell asleep utterly exhausted, to awaken just outside Bulawayo and be landed with a beastly wooden giraffe, all legs and neck!

But for these small contretemps, all had been going smoothly. And then fresh calamity befell.

It was the night of our arrival at the Falls. I was dictating to Miss Pettigrew in my sitting-room, when suddenly Mrs. Blair burst in without a word of excuse and wearing most compromising attire.

"Where's Anne?" she cried.

A nice question to ask. As though I were responsible for the girl. What did she expect Miss Pettigrew to think? That I was in the habit of producing Anne Beddingfeld from my pocket at midnight or thereabouts? Very compromising for a man in my position.

"I presume," I said coldly, "that she is in her bed."

I cleared my throat and glanced at Miss Pettigrew, to show that I was ready to resume dictating. I hoped Mrs. Blair would take the hint. She did nothing of the kind. Instead she sank into a chair and waved a slippered foot in an agitated manner.

"She's not in her room. I've been there. I had a dream—a terrible dream—that she was in some awful danger, and I got up and went to her room, just to reassure myself, you know. She wasn't there and her bed hadn't been slept in."

She looked at me appealingly.

"What shall I do, Sir Eustace?"

Repressing the desire to reply, "Go to bed, and don't worry over nothing. An able-bodied young woman like Anne Beddingfeld is perfectly well able to take care of herself," I frowned judicially.

"What does Race say about it?"

Why should Race have it all his own way? Let him have some of the disadvantages as well as the advantages of female society.

"I can't find him anywhere."

She was evidently making a night of it. I sighed and sat down in a chair.

"I don't quite see the reason for your agitation," I said patiently.

"My dream——"

"That curry we had for dinner!"

"Oh, Sir Eustace!"

The woman was quite indignant. And yet everybody knows that nightmares are a direct result of injudicious eating.

"After all," I continued persuasively, "why shouldn't Anne Beddingfeld and Race go out for a little stroll without having the whole hotel aroused about it?"

"You think they've just gone out for a stroll together? But it's after midnight!"

"One does these foolish things when one is young," I murmured, "though Race is certainly old enough to know better."

"Do you really think so?"

"I dare say they've run away to make a match of it," I continued soothingly, though fully aware that I was making an idiotic suggestion. For, after all, at a place like this, where is there to run away to?

I don't know how much longer I should have gone on making feeble remarks, but at that moment Race himself walked in upon us. At any rate, I had been partly right—*he* had been out for a stroll, but he hadn't taken Anne with him. However, I had been quite wrong in my way of dealing with the situation. I was soon shown that. Race had the whole hotel turned upside-down in three minutes. I've never seen a man more upset.

The thing is very extraordinary. Where did the girl go? She walked out of the hotel, fully dressed, about ten minutes past eleven, and she was never seen again. The idea of suicide seems impossible. She was one of those energetic young women who are in love with life, and have not the faintest intention of quitting it. There was no train either way until midday on the morrow, so she can't have left the place. Then where the devil is she?

Race is almost beside himself, poor fellow. He has left no stone unturned. All the D.C.'s, or whatever they call themselves, for hundreds of miles round have been pressed into the service. The native trackers have run about on all fours. Everything that can be done is being done—but no sign of Anne Beddingfeld. The accepted theory is that she walked in her sleep. There are signs on the path near the bridge which seem to show that the girl must have been dashed to pieces on the rocks below. Unfortunately, most of the footprints were obliterated by a party of tourists who chose to walk that way early on the Monday morning.

I don't know that it's a very satisfactory theory. In my young days, I always was told that sleep-walkers couldn't hurt themselves—that their own sixth sense took care of them. I don't think the theory satisfies Mrs. Blair either.

I can't make that woman out. Her whole attitude towards Race has changed. She watches him now like a cat a mouse, and she makes obvious efforts to bring herself to be civil to him. And they used to be such friends. Altogether she is unlike herself, nervous, hysterical, starting and jumping at the least sound. I am beginning to think that it is high time I went to Jo'burg.

A rumour came along yesterday of a mysterious island somewhere up the river, with a man and a girl on it. Race got very excited. It turned out to be a mare's-nest, however. The man had been there for years, and is well known to the manager of the hotel. He totes parties up and down the river in the season and points out crocodiles and a stray hippopotamus or so to them. I believe that he keeps a tame one which is trained to bite pieces out of the boat on occasions. Then he fends it off with a boat-hook, and the party feel they have really got to the back of beyond at last. How long the girl has been there is not definitely known, but it seems pretty clear that she can't be Anne, and there is a certain delicacy in interfering in other people's affairs. If I were this young fellow, I should certainly kick Race off the island if he came asking questions about my love affairs.

LATER.

It is definitely settled that I go to Jo'burg to-morrow. Race urges me to do so. Things are getting unpleasant there, by all I hear, but I might as well go before they get worse. I dare say I shall be shot by a striker, anyway. Mrs. Blair was to have accompanied me, but at the last minute she changed her mind and decided to stay on at the Falls. It seems as though she couldn't bear to take her eyes off Race. She came to me to-night and said, with some hesitation, that she had a favour to ask. Would I take charge of her souvenirs for her?

"Not the animals?" I asked, in lively alarm. I always felt that I should get stuck with those beastly animals sooner or later.

In the end we effected a compromise. I took charge of two small wooden boxes for her which contained fragile articles. The animals are to be packed by the local store in vast crates and sent to Cape Town by rail, where Pagett will see to their being stored.

The people who are packing them say that they are of a particularly awkward shape (!), and that special cases will have to be made. I pointed out to Mrs. Blair that by the time she has got them home those animals will have cost her easily a pound apiece!

Pagett is straining at the leash to rejoin me in Jo'burg. I shall make an excuse of Mrs. Blair's cases to keep him in Cape Town. I have written him that he must receive the cases and see to their safe disposal, as they contain rare curios of immense value.

So all is settled and I and Miss Pettigrew go off into the blue together. And any one who has seen Miss Pettigrew will admit that it is perfectly respectable.

29

There is something about the state of things here that is not at all healthy. To use the well-known phrase that I have so often read, we are all living on the edge of a volcano. Bands of strikers, or so-called strikers, patrol the streets and scowl at one in a murderous fashion. They are picking out the bloated capitalists ready for when the massacres begin, I suppose. You can't ride in a taxi—if you do, strikers pull you out again. And the hotels hint pleasurably that when the food gives out they will fling you out on the mat!

I meet Reeves, my labour friend of the *Kilmorden*, last night. He has cold feet worse than any man I ever saw. He's like all the rest of these people, they make inflammatory speeches of enormous length, solely for political purposes, and then wish they hadn't. He's busy now going about and saying he didn't really do it. When I met him, he was just off to Cape Town, where he meditates making a three days' speech in Dutch, vindicating himself, and pointing out that the things he said really meant something entirely different. I am thankful that I do not have to sit in the Legislative Assembly of South Africa. The House of Commons is bad enough, but at least we have only one language, and some slight restriction as to length of speeches. When I went to the Assembly before leaving Cape Town, I listened to a gray-haired gentleman with a drooping moustache who looked exactly like the Mock Turtle in *Alice in Wonderland*. He dropped out his words one by one in a particularly melancholy fashion. Every now and then he galvanized himself to further efforts by ejaculating something that sounded like "Platt Skeet," uttered *fortissimo* and in marked contrast to the rest of his delivery. When he did this, half his audience yelled "Whoof, whoof!" which is possibly Dutch for "Hear, hear," and the other half woke up with a start from the pleasant nap they had been having. I was given to understand that the gentleman had been speaking for at least three days. They must have a lot of patience in South Africa.

I have invented endless jobs to keep Pagett in Cape Town, but at last the fertility of my imagination has given out, and he joins me to-morrow in the spirit of the faithful dog who comes to die by his master's side. And I was getting on so well with my Reminiscences too! I had invented some extraordinarily witty things that the strike leaders said to me and I said to the strike leaders.

This morning I was interviewed by a Government official. He was urbane, persuasive and mysterious in turn. To begin with, he alluded to my exalted position and importance and suggested that I should remove myself, or be removed by him, to Pretoria.

"You expect trouble, then?" I asked.

His reply was so worded as to have no meaning whatsoever, so I gathered that they were expecting serious trouble. I suggested to him that his Government were letting things go rather far.

"There is such a thing as giving a man enough rope, and letting him hang himself, Sir Eustace."

"Oh, quite so, quite so."

"It is not the strikers themselves who are causing the trouble. There is some organization at work behind them. Arms and explosives have been pouring in, and we have made a haul of certain documents which throw a good deal of light on the methods adopted to import them. There is a regular code. Potatoes mean 'detonators,' cauliflower, 'rifles,' other vegetables stand for various explosives."

"That's very interesting," I commended.

"More than that, Sir Eustace, we have every reason to believe that the man who runs the whole show, the directing genius of the affair, is at this minute in Johannesburg."

He stared at me so hard that I began to fear that he suspected me of being the man. I broke out into a cold perspiration at the thought, and began to regret that I had ever conceived the idea of inspecting a miniature revolution at first hand.

"No trains are running from Jo'burg to Pretoria," he continued. "But I can arrange to send you over by private car. In case you should be stopped on the way I can provide you with two separate passes, one issued by the Union Government, and the other stating that you are an English visitor who has nothing whatsoever to do with the Union."

"One for your people, and one for the strikers, eh?"

"Exactly."

The project did not appeal to me—I know what happens in a case of that kind. You get flustered and mix the things up. I should hand the wrong pass to the wrong person, and it would end in my being summarily shot by a bloodthirsty rebel, or one of the supporters of law and order whom I notice guarding the streets wearing bowler hats and smoking pipes, with rifles tucked carelessly under their arms. Besides, what should I do with

myself in Pretoria? Admire the architecture of the Union
buildings and listen to the echoes of the shooting round
Johannesburg? I should be penned up there God knows
how long. They've blown up the railway line already, I
hear. It isn't even as if one could get a drink there. They
put the place under martial law two days ago.

"My dear fellow," I said, "you don't seem to realize
that I'm studying conditions on the Rand. How the devil
am I going to study them from Pretoria? I appreciate
your care for my safety, but don't you worry about me.
I shall be all right."

"I warn you, Sir Eustace, that the food question is
already serious."

"A little fasting will improve my figure," I said, with
a sigh.

We were interrupted by a telegram being handed to
me. I read it with amazement:

"Anne is safe. Here with me at Kimberley. Suzanne
Blair."

I don't think I ever really believed in the annihilation
of Anne. There is something peculiarly indestructible
about that young woman—she is like the patent balls
that one gives to terriers. She has an extraordinary knack
of turning up smiling.

I still don't see why it was necessary for her to walk
out of the hotel in the middle of the night in order to
get to Kimberley. There was no train, anyway. She must
have put on a pair of angel's wings and flown there. And
I don't suppose she will ever explain. Nobody does—to
me. I always have to guess. It becomes monotonous after
a while. The exigencies of journalism are at the bottom
of it, I suppose. "How I shot the rapids," by our Special
Correspondent.

I refolded the telegram and got rid of my Governmental friend. I don't like the prospect of being hungry,

but I'm not alarmed for my personal safety. Smuts is perfectly capable of dealing with the revolution. But I would give a considerable sum of money for a drink! I wonder if Pagett will have the sense to bring a bottle of whisky with him when he arrives tomorrow?

I put on my hat and went out, intending to buy a few souvenirs. The curio-shops in Jo'burg are rather pleasant. I was just studying a window full of imposing karosses, when a man coming out of the shop cannoned into me. To my surprise it turned out to be Race.

I can't flatter myself that he looked pleased to see me. As a matter of fact, he looked distinctly annoyed, but I insisted on his accompanying me back to the hotel. I get tired of having no one but Miss Pettigrew to talk to.

"I had no idea you were in Jo'burg," I said chattily. "When did you arrive?"

"Last night."

"Where are you staying?"

"With friends."

He was disposed to be extraordinarily taciturn, and seemed to be embarrassed by my questions.

"I hope they keep poultry," I remarked. "A diet of new-laid eggs and the occasional slaughtering of an old cock will be decidedly agreeable soon from all I hear."

"By the way," I said, when we were back in the hotel, "have you heard that Miss Beddingfeld is alive and kicking?"

He nodded.

"She gave us quite a fright," I said airily. "Where the devil did she go to that night, that's what I'd like to know."

"She was on the island all the time."

"Which island? Not the one with the young man on it?"

"Yes."

"How very improper," I said. "Pagett will be quite shocked. He always did disapprove of Anne Bedding-feld. I suppose that was the young man she originally intended to meet in Durban?"

"I don't think so."

"Don't tell me anything you don't want to," I said, by way of encouraging him.

"I fancy that this is a young man we should all be very glad to lay our hands on."

"Not——?"

He nodded.

"Harry Rayburn, *alias* Harry Lucas—that's his real name, you know. He's given us all the slip once more, but we're bound to rope him in soon."

"Dear me, dear me," I murmured.

"We don't suspect the girl of complicity in any case. On her side it's—just a love-affair."

I always did think Race was in love with Anne. The way he said those last words made me feel sure of it.

"She's gone to Beira," he continued rather hastily.

"Indeed," I said, staring. "How do you know?"

"She wrote to me from Bulawayo, telling me she was going home that way. The best thing she can do, poor child."

"Somehow, I don't fancy she is in Beira," I said meditatively.

"She was just starting when she wrote."

I was puzzled. Somebody was clearly lying. Without stopping to reflect that Anne might have excellent reasons for her misleading statements, I gave myself up to the pleasure of scoring off Race. He is always so cocksure. I took the telegram from my pocket and handed it to him.

"Then how do you explain this?" I asked nonchalantly.

He seemed dumbfounded.

"She said she was just starting for Beira," he said, in a dazed voice.

I know that Race is supposed to be clever. He is, in my opinion, rather a stupid man. It never seemed to occur to him that girls do not always tell the truth.

"Kimberley too. What are they doing there?" he muttered.

"Yes, that surprised me. I should have thought Miss Anne would have been in the thick of it here, gathering copy for the *Daily Budget*."

"Kimberley," he said again. The place seemed to upset him. "There's nothing to see there—the pits aren't being worked."

"You know what women are," I said vaguely.

He shook his head and went off. I have evidently given him something to think about.

No sooner had he departed than my Government official reappeared.

"I hope you will forgive me for troubling you again, Sir Eustace," he apologized. "But there are one or two questions I should like to ask you."

"Certainly, my dear fellow," I said cheerfully. "Ask away."

"It concerns your secretary——"

"I know nothing about him," I said hastily. "He foisted himself upon me in London, robbed me of valuable papers—for which I shall be hauled over the coals—and disappeared like a conjuring trick at Cape Town. It's true that I was at the Falls at the same time as he was, but I was at the hotel, and he was on an island. I can assure you that I never set eyes upon him the whole time that I was there."

I paused for breath.

"You misunderstand me. It was of your other secretary that I spoke."

"What? Pagett?" I cried, in lively astonishment. "He's been with me eight years—a most trustworthy fellow."

My interlocutor smiled.

"We are still at cross-purposes. I refer to the lady."

"Miss Pettigrew?" I exclaimed.

"Yes. She has been seen coming out of Agrasato's Native Curio-shop."

"God bless my soul!" I interrupted. "I was going into that place myself this afternoon. You might have caught *me* coming out!"

There doesn't seem to be any innocent thing that one can do in Jo'burg without being suspected of it.

"Ah! but she has been there more than once—and in rather doubtful circumstances. I may as well tell you—in confidence, Sir Eustace—that the place is suspected of being a well-known rendezvous used by the secret organization behind this revolution. That is why I should be glad to hear all that you can tell me about this lady. Where and how did you come to engage her?"

"She was lent to me," I replied coldly, "by your own Government."

He collapsed utterly.

30

(Anne's Narrative Resumed)

As soon as I got to Kimberley I wired to Suzanne. She joined me there with the utmost dispatch, heralding her arrival with telegrams sent off *en route*. I was awfully surprised to find that she really was fond of me—I thought I had been just a new sensation, but she positively fell on my neck and wept when we met.

When we had recovered from our emotion a little, I sat down on the bed and told her the whole story from A to Z.

"You always did suspect Colonel Race," she said thoughtfully, when I had finished. "I didn't until the night you disappeared. I liked him so much all along and thought he would make such a nice husband for you. Oh, Anne, dear, don't be cross, but how do you know that this young man of yours is telling the truth? You believe every word he says."

"Of course I do," I cried indignantly.

"But what is there in him that attracts you so? I don't see that there's anything in him at all except his rather reckless good looks and his modern Sheik-cum-Stone-Age lovemaking."

I poured out the vials of my wrath upon Suzanne for some minutes.

"Just because you're comfortably married and getting fat, you've forgotten that there's any such thing as romance," I ended.

"Oh, I'm not getting fat, Anne. All the worry I've had about you lately must have worn me to a shred."

"You look particularly well nourished," I said coldly. "I should say you must have put on about half a stone."

"And I don't know that I'm so comfortably married either," continued Suzanne in a melancholy voice. "I've been having the most dreadful cables from Clarence ordering me to come home at once. At last I didn't answer them, and now I haven't heard for over a fortnight."

I'm afraid I didn't take Suzanne's matrimonial troubles very seriously. She will be able to get round Clarence all right when the times comes. I turned the conversation to the subject of the diamonds.

Suzanne looked at me with a dropped jaw.

"I must explain, Anne. You see, as soon as I began to suspect Colonel Race, I was terribly upset about the diamonds. I wanted to stay on at the Falls in case he might have kidnapped you somewhere close by, but didn't know what to do about the diamonds. I was afraid to keep them in my possession——"

Suzanne looked round her uneasily, as though she feared the walls might have ears, and then whispered vehemently in my ear.

"A distinctly good idea," I approved. "At the time, that is. It's a bit awkward now. What did Sir Eustace do with the cases?"

"The big ones were sent down to Cape Town. I heard from Pagett before I left the Falls, and he enclosed the receipt for their storage. He's leaving Cape Town today, by the by, to join Sir Eustace in Johannesburg."

"I see," I said thoughtfully. "And the small ones, where are they?"

"I suppose Sir Eustace has got them with him."

I turned the matter over in my mind.

"Well," I said at last, "it's awkward—but it's safe enough. We'd better do nothing for the present."

Suzanne looked at me with a little smile.

"You don't like doing nothing, do you, Anne?"

"Not very much," I replied honestly.

The one thing I could do was to get hold of a time-table and see what time Guy Pagett's train would pass through Kimberley. I found that it would arrive at 5.40 on the following afternoon and depart again at 6. I wanted to see Pagett as soon as possible, and that seemed to me a good opportunity. The situation on the Rand was getting very serious, and it might be a long time before I got another chance.

The only thing that livened up the day was a wire dispatched from Johannesburg. A most innocent-sounding telegram:

"Arrived safely. All going well. Eric here, also Eustace, but not Guy. Remain where you are for the present. Andy."

Eric was our pseudonym for Race. I chose it because it is a name I dislike exceedingly. There was clearly nothing to be done until I could see Pagett. Suzanne employed herself in sending off a long soothing cable to the far-off Clarence. She became quite sentimental over him. In her way—which of course is quite different from me and Harry—she is really fond of Clarence.

"I do wish he was here, Anne," she gulped. "It's such a long time since I've seen him."

"Have some face cream," I said soothingly.

Suzanne rubbed a little on the tip of her charming nose.

"I shall want some more face cream soon too," she remarked, "and you can only get this kind in Paris." She sighed. "Paris!"

"Suzanne," I said, "very soon you'll have had enough of South Africa and adventure."

"I should like a really nice hat," admitted Suzanne wistfully. "Shall I come with you to meet Guy Pagett to-morrow?"

"I prefer to go alone. He'd be shyer speaking before two of us."

So it came about that I was standing in the doorway of the hotel on the following afternoon, struggling with a recalcitrant parasol that refused to go up, whilst Suzanne lay peacefully on her bed with a book and a basket of fruit.

According to the hotel porter, the train was on its good behaviour to-day and would be almost on time, though he was extremely doubtful whether it would ever get through to Johannesburg. The line had been blown up, so he solemnly assured me. It sounded cheerful!

The train drew in just ten minutes late. Everybody tumbled out on the platform and began walking up and down feverishly. I had no difficulty in espying Pagett. I accosted him eagerly. He gave his usual nervous start at seeing me—somewhat accentuated this time.

"Dear me, Miss Beddingfeld, I understood that you had disappeared."

"I have reappeared again," I told him solemnly. "And how are you, Mr. Pagett?"

"Very well, thank you—looking forward to taking up my work again with Sir Eustace."

"Mr. Pagett," I said, "there is something I want to ask you. I hope that you won't be offended, but a lot hangs on it, more than you can possibly guess. I want to know what you were doing at Marlow on the 8th of January last?"

He started violently.

"Really, Miss Beddingfeld—I—indeed——"

"You *were* there, weren't you?"

"I—for reasons of my own I was in the neighbourhood, yes."

"Won't you tell me what those reasons were?"

"Sir Eustace has not already told you?"

"Sir Eustace? Does he know?"

"I am almost sure that he does. I hoped he had not recognized me, but from the hints he has let drop, and his remarks, I fear it is only too certain. In any case, I meant to make a clean breast of the matter and offer him my resignation. He is a peculiar man, Miss Beddingfeld, with an abnormal sense of humour. It seems to amuse him to keep me on tenter-hooks. All the time, I dare say, he was perfectly well aware of the true facts. Possibly he has known them for years."

I hoped that sooner or later I should be able to understand what Pagett was talking about. He went on fluently:

"It is difficult for a man of Sir Eustace's standing to put himself in my position. I know that I was in the wrong, but it seemed a harmless deception. I would have thought it better taste on his part to have tackled me outright—instead of indulging in covert jokes at my expense."

A whistle blew, and the people began to surge back into the train.

"Yes, Mr. Pagett," I broke in, "I'm sure I quite agree with all you're saying about Sir Eustace. *But why did you go to Marlow?*"

"It was wrong of me, but natural under the circumstances—yes, I still feel natural under the circumstances."

"What circumstances?" I cried desperately.

For the first time Pagett seemed to recognize that I was asking him a question. His mind detached itself from the peculiarities of Sir Eustace and his own justification and came to rest on me.

"I beg your pardon, Miss Beddingfeld," he said stiffly, "but I fail to see your concern in the matter."

He was back in the train now, leaning down to speak to me. I felt desperate. What could one do with a man like that?

"Of course, if it's so dreadful that you'd be ashamed to speak of it to me——" I began spitefully.

At last I had found the right stop. Pagett stiffened and flushed.

"Dreadful? Ashamed? I don't understand you."

"Then tell me."

In three short sentences he told me. At last I knew Pagett's secret! It was not in the least what I expected.

I walked slowly back to the hotel. There a wire was handed to me. I tore it open. It contained full and definite instructions for me to proceed forthwith to Johannesburg, or rather to a station this side of Johannesburg, where I should be met by a car. It was signed, not Andy, but Harry.

I sat down in a chair to do some very serious thinking.

(From the diary of Sir Eustace Pedler)

JOHANNESBURG,
MARCH 7TH.

Pagett has arrived. He is in a blue funk of course. Suggested at once that we should go off to Pretoria. Then, when I had told him kindly but firmly that we were going to remain here, he went to the other extreme, wished he had his rifle here, and began bucking about some bridge he guarded during the Great War. A railway bridge at Little Puddecombe junction, or something of that sort.

I soon cut that short by telling him to unpack the big typewriter. I thought that that would keep him employed for some time, because the typewriter was sure to have gone wrong—it always does—and he would have to take it somewhere to be mended. But I had forgotten Pagett's powers of being in the right.

"I've already unpacked all the cases, Sir Eustace. The typewriter is in perfect condition."

"What do you mean—all the cases?"

"The two small cases as well."

"I wish you wouldn't be so officious, Pagett. Those small cases were no business of yours. They belong to Mrs. Blair."

Pagett looked crestfallen. He hates to make a mistake

"So you can just pack them up again neatly," I continued. "After that you can go out and look around you
Jo'burg will probably be a heap of smoking ruins by
tomorrow, so it may be your last chance."

I thought that that would get rid of him successfully
for the morning, at any rate.

"There is something I want to say to you when you
have the leisure, Sir Eustace."

"I haven't got it now," I said hastily. "At this minute
I have absolutely no leisure whatsoever."

Pagett retired.

"By the way," I called after him, "what was there in
those cases of Mrs. Blair's?"

"Some fur rugs, and a couple of fur—hats, I think."

"That's right," I assented. "She bought them on the
train. They *are* hats—of a kind—though I hardly wonder
at your not recognizing them. I dare say she's going to
wear one of them at Ascot. What else was there?"

"Some rolls of films and some baskets—a lot of baskets——"

"There would be," I assured him. "Mrs. Blair is the
kind of woman who never buys less than a dozen or so
of anything."

"I think that's all, Sir Eustace, except some miscel-
laneous odds and ends, a motor-veil and some odd
gloves—that sort of thing."

"If you hadn't been a born idiot, Pagett, you would
have seen from the start that those couldn't possibly be
my belongings."

"I thought some of them might belong to Miss Pettigrew."

"Ah, that reminds me—what do you mean by picking
me out such a doubtful character as a secretary?"

And I told him about the searching cross-examination I had been put through. Immediately I was sorry, I saw a glint in his eye that I knew only too well. I changed the conversation hurriedly. But it was too late. Pagett was on the war-path.

He next proceeded to bore me with a pointless story about the *Kilmorden*. It was about a roll of films and a wager. The roll of films being thrown through a porthole in the middle of the night by some steward who ought to have known better. I hate horse-play. I told Pagett so, and he began to tell me the story all over again. He tells a story extremely badly, anyway. It was a long time before I could make head or tail of this one.

I did not see him again until lunch-time. Then he came in brimming over with excitement, like a bloodhound on the scent. I never have cared for bloodhounds. The upshot of it all was that he had seen Rayburn.

"What?" I cried, startled.

Yes, he had caught sight of some one whom he was sure was Rayburn crossing the street. Pagett had followed him.

"And who do you think I saw him stop and speak to? Miss Pettigrew!"

"What?"

"Yes, Sir Eustace. And that's not all. I've been making inquiries about her——"

"Wait a bit. What happened to Rayburn?"

"He and Miss Pettigrew went into that corner curio-shop——"

I uttered an involuntary exclamation. Pagett stopped inquiringly.

"Nothing," I said. "Go on."

"I waited outside for ages—but they didn't come out. At last I went in. Sir Eustace, there was no one in the shop! There must be another way out."

I stared at him.

"As I was saying, I came back to the hotel and made some inquiries about Miss Pettigrew." Pagett lowered his voice and breathed hard as he always does when he wants to be confidential. "Sir Eustace, a man was seen coming out of her room last night."

I raised my eyebrows.

"And I always regarded her as a lady of such eminent respectability," I murmured.

Pagett went on without heeding.

"I went straight up and searched her room. What do you think I found?"

I shook my head.

"This!"

Pagett held up a safety razor and a stick of shaving soap.

"What should a woman want with these?"

I don't suppose Pagett ever reads the advertisements in the high-class ladies' papers. I do. Whilst not proposing to argue with him on the subject, I refused to accept the presence of the razor as proof positive of Miss Pettigrew's sex. Pagett is so hopelessly behind the times. I should not have been at all surprised if he had produced a cigarette-case to support his theory. However, even Pagett has his limits.

"You're not convinced, Sir Eustace. What do you say to *this?*"

I inspected the article which he dangled aloft triumphantly.

"It looks like hair," I remarked distastefully.

"It is hair. I think it's what they call a toupee."

"Indeed," I commented.

"Now are you convinced that that Pettigrew woman is a man in disguise?"

"Really, my dear Pagett, I think I am. I might have known it by her feet."

"Then that's that. And now, Sir Eustace, I want to speak to you about my private affairs. I cannot doubt, from your hints and your continual allusions to the time I was in Florence, that you have found me out."

At last the mystery of what Pagett did in Florence is going to be revealed!

"Make a clean breast of it, my dear fellow," I said kindly. "Much the best way."

"Thank you, Sir Eustace."

"Is it her husband? Annoying fellows, husbands. Always turning up when they're least expected."

"I fail to follow you, Sir Eustace. Whose husband?"

"The lady's husband."

"What lady?"

"God bless my soul, Pagett, the lady you met in Florence. There must have been a lady. Don't tell me that you merely robbed a church or stabbed an Italian in the back because you didn't like his face."

"I am quite at a loss to understand you, Sir Eustace. I suppose you are joking."

"I am an amusing fellow sometimes, when I take the trouble, but I can assure you that I am not trying to be funny this minute."

"I hoped that as I was a good way off you had not recognized me, Sir Eustace."

"Recognized you where?"

"At Marlow, Sir Eustace?"

"At Marlow? What the devil were you doing at Marlow?"

"I thought you understood that——"

"I'm beginning to understand less and less. Go back to the beginning of the story and start again. You went to Florence——"

"Then you don't know after all—and you didn't recognize me!"

"As far as I can judge, you seem to have given yourself away needlessly—made a coward of by your conscience. But I shall be able to tell better when I've heard the whole story. Now, then, take a deep breath and start again. You went to Florence——"

"But I didn't go to Florence. That is just it."

"Well, where did you go, then?"

"I went home—to Marlow."

"What the devil did you want to go to Marlow for?"

"I wanted to see my wife. She was in delicate health and expecting——"

"Your wife? But I didn't know you were married?"

"No, Sir Eustace, that is just what I am telling you. I deceived you in this matter."

"How long have you been married?"

"Just over eight years. I had been married just six months when I became your secretary. I did not want to lose the post. A resident secretary is not supposed to have a wife, so I suppressed the fact."

"You take my breath away," I remarked. "Where has she been all these years?"

"We have had a small bungalow on the river at Marlow, quite close to Mill House, for over five years."

"God bless my soul," I muttered. "Any children?"

"Four children, Sir Eustace."

I gazed at him in a kind of stupor. I might have known, all along, that a man like Pagett couldn't have a guilty secret. The respectability of Pagett has always been my bane. That's just the kind of secret he would have—a wife and four children.

"Have you told this to any one else?" I demanded at last, when I had gazed at him in fascinated interest for quite a long while.

"Only Miss Beddingfeld. She came to the station at Kimberley."

I continued to stare at him. He fidgeted under my glance.

"I hope, Sir Eustace, that you are not seriously annoyed?"

"My dear fellow," I said, "I don't mind telling you here and now that you've blinking well torn it!"

I went out seriously ruffled. As I passed the corner curio-shop, I was assailed by a sudden irrestible temptation and went in. The proprietor came forward obsequiously, rubbing his hands.

"Can I show you something? Furs, curios?"

"I want something quite out of the ordinary," I said. "It's for a special occasion. Will you show me what you've got?"

"Perhaps you will come into my back room? We have many specialties there?"

That is where I made a mistake. And I thought I was going to be so clever. I followed him through the swinging *portières*.

32

(Anne's Narrative Resumed)

I had great trouble with Suzanne. She argued, she pleaded, she even wept before she would let me carry out my plan. But in the end I got my own way. She promised to carry out my instructions to the letter and came down to the station to bid me a tearful farewell.

I arrived at my destination the following morning early. I was met by a short black-bearded Dutchman whom I had never seen before. He had a car waiting and we drove off. There was a queer booming in the distance, and I asked him what it was. "Guns," he answered laconically. So there was fighting going on in Jo'burg!

I gathered that our objective was a spot somewhere in the suburbs of the city. We turned and twisted and made several detours to get there, and every minute the guns were nearer. It was an exciting time. At last we stopped before a somewhat ramshackle building. The door was opened by a Kafir boy. My guide signed to me to enter. I stood irresolute in the dingy square hall. The man passed me and threw open a door.

"The young lady to see Mr. Harry Rayburn," he said, and laughed.

Thus announced, I passed in. The room was sparsely furnished and smelt of cheap tobacco smoke. Behind a desk a man sat writing. He looked up and raised his eyebrows.

"Dear me," he said, "if it isn't Miss Beddingfeld!"

"I must be seeing double," I apologized. "Is it Mr. Chichester, or is it Miss Pettigrew? There is an extraordinary resemblance to both of them."

"Both characters are in abeyance for the moment. I have doffed my petticoats—and my cloth likewise. Won't you sit down?"

I accepted a seat composedly.

"It would seem," I remarked, "that I have come to the wrong address."

"From your point of view, I am afraid you have. Really, Miss Beddingfeld, to fall into the trap a second time!"

"It was not very bright of me," I admitted meekly.

Something about my manner seemed to puzzle him.

"You hardly seem upset by the occurrence," he remarked dryly.

"Would my going into heroics have any effect upon you?" I asked.

"It certainly would not."

"My great-aunt Jane always used to say that a true lady was neither shocked nor surprised at anything that might happen," I murmured dreamily. "I endeavour to live up to her precepts."

I read Mr. Chichester-Pettigrew's opinion so plainly written on his face that I hastened into speech once more.

"You really are positively marvellous at make-up," I said generously. "All the time you were Miss Pettigrew I never recognized you—even when you broke your pencil in the shock of seeing me climb upon the train at Cape Town."

He tapped upon the desk with the pencil he was holding in his hand at the minute.

"All this is very well in its way, but we must get to business. Perhaps, Miss Beddingfeld, you can guess why we required your presence here?"

"You will excuse me," I said, "but I never do business with any one but principals."

I had read the phrase or something like it in a moneylender's circular, and I was rather pleased with it. It certainly had a devastating effect upon Mr. Chichester-Pettigrew. He opened his mouth and then shut it again. I beamed upon him.

"My great-uncle George's maxim," I added, as an afterthought. "Great-aunt Jane's husband, you know. He made knobs for brass beds."

I doubt if Chichester-Pettigrew had ever been ragged before. He didn't like it at all.

"I think you would be wise to alter your tone, young lady."

I did not reply, but yawned—a delicate little yawn that hinted at intense boredom.

"What the devil——" he began forcibly.

I interrupted him.

"I can assure you it's no good shouting at me. We are only wasting time here. I have no intention of talking with underlings. You will save a lot of time and annoyance by taking me straight to Sir Eustace Pedler."

"To——"

He looked dumbfounded.

"Yes," I said. "Sir Eustace Pedler."

"I—I—excuse me——"

He bolted from the room like a rabbit. I took advantage of the respite to open my bag and powder my nose thoroughly. Also I settled my hat at a more becoming angle. Then I settled myself to wait with patience for my enemy's return.

He reappeared in a subtly chastened mood.

"Will you come this way, Miss Beddingfeld?"

I followed him up the stairs. He knocked at the door of a room, a brisk "Come in" sounded from inside, and he opened the door and motioned to me to pass inside.

Sir Eustace Pedler sprang up to greet me, genial and smiling.

"Well, well, Miss Anne." He shook me warmly by the hand. "I'm delighted to see you. Come and sit down. Not tired after your journey? That's good."

He sat down facing me, still beaming. It left me rather at a loss. His manner was so completely natural.

"Quite right to insist on being brought straight to me," he went on. "Minks is a fool. A clever actor—but a fool. That was Minks you saw downstairs."

"Oh, really," I said feebly.

"And now," said Sir Eustace cheerfully, "let's get down to facts. How long have you known that I was the 'Colonel'?"

"Ever since Mr. Pagett told me that he had seen you in Marlow when you were supposed to be in Cannes."

Sir Eustace nodded ruefully.

"Yes, I told the fool he'd blinking well torn it. He didn't understand of course. His whole mind was set on whether I'd recognized him. It never occurred to him to wonder what I was doing down there. A piece of sheer bad luck that was. I arranged it all so carefully too, sending him off to Florence, telling the hotel I was going over to Nice for one night or possibly two. Then, by the time the murder was discovered, I was back again in Cannes, with nobody dreaming that I'd ever left the Riviera."

He still spoke quite naturally and unaffectedly. I had to pinch myself to understand that this was all real—that the man in front of me was really that deep-dyed criminal, the "Colonel." I followed things out in my mind.

"Then it was you who tried to throw me overboard on the *Kilmorden*," I said slowly. "It was you that Pagett followed up on deck that night?"

He shrugged his shoulders.

"I apologize, my dear child, I really do. I always liked you—but you were so confoundedly interfering. I couldn't have all my plans brought to naught by a chit of a girl."

"I think your plan at the Falls was really the cleverest," I said, endeavouring to look at the thing in a detached fashion. "I would have been ready to swear anywhere that you were in the hotel when I went out. Seeing is believing in future."

"Yes, Minks had one of his greatest successes as Miss Pettigrew, and he can imitate my voice quite creditably."

"There is one thing I should like to know."

"Yes?"

"How did you induce Pagett to engage her?"

"Oh, that was quite simple. She met Pagett in the doorway of the Trade Commissioner's office or the Chamber of Mines, or wherever it was he went—told him I had phoned down in a hurry, and that she had been selected by the Government department in question. Pagett swallowed it like a lamb."

"You're very frank," I said, studying him.

"There's no earthly reason why I shouldn't be."

I didn't quite like the sound of that. I hastened to put my own interpretation on it.

"You believe in the success of this Revolution? You've burnt your boats."

"For an otherwise intelligent young woman, that's a singularly unintelligent remark. No, my dear child, I do not believe in this Revolution. I give it a couple of days longer and it will fizzle out ignominiously."

"Not one of your successes, in fact?" I said nastily.

"Like all women, you've no idea of business. The job I took on was to supply certain explosives and arms—heavily paid for—to foment feeling generally, and to incriminate certain people up to the hilt. I've carried out my contract with complete success, and I was careful to be paid in advance. I took special care over the whole thing, as I intended it to be my last contract before retiring from business. As for burning my boats, as you call it, I simply don't know what you mean. I'm not the rebel chief, or anything of that kind—I'm a distinguished English visitor, who had the misfortune to go nosing into a certain curio-shop—and saw a little more than he was meant to, and so the poor fellow was kidnapped. To-morrow, or the day after, when circumstances permit, I shall be found tied up somewhere in a pitiable state of terror and starvation."

"Ah!" I said slowly. "But what about me?"

"That's just it," said Sir Eustace softly. "What about you? I've got you here—I don't want to rub it in in any way—but I've got you here very neatly. The question is, what am I going to do with you? The simplest way of disposing of you—and, I may add, the pleasantest to myself—is the way of marriage. Wives can't accuse their husbands, you know, and I'd rather like a pretty young wife to hold my hand and glance at me out of liquid eyes—don't flash them at me so! You quite frighten me. I see that the plan does not commend itself to you?"

"It does not."

Sir Eustace sighed.

"A pity! But I am no Adelphi villain. The usual trouble, I suppose. You love another, as the books say."

"I love another."

"I thought as much—first I thought it was that long-legged, pompous ass, Race, but I suppose it's the young hero who fished you out of the Falls that night. Women have no taste. Neither of those two have half the brains that I have. I'm such an easy person to underestimate."

I think he was right about that. Although I knew well enough the kind of man he was and must be, I could not bring myself to realize it. He had tried to kill me on more than one occasion, he had actually killed another woman, and he was responsible for endless other deeds of which I knew nothing, and yet I was quite unable to bring myself into the frame of mind for appreciating his deeds as they deserved. I could not think of him as other than our amusing, genial travelling companion. I could not even feel frightened of him—and yet I knew he was capable of having me murdered in cold blood if it struck him as necessary. The only parallel I can think of is the case of Stevenson's Long John Silver. He must have been much the same kind of man.

"Well, well," said this extraordinary person, leaning back in his chair. "It's a pity that the idea of being Lady Pedler doesn't appeal to you. The other alternatives are rather crude."

I felt a nasty feeling going up and down my spine. Of course I had known all along that I was taking a big risk, but the prize had seemed worth it. Would things turn out as I had calculated, or would they not?

"The fact of the matter is," Sir Eustace was continuing, "I've a weakness for you. I really don't want to proceed to extremes. Suppose you tell me the whole story, from the very beginning, and let's see what we can make of it. But no romancing, mind—I want the truth."

I was not going to make any mistake over that. I had a great deal of respect for Sir Eustace's shrewdness. It was a moment for the truth, the whole truth, and nothing but the truth. I told him the whole story, omitting nothing, up to the moment of my rescue by Harry. When I had finished, he nodded his head in approval.

"Wise girl. You've made a clean breast of the thing. And let me tell you I should soon have caught you out if you hadn't. A lot of people wouldn't believe your story, anyway, especially the beginning part, but I do. You're the kind of girl who would start off like that— at a moment's notice, on the slenderest of motives. You've had amazing luck, of course, but sooner or later the amateur runs up against the professional and then the result is a foregone conclusion. I am the professional. I started on this business when I was quite a youngster. All things considered, it seemed to me a good way of getting rich quickly. I always could think things out, and devise ingenious schemes—and I never made the mistake of trying to carry out my schemes myself. Always employ the expert—that has been my motto. The one time I departed from it I came to grief—but I couldn't trust any one to do that job for me. Nadina knew too much. I'm an easy-going man, kind-hearted and good tempered so long as I'm not thwarted. Nadina both thwarted me and threatened me—just as I was at the apex of a successful career. Once she was dead and the diamonds were in my possession, I was safe. That idiot Pagett, with his wife and family! My fault—it tickled my sense of humour to employ the fellow, with his Cin-quecento poisoner's face and his mid-Victorian soul. A maxim for you, my dear Anne. Don't let your sense of humour carry you away. For years I've had an instinct that it would be wise to get rid of Pagett, but the fellow was so hard-working and conscientious that I honestly couldn't find an excuse for sacking him. So I left things drift.

"But we're wandering from the point. The question is what to do with you. Your narrative was admirably clear, but there is one thing that still escapes me. Where are the diamonds now?"

"Harry Rayburn has them," I said, watching him.

His face did not change, it retained its expression of sardonic good-humour.

"H'm. I want those diamonds."

"I don't see much chance of your getting them," I replied.

"Don't you? Now I do. I don't want to be unpleasant, but I should like you to reflect that a dead girl or so found in this quarter of the city will occasion no surprise. There's a man downstairs who does those sort of jobs very neatly. Now, you're a sensible young woman. What I propose is this: you will sit down and write to Harry Rayburn, telling him to join you here and bring the diamonds with him——"

"I won't do anything of the kind."

"Don't interrupt your elders. I propose to make a bargain with you. The diamonds in exchange for your life. And don't make any mistake about it, your life is absolutely in my power."

"And Harry?"

"I'm far too tender-hearted to part two young lovers. He shall go free too—on the understanding, of course, that neither of you will interfere with me in future."

"And what guarantee have I that you will keep your side of the bargain?"

"None whatever, my dear girl. You'll have to trust me and hope for the best. Of course, if you're in an heroic mood and prefer annihilation, that's another matter."

This was what I had been playing for. I was careful not to jump at the bait. Gradually I allowed myself to be bullied and cajoled into yielding. I wrote at Sir Eustace's dictation:

DEAR HARRY,
I think I see a chance of establishing your innocence beyond any possible doubt. Please follow my instructions minutely. Go to Agrasato's curio-shop. Ask to see something "out of the ordinary," "for a special occasion." The man will then ask you to "come into the back room." Go with him. You will find a messenger who will bring you to me. Do exactly as he tells you. Be sure and bring the diamonds with you. Not a word to any one."

Sir Eustace stopped. "I leave the fancy touches to your own imagination," he remarked. "But be careful to make no mistakes."

" 'Yours for ever and ever, Anne,' will be sufficient," I remarked.

I wrote in the words. Sir Eustace stretched out his hand for the letter and read it through.

"That seems all right. Now the address."

I gave it to him. It was that of a small shop which received letters and telegrams for a consideration.

He struck the bell upon the table with his hand. Chichester-Pettigrew, *alias* Minks, answered the summons.

"This letter is to go immediately—the usual route."

"Very well, Colonel."

He looked at the name on the envelope. Sir Eustace was watching him keenly.

"A friend of yours, I think?"

"Of mine?"

The man seemed startled.

"You had a prolonged conversation with him in Johannesburg yesterday."

"A man came up and questioned me about your movements and those of Colonel Race. I gave him misleading information."

"Excellent, my dear fellow, excellent," said Sir Eustace genially. "My mistake."

I chanced to look at Chichester-Pettigrew as he left the room. He was white to the lips, as though in deadly terror. No sooner was he outside than Sir Eustace picked up a speaking-tube that rested by his elbow and spoke down it.

"That you, Schwart? Watch Minks. He's not to leave the house without orders."

He put the speaking-tube down again and frowned, slightly tapping the table with his hand.

"May I ask you a few questions, Sir Eustace," I said, after a minute or two of silence.

"Certainly. What excellent nerves you have, Anne. You are capable of taking an intelligent interest in things when most girls would be sniffling and wringing their hands."

"Why did you take Harry as your secretary instead of giving him up to the police?"

"I wanted those cursed diamonds. Nadina, the little devil, was playing off your Harry against me. Unless I gave her the price she wanted, she threatened to sell them back to him. That was another mistake I made—I thought she'd have them with her that day. But she was too clever for that. Carton, her husband, was dead too—I'd no clue whatsoever as to where the diamonds were hidden. Then I managed to get a copy of a wireless message sent to Nadina by some one on board the *Kilmorden*—either Carton or Rayburn, I didn't know which. It was a duplicate of that piece of paper you picked up. 'Seventeen one twenty two,' it ran. I took it to be an appointment with Rayburn, and when he was so desperate to get aboard the *Kilmorden* I was convinced that I was right. So I pretended to swallow his statements, and let him come. I kept a pretty sharp watch upon him and hoped that I should learn more. Then I found Minks trying to play a lone hand and interfering with me. I soon stopped that. He came to heel all right. It was annoying not getting Cabin 17, and it worried me not being able to place you. Were you the innocent young girl you seemed, or were you not? When Rayburn set out to keep the appointment that night, Minks was told off to intercept him. Minks muffed it of course."

"But why did the wireless message say 'seventeen' instead of 'seventy-one'?"

"I've thought that out. Carton must have given that wireless operator his own memorandum to copy off on to a form, and he never read the copy through. The operator made the same mistake we all did, and read it as 17.1.22 instead of 1.71.22. The thing I don't know is how Minks got on to Cabin 17. It must have been sheer instinct."

"And the dispatch to General Smuts? Who tampered with that?"

"My dear Anne, you don't suppose I was going to have a lot of my plans given away, without making an effort to save them? With an escaped murderer as a secretary, I had no hesitation whatever in substituting blanks. Nobody would think of suspecting poor old Pedler."

"What about Colonel Race?"

"Yes, that was a nasty jar. When Pagett told me he
was a Secret Service fellow, I had an unpleasant feeling
down the spine. I remembered that he'd been nosing
around Nadina in Paris during the War—and I had a
horrible suspicion that he was out after *me!* I don't like
the way he's stuck to me ever since. He's one of those
strong, silent men who have always got something up
their sleeve."

A whistle sounded. Sir Eustace picked up the tube,
listened for a minute or two, then answered:

"Very well, I'll see him now."

"Business," he remarked. "Miss Anne, let me show
you your room."

He ushered me into a small shabby apartment, a Kafir
boy brought up my small suit-case, and Sir Eustace, urg-
ing me to ask for anything I wanted, withdrew, the picture of a courteous host. A can of hot water was on the
washstand, and I proceeded to unpack a few necessaries.
Something hard and familiar in my sponge-bag puzzled
me greatly. I untied the string and looked inside.

To my utter amazement I drew out a small pearl-
handled revolver. It hadn't been there when I started
from Kimberley. I examined the thing gingerly. It appeared to be loaded.

I handled it with a comfortable feeling. It was a useful
thing to have in a house such as this. But modern clothes
are quite unsuited to the carrying of fire-arms. In the end
I pushed it gingerly into the top of my stocking. It made
a terrible bulge, and I expected every minute that it
would go off and shoot me in the leg, but it really
seemed the only place.

33

I was not summoned to Sir Eustace's presence until late in the afternoon. Eleven-o'clock tea and a substantial lunch had been served to me in my own apartment, and I felt fortified for further conflict.

Sir Eustace was alone. He was walking up and down the room, and there was a gleam in his eye and a restlessness in his manner which did not escape me. He was exultant about something. There was a subtle change in his manner towards me.

"I have news for you. Your young man is on his way. He will be here in a few minutes. Moderate your transports—I have something more to say. You attempted to deceive me this morning. I warned you that you would be wise to stick to the truth, and up to a certain point you obeyed me. Then you ran off the rails. You attempted to make me believe that the diamonds were in Harry Rayburn's possession. At the time, I accepted your statement because it facilitated my task—the task of inducing you to decoy Harry Rayburn here. But, my dear Anne, the diamonds have been in my possession ever since I left the Falls—though I only discovered the fact yesterday."

"You know!" I gasped.

"It may interest you to hear that it was Pagett who gave the show away. He insisted on boring me with a long pointless story about a wager and a tin of films. It didn't take me long to put two and two together—Mrs. Blair's distrust of Colonel Race, her agitation, her entreaty that I would take care of her souvenirs for her. The excellent Pagett had already unfastened the cases through an excess of zeal. Before leaving the hotel, I simply transferred all the rolls of films to my own pocket. They are in the corner there. I admit that I haven't had time to examine them yet, but I notice that one is of a totally different weight to the others, rattles in a peculiar fashion, and has evidently been stuck down with seccotine, which will necessitate the use of a tin-opener. The case seems clear, does it not? And now, you see, I have you both nicely in the trap. . . . It's a pity that you didn't take kindly to the idea of becoming Lady Pedler."

I did not answer. I stood looking at him.

There was the sound of feet on the stairs, the door was flung open, and Harry Rayburn was hustled into the room between two men. Sir Eustace flung me a look of triumph.

"According to plan," he said softly. "You amateurs *will* pit yourselves against professionals."

"What's the meaning of this?" cried Harry hoarsely.

"It means that you have walked into my parlour— said the spider to the fly," remarked Sir Eustace facetiously. "My dear Rayburn, you are extraordinarily unlucky."

"You said I could come safely, Anne?"

"Do not reproach her, my dear fellow. That note was written at my dictation, and the lady could not help herself. She would have been wiser not to write it, but I did not tell her so at the time. You followed her instructions, went to the curio-shop, were taken through the secret passage from the back room—and found yourself in the hands of your enemies!"

Harry looked at me. I understood his glance and edged nearer to Sir Eustace.

"Yes," murmured the latter, "decidedly you are not lucky! This is—let me see, the third encounter."

"You are right," said Harry. "This is the third encounter. Twice you have worsted me—have you never heard that the third time the luck changes? This is my round—cover him, Anne."

I was all ready. In a flash I had whipped the pistol out of my stocking and was holding it to his head. The two men guarding Harry sprang forward, but his voice stopped them.

"Another step—and he dies! If they come any nearer, Anne, pull the trigger—don't hesitate."

"I shan't," I replied cheerfully. "I'm rather afraid of pulling it, anyway."

I think Sir Eustace shared my fears. He was certainly shaking like a jelly.

"Stay where you are," he commanded, and the men stopped obediently.

"Tell them to leave the room," said Harry.

Sir Eustace gave the order. The men filed out, and Harry shot the bolt across the door behind them.

"Now we can talk," he observed grimly, and coming across the room, he took the revolver out of my hand.

Sir Eustace uttered a sigh of relief and wiped his forehead with a handkerchief.

"I'm shockingly out of condition," he observed. "I think I must have a weak heart. I am glad that revolver is in competent hands. I didn't trust Miss Anne with it. Well, my young friend, as you say, now we can talk. I'm willing to admit that you stole a march upon me. Where the devil that revolver came from I don't know. I had the girl's luggage searched when she arrived. And where did you produce it from now? You hadn't got it on you a minute ago?"

"Yes, I had," I replied. "It was in my stocking."

"I don't know enough about women. I ought to have studied them more," said Sir Eustace sadly. "I wonder if Pagett would have known that?"

Harry rapped sharply on the table.

"Don't play the fool. If it weren't for your grey hairs, I'd throw you out of the window. You damned scoundrel! Grey hairs, or no grey hairs, I——"

He advanced a step or two, and Sir Eustace skipped nimbly behind the table.

"The young are always so violent," he said reproachfully. "Unable to use their brains, they rely solely on their muscles. Let us talk sense. For the moment you have the upper hand. But that state of affairs cannot continue. The house is full of my men. You are hopelessly outnumbered. Your momentary ascendency has been gained by an accident——"

"Has it?"

Something in Harry's voice, a grim raillery, seemed to attract Sir Eustace's attention. He stared at him.

"Has it?" said Harry again. "Sit down, Sir Eustace, and listen to what I have to say." Still covering him with the revolver, he went on: "The cards are against you this time. To begin with, listen to *that!*"

That was a dull banging at the door below. There were shouts, oaths, and then a sound of firing. Sir Eustace paled.

"What's that?"

"Race—and his people. You didn't know, did you, Sir Eustace, that Anne had an arrangement with me by which we should know whether communications from one to the other were genuine? Telegrams were to be signed 'Andy,' letters were to have the word 'and' crossed out somewhere in them. Anne knew that your telegram was a fake. She came here of her own free will, walked deliberately into the snare, in the hope that she might catch you in your own trap. Before leaving Kimberley she wired both to me and to Race. Mrs. Blair has been in communication with us ever since. I received the letter written at your dictation, which was just what I expected. I had already discussed the probabilities of a secret passage leading out of the curio-shop with Race, and he had discovered the place where the exit was situated."

There was a screaming, tearing sound, and a heavy explosion which shook the room.

"They're shelling this part of the town. I must get you out of here, Anne."

A bright light flared up. The house opposite was on fire. Sir Eustace had risen and was passing up and down. Harry kept him covered with the revolver.

"So you see, Sir Eustace, the game is up. It was you yourself who very kindly provided us with the clue of your whereabouts. Race's men were watching the exit of the secret passage. In spite of the precautions you took, they were successful in following me here."

Sir Eustace turned suddenly.

"Very clever. Very creditable. But I've still a word to say. If I've lost the trick, so have you. You'll never be able to bring the murder of Nadina home to me. I was in Marlow on that day, that's all you've got against me. No one can prove that I even knew the woman, your record's against you. You're a thief, remember, a thief. There's one thing you don't know, perhaps. *I've got the diamonds.* And here goes——"

With an incredibly swift movement, he stooped, swung up his arm and threw. There was a tinkle of breaking glass, as the object went through the window and disappeared into the blazing mass opposite.

"There goes your only hope of establishing your innocence over the Kimberley affair. And now we'll talk. I'll drive a bargain with you. You've got me cornered. Race will find all he needs in this house. There's a chance for me if I can get away. I'm done for it if I stay, but so are you, young man! There's a skylight in the next room. A couple of minutes' start and I shall be all right. I've got one or two little arrangements all ready made. You let me out that way, and give me a start— and I leave you a signed confession that I killed Nadina."

"*Yes*, Harry," I cried. "Yes, yes, yes!"

He turned a stern face on me.

"No, Anne, a thousand times, no. You don't know what you're saying."

"I do. It solves everything."

"I'd never be able to look Race in the face again. I'll take my chance, but I'm damned if I'll let this slippery old fox get away. It's no good, Anne. I won't do it."

Sir Eustace chuckled. He accepted defeat without the least emotion.

"Well, well," he remarked. "You seem to have met your master, Anne. But I can assure you both that moral rectitude does not always pay."

There was a crash of rending wood, and footsteps surged up the stairs. Harry drew back the bolt. Colonel Race was the first to enter the room. His face lit at the sight of us.

"You're safe, Anne. I was afraid——" He turned to Sir Eustace. "I've been after you for a long time, Pedler—and at last I've got you."

"Everybody seems to have gone completely mad," declared Sir Eustace airily. "These young people have been threatening me with revolvers and accusing me of the most shocking things. I don't know what it's all about."

"Don't you? It means that I've found the 'Colonel.' It means that on January 8th last you were not at Cannes, but at Marlow. It means that when your tool, Madame Nadina, turned against you, you planned to do away with her—and at last we shall be able to bring the crime home to you."

"Indeed? And from whom did you get all this interesting information? From the man who is even now being looked for by the police? His evidence will be very valuable."

"We have other evidence. There is some one else who knew that Nadina was going to meet you at the Mill House."

Sir Eustace looked surprised. Colonel Race made a gesture with his hand. Arthur Minks *alias* the Rev. Edward Chichester *alias* Miss Pettigrew stepped forward. He was pale and nervous, but he spoke clearly enough:

"I saw Nadina in Paris the night before she went over to England. I was posing at the time as a Russian Count. She told me of her purpose. I warned her, knowing what kind of man she had to deal with, but she did not take my advice. There was a wireless message on the table. I read it. Afterwards I thought I would have a try for the diamonds myself. In Johannesburg, Mr. Rayburn accosted me. He persuaded me to come over to his side."

Sir Eustace looked at him. He said nothing, but Minks seemed visibly to wilt.

"Rats always leaving a sinking ship," observed Sir Eustace. "I don't care for rats. Sooner or later, I destroy vermin."

"There's just one thing I'd like to tell you, Sir Eustace," I remarked. "That tin you threw out of the window didn't contain the diamonds. It had common pebbles in it. The diamonds are in a perfectly safe place. As a matter of fact, they're in the big giraffe's stomach. Suzanne hollowed it out, put the diamonds in with cotton wool so they wouldn't rattle, and plugged it up again."

Sir Eustace looked at me for some time. His reply was characteristic:

"I always did hate that blinking giraffe," he said. "I must have been instinct."

34

We were not able to return to Johannesburg that night. The shells were coming over pretty fast, and I gathered that we were now more or less cut off, owing to the rebels having obtained possession of a new part of the suburbs.

Our place of refuge was a farm some twenty miles or so from Johannesburg—right out on the veld. I was dropping with fatigue. All the excitement and anxiety of the last two days had left me little better than a limp rag.

I kept repeating to myself, without being able to believe it, that our troubles were really over. Harry and I were together and we should never be separated again. Yet all through I was conscious of some barrier between us—a constraint on his part, the reason of which I could not fathom.

Sir Eustace had been driven off in an opposite direction accompanied by a strong guard. He waved his hand airily to us on departing.

I came out on to the *stoep* early on the following morning and looked across the veld in the direction of Johannesburg. I could see the great dumps glistening in the pale morning sunshine, and I could hear the low rumbling mutter of the guns. The Revolution was not over yet.

The farmer's wife came out and called me in to breakfast. She was a kind, motherly soul, and I was already very fond of her. Harry had gone out at dawn and had not yet returned, so she informed me. Again I felt a stir of uneasiness pass over me. What was this shadow of which I was so conscious between us?

After breakfast I sat out on the *stoep*, a book in my hand which I did not read. I was so lost in my own thoughts that I never saw Colonel Race ride up and dismount from his horse. It was not until he said "Good morning, Anne," that I became aware of his presence.

"Oh," I said, with a flush, "it's you."

"Yes. May I sit down?"

He drew a chair up beside me. It was the first time we had been alone together since that day at the Matoppos. As always, I felt that curious mixture of fascination and fear that he never failed to inspire in me.

"What is the news?" I asked.

"Smuts will be in Johannesburg to-morrow. I give this outbreak three days more before it collapses utterly. In the meantime the fighting goes on."

"I wish," I said, "that one could be sure that the right people were the ones to get killed. I mean the ones who wanted to fight—not just all the poor people who happen to live in the parts where the fighting is going on."

He nodded.

"I know what you mean, Anne. That's the unfairness of war. But I've other news for you."

"Yes?"

"A confession of incompetency on my part. Pedler has managed to escape."

"What?"

"Yes. No one knows how he managed it. He was securely locked up for the night—in an upper-story room of one of the farms roundabouts which the Military have taken over, but this morning the room was empty and the bird had flown."

Secretly I was rather pleased. Never, to this day, have I been able to rid myself of a sneaking fondness for Sir Eustace. I dare say it's reprehensible, but there it is. I admired him. He was a thorough-going villain, I dare say—but he was a pleasant one. I've never met any one half so amusing since.

I concealed my feelings, of course. Naturally Colonel Race would feel quite guilty about it. He wanted Sir Eustace brought to justice. There was nothing very surprising in his escape when one came to think of it. All round Jo'burg he must have innumerable spies and agents. And, whatever Colonel Race might think, I was exceedingly doubtful that they would ever catch him. He probably had a well-planned line of retreat. Indeed, he had said as much to us.

I expressed myself suitably, though in a rather lukewarm manner, and the conversation languished. Then Colonel Race asked suddenly for Harry. I told him that he had gone off at dawn and that I hadn't see him this morning.

"You understand, don't you, Anne, that apart from formalities, he is completely cleared? There are technicalities, of course, but Sir Eustace's guilt is well assured. There is nothing now to keep you apart."

He said this without looking at me, in a slow, jerky voice.

"I understand," I said gratefully.

"And there is no reason why he should not at once resume his real name."

"No, of course not."

"You know his real name?"

The question surprised me.

"Of course I do. Harry Lucas."

He did not answer, and something in the quality of his silence struck me as peculiar.

"Anne, do you remember that, as we drove home from the Matoppos that day, I told you that I knew what I had to do?"

"Of course, I remember."

"I think that I may fairly say I have done it. The man you love is cleared of suspicion."

"Was that what you meant?"

"Of course."

I hung my head, ashamed of the baseless suspicion I had entertained. He spoke again in a thoughtful voice:

"When I was a mere youngster, I was in love with a girl who jilted me. After that I thought only of my work. My career meant everything to me. Then I met you, Anne—and all that seemed worth nothing. But youth's call to youth. . . . I've still got my work."

I was silent. I suppose one can't really love two men at once—but you can feel like it. The magnetism of this man was very great. I looked up at him suddenly.

"I think that you'll go very far," I said dreamily. "I think that you've got a great career ahead of you. You'll be one of the world's big men."

I felt as though I was uttering a prophecy.

"I shall be alone, though."

"All the people who do really big things are."

"You think so?"

"I'm sure of it."

He took my hand and said in a low voice:

"I'd rather have had—the other."

Then Harry came striding round the corner of the house. Colonel Race rose.

"Good morning—Lucas," he said.

For some reason Harry flushed up to the roots of his hair.

"Yes," I said gaily, "you must be known by your real name now."

But Harry was still staring at Colonel Race.

"So you know, sir," he said at last.

"I never forget a face. I saw you once as a boy."

"What's this all about?" I asked, puzzled, looking from one to the other.

It seemed a conflict of wills between them. Race won. Harry turned slightly away.

"I suppose you're right, sir. Tell her my real name."

"Anne, this isn't Harry Lucas. Harry Lucas was killed in the War. This is John Harold Eardsley."

With his last words Colonel Race had swung away and left us. I stood staring after him. Harry's voice recalled me to myself.

"Anne, forgive me, say you forgive me."

He took my hand in his and almost mechanically I drew it away.

"Why did you deceive me?"

"I don't know that I can make you understand. I was afraid of all that sort of thing—the power and fascination of wealth. I wanted you to care for me just for myself— for the man I was—without ornaments and trappings."

"You mean you didn't trust me?"

"You can put it that way if you like, but it isn't quite true. I'd become embittered, suspicious—always prone to look for ulterior motives—and it was so wonderful to be cared for in the way you cared for me."

"I see," I said slowly. I was going over in my own mind the story he had told me. For the first time I noted discrepancies in it which I had disregarded—an assurance of money, the power to buy back the diamonds of Nadina, the way in which he had preferred to speak of both men from the point of view of an outsider. And when he said "my friend" he had meant, not Eardsley, but Lucas. It was Lucas, the quiet fellow, who had loved Nadina so deeply.

"How did it come about?" I asked.

"We were both reckless—anxious to get killed. One night we exchanged identification discs—for luck! Lucas was killed the next day—blown to pieces."

I shuddered.

"But why didn't you tell me now? This morning? You couldn't have doubted my caring for you this time?"

"Anne, I didn't want to spoil it. I wanted to take you back to the island. What's the good of money? It can't buy happiness. We'd have been happy on the island. I tell you I'm afraid of that other life—it nearly rotted me through once."

"Did Sir Eustace know who you really were?"

"Oh, yes."

"And Carton?"

"No. He saw us both with Nadina at Kimberley one night, but he didn't know which was which. He accepted my statement that I was Lucas, and Nadina was deceived by his cable. She was never afraid of Lucas. He was a quiet chap—very deep. But I always had the devil's own temper. She'd have been scared out of her life if she'd known that I'd come to life again."

"Harry, if Colonel Race hadn't told me, what did you mean to do?"

"Say nothing. Go on as Lucas."

"And your father's millions?"

"Race was welcome to them. Anyway, he would make a better use of them than I ever shall. Anne, what are you thinking about? You're frowning so."

"I'm thinking," I said slowly, "that I almost wish Colonel Race hadn't made you tell me."

"No. He was right. I owed you the truth."

He paused, then said suddenly:

"You know, Anne, I'm jealous of Race. He loves you too—and he's a bigger man than I am or ever shall be."

I turned to him, laughing.

"Harry, you idiot. It's you I want—and that's all that matters."

As soon as possible we started for Cape Town. There Suzanne was waiting to greet me, and we disembowelled the big giraffe together. When the Revolution was finally quelled, Colonel Race came down to Cape Town and at his suggestion the big villa at Muizenberg that had belonged to Sir Lawrence Eardsley was reopened and we all took up our abode in it.

There we made our plans. I was to return to England with Suzanne and to be married from her house in London. And the trousseau was to be bought in Paris! Suzanne enjoyed planning all these details enormously. So did I. And yet the future seemed curiously unreal. And sometimes, without knowing why, I felt absolutely stifled—as though I couldn't breathe.

It was the night before we were to sail. I couldn't sleep. I was miserable, and I didn't know why. I hated leaving Africa. When I came back to it, would it be the same thing? Would it ever be the same thing again?

And then I was startled by an authoritative rap on the shutter. I sprang up. Harry was on the *stoep* outside.

"Put some clothes on, Anne, and come out. I want to speak to you."

I huddled on a few garments, and stepped out into the cool night air—still and scented, with its velvety feel. Harry beckoned me out of earshot of the house. His face looked pale and determined and his eyes were blazing.

"Anne, do you remember saying to me once that women enjoyed doing the things they disliked for the sake of some one they liked?"

"Yes," I said, wondering what was coming.

He caught me in his arms.

"Anne, come away with me—now—to-night. Back to Rhodesia—back to the island. I can't stand all this tomfoolery. I can't wait for you any longer."

I disengaged myself a minute.

"And what about my French frocks?" I lamented mockingly.

To this day Harry never knows when I'm in earnest and when I'm only teasing him.

"Damn your French frocks. Do you think I want to put frocks on you? I'm a damned sight more likely to want to tear them off you. I'm not going to let you go, do you hear? You're my woman. If I let you go away, I may lose you. I'm never sure of you. You're coming with me now—to-night—and damn everybody."

He held me to him, kissing me until I could hardly breathe.

"I can't do without you any longer, Anne. I can't indeed. I hate all this money. Let Race have it. Come on. Let's go."

"My toothbrush?" I demurred.

"You can buy one. I know I'm a lunatic, but for God's sake, *come!*"

He stalked off at a furious pace. I followed him as meekly as the Barotsi woman I had observed at the Falls. Only I wasn't carrying a frying-pan on my head. He walked so fast that it was very difficult to keep up with him.

"Harry," I said at last, in a meek voice, "are we going to walk all the way to Rhodesia?"

He turned suddenly and with a great shout of laughter gathered me up in his arms.

"I'm mad, sweetheart, I know it. But I do love you so."

"We're a couple of lunatics. And, oh, Harry, you never asked me, but I'm not making a sacrifice at all! I *wanted* to come!"

36

That was two years ago. We still live on the island. Before me, on the rough wooden table, is the letter that Suzanne wrote me.

DEAR BABES IN THE WOOD—DEAR LUNATICS IN
    LOVE,

I'm not surprised—not at all. All the time we've been talking Paris and frocks I felt that it wasn't a bit real—that you'd vanish into the blue some day to be married over the tongs in the good old gipsy fashion. But you *are* a couple of lunatics! This idea of renouncing a vast fortune is absurd. Colonel Race wanted to argue the matter, but I have persuaded him to leave the argument to time. He can administer the estate for Harry—and none better. Because, after all, honeymoons don't last forever—you're not here, Anne, so I can safely say that without having you fly out at me like a little wild-cat—Love in the wilderness will last a good while, but one day you will suddenly begin to dream of houses in Park Lane, sumptuous furs, Paris frocks, the largest thing in motors and the latest thing in perambulators, French maids and Norland nurses! Oh, yes, you will!

But have your honeymoon, dear lunatics, and let it be a long one. And think of me sometimes, comfortably putting on weight amidst the fleshpots!

Your loving friend,
SUZANNE BLAIR.

P.S.—I am sending you an assortment of frying-pans as a wedding present, and an enormous *terrine* of *pâté de foie gras* to remind you of me.

There is another letter that I sometimes read. It came a good while after the other and was accompanied by a bulky packet. It appeared to be written from somewhere in Bolivia.

MY DEAR ANNE BEDDINGFELD,

I can't resist writing to you, not so much for the pleasure it gives me to write, as for the enormous pleasure I know it will give you to hear from me. Our friend Race wasn't quite as clever as he thought himself, was he?

I think I shall appoint you my literary executor. I'm sending you my diary. There's nothing in it that would interest Race and his crowd, but I fancy that there are passages in it which may amuse you. Make use of it in any way you like. I suggest an article for the *Daily Budget*, "Criminals I have met." I only stipulate that I shall be the central figure.

By this time I have no doubt that you are no longer Anne Beddingfeld, but Lady Eardsley, queening it in Park Lane. I should just like to say that I bear you no malice whatever. It is hard, of course, to have to begin all over again at my time of life, but, *entre nous*, I had a little reserve fund carefully put aside for such a contingency. It has come in very usefully and I am getting together a nice little connection. By the way, if you ever come across that funny friend of yours, Arthur Minks, just tell him that I haven't forgotten him, will you? That will give him a nasty jar.

On the whole I think I have displayed a most Christian and forgiving spirit. Even to Pagett. I happened to hear that he—or rather Mrs. Pagett—had brought a sixth child into the world the other day. England will be entirely populated by Pagetts soon. I sent the child a silver mug, and, on a post card, declared my willingness to act as god-father. I can see Pagett taking both mug and post card straight to Scotland Yard without a smile on his face!

Bless you, liquid eyes. Some day you will see what a mistake you have made in not marrying me.

Yours ever,
EUSTACE PEDLER

Harry was furious. It is the one point on which he and I do not see eye to eye. To him, Sir Eustace was the man who tried to murder me and whom he regards as responsible for the death of his friend. Sir Eustace's attempts on my life have always puzzled me. They are not in the picture, so to speak. For I am sure that he always had a genuinely kindly feeling towards me.

Then why did he twice attempt to take my life? Harry says "because he's a damned scoundrel," and seems to think that settles the matter. Suzanne was more discriminating. I talked it over with her, and she put it down to a "fear complex." Suzanne goes in rather for psycho-analysis. She pointed out to me that Sir Eustace's whole life was actuated by a desire to be safe and comfortable. He had an acute sense of self-preservation. And the murder of Nadina removed certain inhibitions. His actions did not represent the state of his feeling towards me, but were the result of his acute fears for his own safety. I think Suzanne is right. As for Nadina, she was the kind of woman who deserved to die. Men do all sorts of questionable things in order to get rich, but women shouldn't pretend to be in love when they aren't for ulterior motives.

I can forgive Sir Eustace easily enough, but I shall never forgive Nadina. Never, never, never!

The other day I was unpacking some tins that were wrapped in bits of an old *Daily Budget*, and I suddenly came upon the words, "The Man in the Brown Suit." How long ago it seemed! I had, of course, severed my connection with the *Daily Budget* long ago—I had done with it sooner than it had done with me. MY ROMANTIC WEDDING was given a halo of publicity.

My son is lying in the sun, kicking his legs. There's a "man in a brown suit" if you like. He's wearing as little as possible, which is the best costume for Africa, and is as brown as a berry. He's always burrowing in the earth. I think he takes after Papa. He'll have that same mania for Pleiocene clay.

Suzanne sent me a cable when he was born:

"Congratulations and love to the latest arrival on Lunatics' Island. Is his head dolichocephalic or brachycephalic?"

I wasn't going to stand that from Suzanne. I sent her a reply of one word, economical and to the point:

"Platycephalic!"

m a